I0891576

The Dead Shall Inherit

Also by Raye Anderson

The Roxanne Calloway Mystery series

And We Shall Have Snow

And Then Is Heard No More

Down Came the Rain

Sing a Song of Summer

The Dead *Shall* Inherit

AN *Elspeth Laird* MYSTERY

RAYE ANDERSON

Signature
EDITIONS

Cover design by Doowah Design.
Photo of Raye Anderson by Michael Long

This book was printed on Ancient Forest Friendly paper.
Printed and bound in Canada by Hignell Book Printing Inc.

Library and Archives Canada Cataloguing in Publication

Title: The dead shall inherit / Raye Anderson.
Names: Anderson, Raye, 1943- author.
Description: Series statement: An Elspeth Buchanan mystery
Identifiers: Canadiana (print) 20240419227
| Canadiana (ebook) 20240419235
| ISBN 9781773241463 (softcover) | ISBN 9781773241470 (EPUB)
Subjects: LCGFT: Detective and mystery fiction. | LCGFT: Novels.
Classification: LCC PS8601.N44725 D43 2024
| DDC C813/.6—dc23

We acknowledge the support of the Canada Council for the Arts the Manitoba Arts Council, and the Manitoba Government for our publishing program.

Canada Council for the Arts Conseil des arts du Canada
Manitoba Arts Council Conseil des arts du Manitoba
Manitoba

Signature Editions
P.O. Box 206, RPO Corydon, Winnipeg, Manitoba, R3M 3S7
www.signature-editions.com

For Diann, Sylvia, and Jill,
my friends back home

Cast of Characters

Elspeth Laird

Elspeth's family:

Margaret Laird (née Balfour)—Elspeth's mother, in Winnipeg, Manitoba

Dave Bueller—Elspeth's partner, in Winnipeg, Manitoba

Deirdre MacPhail (née Balfour)—Elspeth's aunt and Margaret's sister. A writer.

Granny Balfour—From Carnoustie, Scotland, Elspeth's birthplace

Iain Balfour—Deirdre's nephew and Elspeth's cousin, in Edinburgh

Shona Balfour—Iain's daughter, in Edinburgh

Ewan Balfour—Iain's brother, in Australia

On the Isle of Sulla

Skipper Rob MacPhail—A ship's captain

Megan MacPhail—His wife, a teacher

Alasdair MacPhail—Deirdre's husband and Skipper MacPhail's nephew

Norman MacPhail—Alasdair's cousin and Skipper MacPhail's nephew

Chrissie MacPhail (née McFee)—Norman's wife

Young Norman MacPhail—Norman and Chrissie's older son, a crofter

Rob MacPhail (Rob the Garage)—Norman and Chrissie's younger son

Lachlan (Lachie) MacKinnon—A crofter

Cath MacKinnon (née McFee)—His wife

Isa McFee (nee McQuarrie)—Cath's mother

John McFee—Cath's father

Murdo McFee (deceased)—John's brother

Donalda McFee—Murdo's wife

Calum McFee—Murdo and Donalda's son, a lawyer, Oban and Sulla

Annabel McQuarrie—Co-owner of Annabel's Café and Bookshop

Sandy McQuarrie—Co-owner of Annabel's Café and Bookshop

Jan MacLeod—An artist and craft shop owner

Kate Mary MacLeod—Jan's mother

Angus MacLeod —Jan's father and Kate Mary's husband

Skye MacLeod—Jan's daughter, in Oban

Donald (Donnie) MacPherson—Owner of the Sulla Hotel and barman

Frieda MacPherson—Donnie's wife and the hotel's chef

PC Jackie Buchanan—Sulla's only police constable

Doug Buchanan —Jackie's husband and owner of a watersport centre

Other characters

Liz Fraser—Deirdre MacPhail's literary agent, in Edinburgh

Inga Hansen—Liz's partner, also in Edinburgh

DI Fergus Alexander—Police Scotland

DS Julie Lawson—Police Scotland

Bernard (Bernie) Baxter—A summer house owner from Glasgow

Kimmy MacLeod—Deirdre's house cleaner

Colin the Harbour—The harbourmaster

Sally Kerr—A friend of Calum McFee, in Oban

Geordie MacLeod—An elderly crofter

Mike Nicolson—A contractor

Ainslie Goertzen—A Canadian visitor

Dr. Thomson—Sulla's part-time doctor

1

Deirdre MacPhail was dead, and Scotland mourned her loss, at least those Scots who had read and admired her many books did. She was, after all, one of their own, a fixture in the Scottish literary landscape as long as many of them could remember, ever since she'd written the first Sulla stories, back in the sixties. Those books, about the island off the West Coast where she'd set up home, were still in print. She had been prolific. There had been plays as well, and historical novels, but the stories she had told about Sulla were the ones that had made her and her island famous and provided her with a steady income.

She had been a fixture at book festivals, up and down the land, for years. The books had paid for a flat in Edinburgh, in the seventies when those were still affordable, as well as the house on Sulla. She could be relied upon to show up at the Edinburgh Book Festival each year, although she hadn't been seen there recently. She was, after all, over eighty, and she had preferred to remain in her island home as she got older. She still wrote. She'd ventured into crime fiction in the past few years, with some success. Her books were translated into other languages. She was as well-known, internationally, as many of the other writers who now made Edinburgh their home, and she certainly had staying power.

She had founded the Sulla Book Festival, five years earlier. That had brought a galaxy of Scottish writers to the island. If travelling to other festivals was beginning to be too much for her creaky bones, she could bring them to her own door, she had said. Then the pandemic had happened. The festival had gone online and Deirdre had stayed on her island for the duration, still figuring out new stories, seemingly unstoppable, until the day she tripped on a rug and toppled down the stairs. She had been alone in her house when it happened. Her body had not been found until two days later.

A tragic loss, *The Scotsman* pronounced, and did a half-page article about her in the weekend arts edition. There were many tributes to her memory online and *The Guardian* published an obituary. Deirdre would have been gratified, pleased to be so well noticed and praised.

Elspeth Laird was her niece. She lived half the world away, in Winnipeg, Manitoba, Canada. Elspeth was surprised to receive an email from her cousin in Edinburgh, Iain Balfour, informing her that their aunt had left the house on the Isle of Sulla and its contents to her. Not only that, she was to be the inheritor of her aunt's literary legacy, and would be the recipient of any future royalties earned by the books.

Elspeth's mother, Margaret, invited her to lunch, as soon as she heard. They sat at a window on the third floor of a building that housed the elderly, those with the means to afford it and its amenities. It was well-appointed, stuffed full of furnishings that Elspeth remembered from the house where she had grown up, in an equally respectable Winnipeg neighbourhood. It overlooked a frozen river, bare trees and snowy streets. This was March and the long Manitoba winter was not over, but the heating was turned up high in Margaret's residence and her room was warm. She was younger than Deirdre, still in her late seventies, white haired and in need of a hip replacement, but otherwise, like her sister, she was spry and had all her wits about her.

She remembered the house on Sulla. She'd visited it once, a long time ago. Margaret hadn't seen Deirdre in years. They'd never been close; exchanged Christmas cards, that was all. Elspeth got one of those too, every year, usually one that looked like it had been made by an islander featuring seals or boats, tartan and a cute Scottish greeting. Signed *Cheers, Deirdre*, that was all.

"It's a rectangular stone pile with thick walls," Margaret reported, over bowls of tomato soup and grilled cheese sandwiches. The soup came from a can. Cooking was not her strong point. "Not pretty. But it does have a view, on the landward side. Mull. Iona. You can see Islay to the south when it's not raining. Otherwise, it's the Atlantic. Not a spot of land between it and Canada. There's a pier right beside it, too. It's called the Skipper's House because it once belonged to a ship's captain that came from Sulla. A MacPhail, like Deirdre's husband, Alasdair. She got it when he died." Elspeth knew how that had happened. It was family lore. Alasdair MacPhail had gone out in a boat one day and drowned. Her aunt had been left a widow when she was barely thirty.

"The house was crammed full of junk that Skipper MacPhail brought back from his trips overseas. A damp place. It rained all the time I was there. Wind howling in off the Atlantic. I've no idea why she kept it, not after she bought that flat in Edinburgh, too." Margaret poured tea and spoke with the precise accent of an educated Scot. "I can't imagine why she thought she needed two houses, or how she could afford them both. I suppose the flat in Bruntsfield has been left to your cousin, Iain. Deirdre bought it years ago, when she started making money off the books. It's got to be worth three times what she paid for it, now. More than that old house on Sulla. Are you going to have to go over there?"

"I don't think I can. Iain's the executor and according to him the estate has to be valued. It's Scottish law. It will all be tied up for about six months."

Elspeth was broke, and her mother knew it. She designed theatre sets. Business had been shut down for the past two years because of the pandemic. She'd got by on a government support program and there had been a couple of video productions that she'd been asked to design, but they had paid very little. Theatre companies were getting back on their feet again, but there wouldn't be much in the way of real work until the fall. Having to wait six months for an inheritance was frustrating. And it meant she didn't have the money for a trip to the U.K., to see this house that she had inherited.

"You'll just have to wait then," her mother advised. "Don't get your hopes up. That house is probably worth nothing. And it's years since Deirdre wrote those books about Sulla. I can't imagine many people are buying them nowadays, so don't expect much from those either."

Margaret had money, but it was obvious she wasn't going to pay for a plane ticket and Elspeth knew better than to ask. She had had to borrow from her mother, twice, years ago, when she was starting out in her career and contracts had been few and far between. Both debts had been repaid but she'd been reminded of them, many times.

There was a row of Deirdre's books on a shelf, over by a window, old ones from the days when Margaret had made an annual trip back to Scotland to visit Elspeth's grandmother. Those had stopped once Granny Balfour was dead and buried. Margaret hadn't seen her sister since then and that was twenty years ago. She was matter-of-fact about the death. As far as Elspeth knew, she hadn't shed a single tear.

"Deirdre and I went our separate ways," she remarked. It wasn't surprising that the two of them had drifted apart. She and her sister had been very different. Margaret had gone into science, become a biologist. It was a job at a prestigious lab in Winnipeg that had brought the family to Canada. Elspeth's father had been an architect and they had prospered here in Winnipeg. Worked hard and been careful with their money. Deirdre had always been more of a dreamer, she mused now, over her teacup. "A bit like you, Elspeth. Maybe that's why she's left you a little something or two."

Elspeth borrowed a half dozen of the first books that Deirdre had written. She'd never read them. If she was to receive the proceeds from any sales, she should get acquainted.

"The obituary said something about mystery novels?" she asked as she pulled on her parka and boots, ready for the freezing cold outside.

Margaret knew nothing about that. "To be honest, I haven't read more than one or two of the ones about Sulla myself." She watched Elspeth tuck the books under her arm as she waited to see her out the door. "They're not my kind of reading, but some people like them. There's no accounting for taste. Your grandfather was so disappointed when she turned to writing those. He was proud when Deirdre got into Edinburgh University. She was doing well, on track to get first class honours until she met Alasdair MacPhail and his art school friends. That was back in the early sixties, you know. They were all a bit wild. In the end she barely scraped a second."

Elspeth recognized the judgmental tone. She herself had started in architecture, following in her father's footsteps, but she had discovered theatre, second year of university, and changed direction. Margaret had made her disapproval clear, although her dad had understood. He hadn't minded paying for her to go train in stage design instead, in Montreal. She was thankful for that.

"I suppose we should be glad the books were popular enough to pay the bills." Margaret hurried Elspeth to the elevator, eager to get downstairs in time for her weekly bridge game. The door slid open to reveal two of her elderly friends. Their conversation about Deirdre MacPhail ceased.

2

That evening, Elspeth sat at a table in the living room of her own house, logs burning in the hearth. Outside, the night was starry clear, the air crisp and cold. The icy road gleamed in the street lights, the branches of elm trees reaching black fingers across it in a skeletal arch.

She flipped through the stack of paperbacks. They had all been written before the 1980s. Deirdre had a Wikipedia entry with a list of her publications. Fifteen books had been written about Sulla, between 1970 and 2000. Six plays, throughout Deirdre's long career, all produced to some acclaim in Glasgow and Edinburgh, and five books about women in Scottish history. They had done reasonably well, too, but had not been as popular as the ones about the island. The first of the Mairi MacIntosh crime novels was recent, published in 2017. They had been an instant hit. The year before the pandemic, Deirdre had been a guest author at Bloody Scotland, a crime fiction conference in Stirling. She'd been interviewed by Nicola Sturgeon, then Scotland's First Minister. The recording was available on YouTube. She turned it on.

She watched her aunt breeze onto the stage, fair hair, probably dyed, pinned up in a messy bun, wearing a long floaty skirt and scarves, bangles at her wrists and a pendant around her neck with a large, polished green stone dangling in front. She looked and sounded exactly as Elspeth remembered her the few times that she had met her, years ago, happy to talk about herself with a gravelly laugh, a bit of a performer. The interview was lively and the audience applauded when she was done.

Elspeth walked through to the kitchen.

"I might get a bit of cash from Deirdre's books after all," she said. "She's been writing mysteries and they've been doing well." Her partner, Dave, looked up from the other side of the table. He had a job with a steady income, as vice principal of a local elementary school. His salary had kept them afloat during the pandemic years. Dave Bueller helped coach basketball in the winter, soccer in the summer and was busy working on schedules. They had developed the habit of working in separate rooms during the pandemic when they had been cooped up together for months.

"That right? She's dead, though. There won't be any more, will there?" He returned to looking at his own screen, making it clear he was busy and did not want to be distracted. She looked down at the top of his head. Dave's hair had receded and was turning grey. He looked tired and he worked hard. He obviously wasn't prepared to talk right now. She went back to her own computer.

Elspeth had no idea what a literary legacy entailed. She googled that next. It made sense that the income from existing books continued to come in after an author died. Those royalties, it seemed, would go directly to her. But Dave was right. There would be no more books now that Deirdre was dead. That money would dwindle fast. She found a page on houses for sale in the Hebrides, instead.

They were worth much more than she, or her mother, had thought. Prices had risen dramatically, post pandemic. After two years of being shut in, not able to spend money as much as usual, people hankered for open spaces where the air was fresh and clean, and some of them had cash to spare, one site reported. Tiny two-bedroom cottages on the islands were listed at £250,000; £450,000 got you a restored croft house, especially one with a sea view, and Elspeth's mother had said the house on Sulla looked right out over the water to the mainland.

Elspeth wasn't sure what a croft house was. It seemed that farming land was leased on the islands according to what were called crofting laws, but a house could be owned outright by the tenant. So the Skipper's House must have been a MacPhail house originally. Then ownership had passed to Deirdre.

"Look at this, Dave. I might get some real money after all." Elspeth walked back into the kitchen and laid her laptop on the tabletop so he could see the screen. She watched Dave grow more interested as he scanned the house prices.

"Maybe I should go over there," Elspeth hinted. "Find out how much it's really worth and arrange for someone to sell it for me."

"Do you need to do that?" he asked. "It sounds like your cousin's got everything under control. Can't he arrange to sell it as part of the estate and send you the money?"

She was contracted to design a show in Winnipeg in the fall, a musical, and there was one other prospect, but nothing signed as yet. That was all. The government funding had dried up. She had time on her hands. Elspeth wanted to go.

"If I own a house on a Hebridean island, I want to see it before it gets sold. I just need enough to buy a plane ticket and cover basic expenses. I can probably stay in the house on Sulla, for free. Find out if there was anything in it that I want to keep. Deirdre's left me all this and I barely knew her. I should find more about who she was," she wheedled, hating that she needed to ask.

She'd been stuck in this house with Dave for two long years while he worked from home and she had struggled to keep herself from dying of boredom, with no work projects to hold her interest. Now she had the chance to go somewhere, meet some new people, do something different. See a part of Scotland where she had never been. It wasn't just the house that interested her. She could meet the people who had published Deirdre's books and find out how the whole literary inheritance thing worked.

"See what those houses are going for?" She pointed to a photo of a restored house beside a beach on Colonsay, not far from Sulla. The asking price was £425,000. "I might not get that much for it but it'll be enough to reshingle this house. Buy us a new car. The trip's an investment! I only need to be gone for a month. I'll find someone to sell the house for me and arrange what's to be done with whatever is in it. Deirdre must have had a publisher or an agent. I should find out how much money's likely to come in from the books. It'll be worth going. I'll be back in Winnipeg by the time the snow's melted."

"Margaret didn't say that she'd buy you a ticket?"

"She didn't offer and I'm not going to ask."

Dave looked up at her through his glasses. She could almost see figures clicking through his head. "Alright then. Put the ticket on Visa and take a couple of grand out of our line of credit. Let's hope you're right."

"Thanks, Dave." She wished he didn't sound so grudging, but at least he had agreed.

She booked her flight, emailed Iain Balfour in Edinburgh to let him know that she was coming, and three days later, she was on her way.

3

Air travel was never reliable in Canada in March. Weather was unpredictable, beset by Alberta clippers and Colorado lows that could swoop in and dump heaps of snow at very little notice. A storm could encase a city with ice, halt traffic, bring down trees and power lines. On this day, Toronto had been hit by a storm. It had brought several inches of wet, heavy snow. People could travel freely, post pandemic, at last and airlines were having trouble coping with an unexpected flood of bookings. The plane from Winnipeg sat for over an hour on the tarmac after it landed at Pearson Airport, waiting for a ground crew to come so the passengers could disembark, and Elspeth knew she would miss her connection to London.

The airport was in chaos, full of frustrated passengers who, like her, had missed their flights. Lineups were everywhere. A woman was in tears, her baby wailing. A man yelled at the ticket counter. Another plane was scheduled to leave for London that evening. After a long wait, Elspeth was put on standby. Passengers with bookings were cancelling, unable to get to the airport because of snowy roads that were icing up as the day progressed. With a bit of luck she might get on.

She waited in another line, to buy what was available at a food outlet. A muffin, an energy bar, bottled water was the best she could get. Then she found a corner in the departure lounge, made her jacket into a mat and her carry-on bag into a back rest, took out the first of Deirdre's books about the Isle of Sulla and read.

Each chapter was a separate anecdote, told about an islander. The characters were interesting. Funny things happened. Practical jokes. Mistakes. They were interspersed with sadder chapters too, ones that told of hardship and loss. It had never been easy to scrape a living from the windblown land or the sea, but Deirdre had managed to tell those stories with a light touch, and things always ended well. She wrote with affection and humour, making the island sound charming and idyllic. Elspeth could see why the books were popular, why they had drawn people to Sulla. How they had helped put that little island on the map.

She checked the departures board. There was no sign of her upcoming flight. She had yet more time to wait, so spent it alternating between reading and thinking about what she now knew about Deirdre and the house on Sulla.

Alasdair MacPhail, Deirdre's husband, had come from an island family. He'd shown artistic talent so he'd gone off to art school in Edinburgh. They'd married the year they had both graduated and moved into the vacant MacPhail house on Sulla. She'd been writing and he'd been trying to make a living as an artist. They had no money, and the house came rent free. Some of the funniest episodes that Deirdre wrote about described their attempts to fit in. She had tried keeping chickens, not a success, and Alasdair MacPhail had gone fishing. One day, that had ended in tragedy. He'd set out by himself on a boat one summer's afternoon and fallen overboard. His body had been washed out to sea and had never been recovered. They were both thirty-two years old when it had happened.

By then, Deirdre had published the book that Elspeth had just read and the one that followed. Alasdair, it turned out, had owned the Skipper's House. He had left it to her and she had kept it as a summer home. Elspeth couldn't find a photograph but Google Maps showed her a dark rectangular roof near a long stretch of sandy beach, a stone wall surrounding the house and a couple of outbuildings. A rocky outcrop jutted into the sea, a structure of some sort sticking out into the water. Her mother had mentioned a pier. Deirdre had split her time between Edinburgh and the island until the pandemic but she had stayed on Sulla when that hit, and that was where she had died, three weeks ago.

By the time Elspeth found herself on a plane to Heathrow, hours later, she had browsed two more of the books she had borrowed from her mother. They were easy reading and continued in the same vein as the first. She checked her messages. Iain Balfour had responded to the email she had sent, surprised that she was on her way. It was too bad she wasn't coming to Edinburgh to talk to him first, he said. He could have told her most of what she needed to know. A couple called MacKinnon had a key to the house on Sulla. He sent their phone number and an email address.

Elspeth hadn't considered going to Edinburgh. She had limited time and she wanted to get to the island. Deirdre had been cremated already and there had been no mention of a funeral to attend. She could talk to her cousin online if she had to. Maybe she would visit later, if she had time, though. She hadn't been in that grey city for a very long time.

Elspeth had been born in Scotland, and had emigrated with her parents when she was two years old. There had been trips "back home" every couple of years when she was a child. She remembered Iain Balfour from then, an earnest boy who didn't have much time for a young girl cousin from Canada. He had bragged about going to a prestigious school and thought she should be impressed because he played on the rugby team. His younger brother, Ewan, had been way more fun. She and Iain had never been close.

She'd met Deirdre then, too. She remembered going for tea at Jenners tea room in Edinburgh, cakes and scones on tiered plates, her mother insisting that she sit up straight and mind her manners, Deirdre telling her to go ahead and have another éclair. And to call her that, Deirdre. Never "Aunty." "Too stuffy," she had said, though a cloud of smoke. Cigarettes were still allowed at the table in those days.

Elspeth had been quite mesmerized by her aunt when she was little, but a bit embarrassed, too. Deirdre had been loud and attracted attention. She hadn't changed the way she dressed over the years, based on what Elspeth had seen online. "Like a hippy," her mother had commented. Long hair, long skirts, socks with boots. Not Margaret Laird's style at all. She had favoured a trim skirt and matching jacket for a trip to Edinburgh. Shoes with heels. Elspeth had worn a dress and coat, knee-high white socks, brown polished shoes, nothing at all like the shorts and sneakers she wore in Canada in the summertime. There had been a visit to the zoo on another occasion. Penguins going for a walk. Ice cream. Those visits had dwindled as Elspeth grew older. Eventually it had only been Margaret who had made the annual trek back to Scotland to visit Granny Balfour.

It was twenty-two years since Elspeth had last set foot in Scotland and that trip had been a fluke. Winnipeg's Prairie Theatre Centre had set up an exchange of plays with Edinburgh's Traverse Theatre. A play that Elspeth had designed had been sent to Scotland for that year's Fringe Festival. One of the stage crew got sick at the last minute and she had been invited to step in. She was Scottish, after all, and she had a valid passport. A free trip to Edinburgh and the opportunity to find out what was going on in Scottish theatre had been an unexpected treat and it had meant she could connect with Deirdre once again.

They had met in the theatre bar one afternoon. Deirdre had breezed in and greeted the barman by name. She was well known there. The company had produced a play she had written the previous year. The artistic director had walked by with a couple of actors and there had been hugging and kissing.

Deirdre had resembled Annie Lennox with a lot more hair. She had the same wide mouth, the cheekbones, bright blue eyes and she was just as colourful, but with an entirely different look. That day she had worn a loose jacket over a long, patchwork dress, a scarf, red shoes. Lots of jewellery, too, of hammered silver and beads. Hooped earrings, bangles and another big stone pendant.

She drank Bowmore, she reminded the bartender, with a splash of water, and still smoked while she talked, mainly about herself. She had a new book, just out, and she would be doing a reading at the Edinburgh Book Festival later that week. She fished a copy out of a capacious tote bag and signed it for Elspeth. She'd be on a panel, too, called, "Writing Scotland's Landscape." Could Elspeth come? But Elspeth had a meeting with a Scottish theatre designer that day, and had promised to take some of the Winnipeg cast sightseeing later. She also wanted to catch as much theatre as she could while she was in Edinburgh. Other family visits had to be made as well. Granny Balfour was still alive, living in Carnoustie, in Angus, on the North Sea coast, the town where Deirdre, Margaret and Angus, Iain Balfour's father, had grown up. That was where Elspeth had been born.

"You'd have a much better time with me," Deirdre had said. "Tell you what, why don't you stay a couple of weeks longer? Change your ticket and come with me to Sulla. I'm going right back after the book festival. I'll drive you to Oban then we'll take the boat. You'll love it." Elspeth had been tempted but she couldn't. She had to be in Toronto to design a show for the Canadian Opera Company as soon as she returned. "Well, then. Can't be helped," her aunt had shrugged and lit another cigarette.

Elspeth had given Deirdre tickets to come and see the Manitoba play being produced at the Traverse, but she didn't know if she had ever come. She hadn't read the book, either. She thought she might have lost it. She knew it hadn't gone back to Canada with her. She felt a pang of guilt, now that Deirdre had left her a house and the proceeds from her writing. She had liked her aunt, been quite fascinated by her in those few brief meetings, but she barely knew her. She hadn't thought much about her in the years that followed either.

"I wonder why she left the house to you?" Dave had commented, as he had driven her to the airport in Winnipeg. "Is it just because you work in the arts?"

That was likely. All of Deirdre and Elspeth's Balfour relatives inclined towards sports and science. Elspeth's grandfather had been a well-respected Scottish GP and a fixture on the Carnoustie golf course. Iain Balfour was his grandson, a practising orthopedic surgeon, married to a dentist. Iain's brother, Ewan, now living in Australia, was a vet. Margaret herself had earned some renown in her field of science. Granny Balfour had approved of them all, but not of her eldest daughter.

Deirdre, as far as the rest of the Balfour clan was concerned, had been an anomaly.

"Almost enough to make you believe in changelings, quite away with the fairies," Elspeth had heard her grandmother say as she and Margaret washed up dishes in the big stone-built house where her grandfather had maintained a surgery for over forty years. Deirdre had gone adrift somehow. Granny Balfour had no idea where she got her ideas from. Such a shame, she could have had a good, steady job as an English teacher but she'd thrown it all away. She hardly ever visited the old lady, not even when she was staying in Edinburgh, in that flat of hers. Buying that was the only sensible thing that Deirdre had ever done. At least she'd have that to fall back on when the money she got from writing those books ran out.

But Granny Balfour had been wrong. Deirdre had managed quite well. It was true that she hadn't paid for the house on Sulla.

She had inherited it, but she'd managed to buy the flat in Edinburgh and kept herself afloat through the years. As had Elspeth, until the pandemic had stalled her career.

Elspeth wished now that she had gone to the island when she'd been invited all those years ago. The truth was, she'd been too swept up in her own work at the time. She hadn't paid much attention to her Scottish aunt back then. And now she was going to benefit from her death. Maybe this trip was about making amends.

The plane throbbed its way eastwards, and she eventually slept. More pandemonium and another wait at Heathrow delayed her again before she finally caught a plane north, more than a day late.

It was morning, but Glasgow was drenched in rain. Elspeth only had a spring jacket and sneakers on her feet. She was travelling light, had left her parka and boots with Dave at the airport in Winnipeg. She changed some money and dragged her carry-on to the door.

"See thon bus," a small man in a raincoat with a hat pulled down to his ears answered when she asked directions. He pointed at a large purply-pink double decker, parked outside. "Tell the man tae drop ye off at Queen Street station."

Elspeth barely understood what he was saying but she got the gist. The bus wasn't far away. She turned up her collar and ran for it.

Scotland smelled wet and green. She peered through the rainy windows at leafy trees, fresh grass, flowerbeds that were actually blooming as the bus lumbered its way through city streets. Spring had arrived long since, unlike in snowy Canada. Trains ran from here, every day, to Oban, on the West Coast. From there she could take a small plane out to the island, but it left early in the afternoon. She doubted she'd get there in time to catch it today. She'd have to splurge on an Airbnb and catch the ferry in the morning. That was okay, she told herself. Approaching a Hebridean island for the first time from the sea seemed the right way to go.

4

The train chugged its way north, a scenic route according to the tourism websites, but today the view outside the windows was blurred with rain. Clouds had descended almost to ground level, swallowing buildings, trees and hills.

When they reached it, famous Loch Lomondside was barely visible except for patches of grey water and glimpses of equally grey hillsides. Elspeth was still damp from running to and from the bus but she was drying out on the train; she had bought a sandwich and a coffee, her window seat was comfortable and there was Wi-Fi.

The ferry that left Oban for Sulla sailed at eight the next morning. Buying a ticket online was easily done. She trawled through the many Airbnb listings for Oban and found one that was close to the harbour and reasonably priced. Booking it was straightforward, too. Then she emailed C. MacKinnon, the name that Iain Balfour had provided, to say that she would be arriving and needed to get the key to the Skipper's House. Once that was done, she closed her eyes and slept, lulled by the rocking rhythm of the train.

When she woke, the rain had stopped and they were passing a loch. A castle sat out on the water, on an island maybe, or a peninsula. She had seen another one like that before, on the train between Carnoustie and Edinburgh, on one of her childhood visits. Mary, Queen of Scots, had been imprisoned there, her mother had told her. She had managed to escape, Elspeth didn't remember how. This country must be dotted with ruins, each with its own story, romantic on misty days like these but tied to a violent and stormy past. Deirdre had written a book about the doomed Mary, she was sure. And a play. Maybe there would be a copy in the house on Sulla and she could bone up on some Scottish history while she was here.

She had never been in this part of the country. Her mother had never brought her to visit Deirdre on any of those visits back to their homeland. They had always stayed in Carnoustie, on the eastern shore of the North Sea, never gone further than Edinburgh. They'd never been to Deirdre's flat there, either. They had always met her in a place like a tearoom. Elspeth had been married once before, when she was young, long before she'd met Dave. She and her then husband had met in restaurants while they negotiated a divorce, so that they would both behave themselves. No yelling in public. Perhaps Deirdre and Margaret had been doing something similar, choosing to get together in places where they had to be polite to one another.

The clouds parted as they approached the West Coast. She could finally see the tops of mountains, quite unlike the Canadian Rockies, smooth sided, covered with vegetation almost to the summit where they broke off into craggy rock faces like those of very old men and women. Water streamed down narrow crevasses. Lochs opened up toward the sea; the trees were thick and green. Scotland finally looked like it was bonnie.

She checked her email again. Someone called Calum McFee had written:

Heard from Cath MacKinnon that you'll be in Oban tonight. I was Deirdre's solicitor. Meet this evening?

That was a welcome invitation. She could do that. There was a message from the same Catherine MacKinnon.

Meet you off the ferry, with key.

Elspeth wondered how she would get around on the island. Presumably Deirdre had owned a car, but would she be able to drive it? Maybe this Calum McFee could tell her. Or maybe she could find a bike?

She emailed back to both. By the time the train pulled into the station at Oban she knew that Calum McFee would pick her up at the Airbnb at six that evening. He'd offered to buy her dinner. She stepped off the train and found herself near a bay, surrounded by hills. Houses wrapped around a harbour full of boats. A strange, round pillared structure stood up on a hillside. Two big black-hulled ferryboats were moored at a terminal, one of them most likely the one she would take tomorrow. A large island lay off shore and behind it she could see blue hills, farther out over the water. Those must be on the Isle of Mull. Sulla lay on the other side, near the south end of Mull, all by itself in the middle of the Atlantic.

Finding the Airbnb was easy. She pulled her carry-on up a steep incline to a house with a hedge. Daffodils and tulips flowered in the garden. The top floor of the house was hers for the night, the home owner told her, and gave her a key. The wallpaper was flowery, the bedroom pink, but it was clean and convenient. She could see the harbour and the ferry boats from the front window.

She went for a walk. Shops lined the front, mainly selling Scottish woollens and souvenirs of "Bonnie Oban Bay." Rain jackets were for sale, but they were more expensive than she needed for a quick trip to a rainy island, well-made oilskins more suited for hunting or fishing. She did find a cheap umbrella, one she could fold up and tuck in her bag. That would have to do. A small bookstore had copies of the Mairi MacIntosh crime novels. There would probably be some in Deirdre's house but she bought one anyway to read on the boat as a change from the books about Sulla.

Calum McFee drove up at six, as he had promised, in a grey Range Rover of some vintage, a large man, about her own age, late forties, maybe fifty, big boned, looking more like a farmer than a lawyer. He wore corduroys, a plaid shirt and one of those thick oilskin jackets. He had an unruly head of light brown hair and the hand that gripped Elspeth's was like a bear paw.

"What would you like to eat?" he asked her.

"Could we go to a pub?" Elspeth suggested. She remembered that she had liked Scottish pub food when she had visited Edinburgh, years ago.

"We can do that." He drove to the far end of the bay, across from the ferry terminal, and parked at a hotel. The pub was attached to the side of the building. "The food's good here," he assured her, "And they have a nice ale made by a microbrewery out on Colonsay if you fancy a local beer." A trio of men at a table nodded at him as they walked in.

"Evening, Calum," said the barman.

One whole wall was papered in tartan. Glass cases holding stuffed dead fish hung around the room, with brass labels explaining what they were, their weight, where and when they had been caught and by whom.

"See that one over there?" Calum McFee pointed at one of them. "I caught that myself, ten years ago." There was a case containing large fishhooks with coloured feathers. "Those are for salmon," he explained, leading her to the table below it. He went to fetch beer and brought over a menu. Elspeth was surprised to see curry listed, and fettuccine, alongside more predictable offerings, like fish and chips.

"Go for the salmon," her host advised her, but Elspeth chose shepherd's pie instead. The beer came with a head of creamy foam. It was bitter but refreshing.

"How long will you be staying on Sulla?" Calum McFee had a deep voice but the accent was soft and fluid, quite unlike the ones that she had heard in Glasgow. "I need to get out there myself, soonish."

"I'm not sure. I have a ticket back to Canada in four weeks. I've been told that I inherit my aunt's house so I thought I could find someone to sell it for me and maybe get it cleared out."

Calum McFee had thick brown eyebrows to match his thatch of hair. They shot up in surprise. "You do know you won't get it for at least six months?" he said. "Or be able to sell anything that's in it?"

"Iain Balfour told me that. But I wanted to see it for myself and I thought I could get everything organized." They waited while a girl brought plates to the table.

"You could do that," he agreed. "Have you seen a copy of the will?"

Elspeth shook her head.

"Not to worry. I wrote it up. I can tell you what it says."

Deirdre had left her the house and all of her property on Sulla, he told her. That included the pier beside it. Any proceeds from her books that came in after Deirdre died were Elspeth's too. The flat in Edinburgh and any money in her accounts were to be split between Iain Balfour and his brother, Ewan, in Australia. There were small bequests to their kids, four in all, and Balfour got some money for being the executor. She had also left some cash to help support the Sulla Book Festival, but that was basically it.

"She made the will years ago," he said. "She thought she was doing an even split between you and your two cousins, and it was, back when she signed it. Old houses on the island weren't worth all that much then. But with tourism and Airbnb, prices have risen, and now, after the pandemic, everybody seems to want to run away to a quiet piece of paradise like Sulla. So you've struck it lucky.

"You look like you're hungry." He watched her devour the plateful of food. "Are you sure that's all you want to eat?" She was fine, she said. He went to fetch more beer.

"Do you know about inheritance tax over here?" he asked when he came back. "It's forty percent of everything above £325,000. Too bad Deirdre didn't give some of what she owned to all of you sooner, but she wasn't expecting to die yet. You'll do all right, though. The house should fetch about £400,000 and all the stuff that's in it will get you another £50,000 or so. All in all, you should clear close to £300,000 by the end of the day. And that's not counting what you'll get from the books."

Elspeth blinked. In Canadian money, that was about half a million bucks.

The young server had come to clear their empty plates. "Bring us back the menu, Becky," Calum said. "We'll need a pudding."

"The blackcurrant pie's good today," Becky told them. "I can bring it with ice cream."

Elspeth opted for some cheese but Calum McFee ordered the pie.

"You don't look much like Deirdre." He tipped his head sideways, examining Elspeth across the table. She didn't. She was little and dark. She wore her hair short and suspected it was curling in the damp, Scottish air.

"I take after my dad," she told him.

"But Deirdre told me that you were the only one in the family that was like her."

"She wrote, plays sometimes. I work in theatre. Was that the connection? The reason that she left me the books?" Elspeth asked.

"Probably. She said none of the rest of her relatives had ever bothered to read them."

Elspeth felt a twinge of guilt. She wished she had taken the time to do that herself long before now.

"Deirdre had an agent called Liz Fraser," Calum McFee continued. "She appointed her as literary executor so she'll continue to manage that business. I'll give you her email. We're both on the committee for the Book Festival. You can't stay for that? It happens near the end of May. We'll have to do something to honour Deirdre at it."

Dessert and cheese arrived. Beer and a chunk of Stilton was a great combination.

"I can't stay that long," Elspeth said. "I've only got enough cash to last me a month. There's been no work in theatre for the last two years"

"Really?" He screwed up his eyes, thinking, as he scooped up some pie. "We could see if your trip here could be charged to the estate, as a funeral expense, if you stay. It should be you that scatters Deirdre's ashes. She wanted them put into the sea off Sulla."

"Do you think so? My cousin hasn't mentioned it." But Elspeth hadn't thought to ask.

"Well." He put down his fork and crossed the fingers of his big hands in front of him. It made him look more like the lawyer that he really was. "I could help you with that if you want. Balfour's hired some Edinburgh solicitor to take care of things from his end but you're going to need someone to help you with the house sale and dealing with everything inside it, especially if you're going straight back to Canada. I can do that for you, if you want. I keep an office on Sulla and I handle most of the house sales over there."

"What is inside it? Besides furniture?" She remembered that her mother had said something about the house being full of junk. Hadn't he said something earlier about the contents being worth £50,000?

"Nobody told you what Skipper MacPhail brought home to Sulla?" he laughed. "Just you wait and see all what's waiting for you over there."

5

Elspeth had thought she wouldn't sleep after her conversation with Calum McFee, but she did, knocked out by the long journey, sea air and jet lag. She woke to her phone alarm, left the house key on the kitchen table and walked to the ferry as the sun began to break behind the town.

She spent the first half hour of the voyage on the aft deck, watching Oban disappear into the distance, gulls screeching in the wake of the boat, hills on one side, an island called Kerrera on the other, becoming more visible as the sun rose.

It was cool out and she retreated to the observation deck. She found a seat on the port side, where she could watch as they passed Mull. This boat didn't stop there. There were a few tourists on board, some backpackers, an elderly couple who sounded Scandinavian, maybe Swedish. A family had driven up from the south of England and there was a scattering of people who seemed local. They kept to themselves. Some of them spoke to one another in Gaelic. All the signage and the announcements on the boat were in both Gaelic and English.

She wondered if Calum McFee was right. Could she stay longer than she had planned and be on Sulla for the Book Festival? Be there for the memorial to Deirdre? That was possible if her ticket could be charged to the estate, as Calum McFee had suggested. She doubted that the cash she had available would last her for an extra month, but it was frustrating that she couldn't stay because all the money that was coming to her was tied up for now. She had been surprised to discover that the "junk" that her mother had said filled Deirdre's house on Sulla, was, in fact, valuable. They were antiques, Calum McFee had told her. From India. China. Tokyo.

"Rob MacPhail was a younger son that had to go to sea because he wasn't going to get the family croft."

"Those are kind of like what I would call a homestead?" she asked.

"I suppose so," he had explained last night as the sky turned darker and they had progressed to a post-dinner glass of a local single malt. "They're small farms that need to be worked and they usually get passed down to the eldest son. There wasn't much else to do out there except keep sheep and fish back then. Lots of island boys went off to sea instead. Rob MacPhail did well. Worked his way up and got his skipper's ticket. Captained some big boats that took him right around the world.

"Once, when he was docked in Cardiff, he met a Welshwoman called Megan. Fell in love, married her and brought her home to the island. The MacPhails gave him a patch of land and he built that house for her. That was right after the First World War."

"So the house was built in the 1920s?" asked Elspeth. "It's over a hundred years old?"

"It was built by islanders the traditional way, with thick walls to withstand the elements," he told her. "It's weathered well. Megan stayed there and taught school while he went off back to sea. They'd no children of their own but my mother says old Mrs. MacPhail was still teaching when she first went to school. She used to take things that Skipper MacPhail had brought home from his travels to class and tell the kids where they came from. Little objects that she could pass around and let them hold in their hands while she told them stories about the places they came from. Bowls with dragons painted on them. Bits of jade carved to look like little people going about their work. There's Indian carpets in that house that were made to size. He ordered them on the way out and picked them up on the way back. Bought her the best of everything."

"Your mother came from Sulla?"

"I grew up there myself," he said. "Then I came here, to Oban, for high school. I'm Sulleach, born and bred.

"Rob MacPhail died of a heart attack just after he retired from the sea," he continued, "but Megan lived on in the house for another fifteen years or so. They're both buried in the kirkyard on the island. And she left the house and all those fine things that he had brought home for her to her favourite nephew, Alasdair. Deirdre kept it all.

It's still there. Iain Balfour will need to send a valuer to find out what it's all worth, but if I was you I'd get some art expert from Glasgow to have a look at it for yourself."

The boat was passing the town of Tobermory, bright-coloured houses lining the harbour. A man passed Elspeth his binoculars so she could look closer. He and his wife were German, lean and fit, eager to strike up a conversation and practise their English. They had a motorhome down on the car deck, with bikes, and planned to stay overnight on Sulla, they enthused, then they would take the boat to the Isle of Tiree. They had heard that the windsurfing was good there. After that they would go to Barra and then travel up through the Outer Hebrides to the Isle of Lewis.

The ferryboat reached open water.

"We should go to the other side," said the man, "So we can see the island as soon as it comes into view." That was not going to happen for a while. Elspeth decided to stay where she was for now, comfortable and out of the wind. She reached into her bag and took out the Mairi MacIntosh book that she had bought. All she could see out the window was heaving sea and blue sky, the occasional white cloud scuttling across it. She could spend some time reading again.

The book told the story of a man who had gone fishing one day and not come back, just as Alasdair MacPhail had done, fifty years ago. All the Sulla books that she had read were based on stories that Deirdre had been told, or events that had actually taken place. Deirdre had added to them, made them into fiction, but they were grounded in fact. Had she done that again, when she wrote in this different genre? Had she built her story on what had happened when her own husband died? Was it fiction with a kernel of truth?

Elspeth read on for almost an hour, enough to know that the story evolved into a traditional whodunit. A family wanted the victim's house and land. His wife was having an affair and felt trapped in the marriage. He had a drinking habit and a past history with cocaine. All of that must have been dreamed up by Deirdre. PC Mairi MacIntosh, her sleuth, was the only police officer on the island, young, energetic and ambitious, destined to solve the case, but Elspeth wasn't close to finding out how when they reached the north end of Sulla and she closed the book.

She went back up on deck to look. Her German acquaintances were already there, standing by the rail. Elspeth had seen the outline of the island from above, on the online map. It lay at a northeast to southwest angle, about seven miles long, only three miles wide at this end but widening to about five miles about halfway further south. Coming at it from the sea, while the boat rocked under her feet, was entirely different. At first she saw treeless hills, a rocky coast, then a house tucked into a tiny bay, a small boat pulled up on some shingle.

"Will we pass your house?" the German husband asked. Elspeth supposed they would but she wasn't sure she would recognize it. Birds flew by. A pair of large black ones perched on a rock and sat, watching. "Cormorants." The man passed the glasses to his wife. It was birding that had brought the couple to the island. There were cliffs at the far end, to the south, where sea birds nested. Puffins would be arriving soon. They hoped to see some.

The land levelled out as the boat pulsed its way steadily southward. Soon it turned grassy green with rocks and sandy beaches edging the shore.

"Could that be it?" The woman pointed and passed the binoculars to Elspeth.

A long, white beach formed a sweeping curve. The land rose at the north end, closest to where the boat was passing and a spit of land jutted out into the water, rocks at the end, waves rolling against them, throwing up sea spray. A stone pier had been built out from it. The house was up above, whitewashed stone with a dark grey slate roof, the windows set deep into the walls. Apart from those, it was plain and rectangular, as Elspeth's mother had described, two windows downstairs, one bigger than the other, three upstairs. Those reached to the roof, with gables arched over them. There was a chimney stack, with four chimneypots. No door was visible on that side, the one that faced the water. A stone wall enclosed the house, a wooden gate facing the sea. An outbuilding stood on the north side and she could just see the edge of another at the other end. It conformed to what she had seen on the Google map.

"The islanders call it the Skipper's House," she told the couple.

"You're very fortunate to have it," said the German woman.

Before long, they approached another bay, one that cut deeper into the island. An announcement, in English and Gaelic, told all drivers to return to their vehicles and her travelling acquaintances hurried off to their motorhome.

Some buildings lay around the harbour. Torbost was the island's closest thing to a town, more like a village, just a cluster of buildings, scattered around an inlet. There was a harbour wall, built of old stone, stained green with weed and moss up to high tide level. It looked like it had been there for centuries. The boat drew into a large pier where cars could drive off. Elspeth walked out onto dry land and dragged her carry-on bag toward a building with a sign that said "Harbourmaster," with the same written in Gaelic.

A woman waved to her from beside an old white van.

"Hello!" she called as Elspeth drew nearer. "I'm Cath! Calum sent me a message this morning telling me what you looked like so I knew it must be you. Welcome to Sulla! Let's get you to the Skipper's House. You must be dying to see it."

All the roads on Sulla were single-track. There were passing places, where one car could pull over to let another one through. There didn't seem to be any rule as to which should give way. "Och, we manage," said her driver. Elspeth sat in the passenger seat, the opposite side from what she was used to. Flat green land lay inland, dotted with sheep. On Cath MacKinnon's side there was blue water that stretched over to the hills of Mull.

"Terrible thing, what happened to your aunty," Cath MacKinnon said. She had the same soft accent as Calum McFee. "I know she was getting on in years but we didn't expect her to leave us just yet."

A small van was approaching. It tucked itself in to a passing place up ahead. Cath drove past and each driver raised a hand in greeting. The man in the van watched over his shoulder so he could get a good look at Cath MacKinnon's passenger.

The road bent and curved, following the shoreline. More sparkly blue sea, a glimpse of white sand, hillier land up ahead. Not a tree in sight. Or fencing. Elspeth could see a building across an open field, some black cows grazing near it.

"Those belong to the MacPhails. Your neighbours," she was told. So there were still members of Alasdair MacPhail's family living here.

She knew it was Deirdre MacPhail's house the minute she saw it. There was no driveway but worn tracks ran across grass towards a wooden garage built at the side of the house. A solid stone wall ran all around, with a double metal gate. A small brown dog sat beside it.

"Wilma, is that you!" Cath MacKinnon stopped the van and got out. The dog came to her with a slow wag of her tail. "This is Deirdre's dog," she said. "She got her from us when she was a pup and we said we'd hang onto her until someone can give her a home but she keeps wandering back. Maybe you could keep her, now that you're here?"

"I'm only here for four weeks." Elspeth liked dogs well enough but she couldn't keep this one.

"That's all? But aren't you going to be here for the book festival?" Cath had pulled the car onto the verge of the road. "There's going to be a big send-off for Deirdre at it."

"I can't. I've got to get back to Canada." Elspeth retrieved her bag from the van and followed her through the gate. The dog raced past them to the front door and waited to get in.

Cath handed her a heavy metal key.

"You can open it yourself," she said. "After all, it's your house now."

The lock slid smoothly and Elspeth stepped inside. Cath threw a switch and the hallway was illuminated with coloured light. The central lampshade was made of stained glass, red, white and blue. A flight of stairs rose at the end of the hall and turned halfway up. A window above it was made of the same colours. Wilma bounded up there and sniffed around.

"That's where Deirdre was lying. Wilma watched over her for two whole days."

"Who found her?" Elspeth asked.

"I did. She usually dropped by to get milk and I hadn't seen her. She wasn't answering her phone so I came by. It was a shock, I can tell you."

A row of coat hooks, hung with jackets and coats, ran along a wall. There were plenty of them. Elspeth might find a rain jacket that would do. A hallstand held sticks and umbrellas. She needn't have bought one. A rack was filled with shoes and boots, all too big for her. Pictures hung on the walls, some hangings, too, all apparently Asian. A long narrow wooden chest that looked like it might be Chinese doubled as a bench. The floor was varnished wood and was covered by an Indian rug. The dog had flopped down on the landing and was staying there, not budging.

"It's a fine house. You're lucky to have it." Cath MacKinnon hovered by the door. "I've left milk and eggs in the fridge. You'll find food for Wilma in the pantry."

"I can't keep her," Elspeth protested, to no avail.

"Och, she'll be no bother. She likes being home and it's just while you're here. I've left you a map of Sulla that we give to visitors. You've got my phone number. Lachie and I live only minutes away from here if you need anything."

She left and the door closed behind her. Elspeth and the dog looked at each other. She had once wanted a dog but had never had one. Her mother had refused to buy a puppy, then work had taken Elspeth away from home and Dave was busy with his own job. Now she might have inherited one that she couldn't keep. She walked through a door into a kitchen. It was time to find out for herself what else Deirdre had left her.

6

A long wooden table stood in the middle of the kitchen, a plate of scones covered with wrap on it, next to the promised map, and jar of jam that looked homemade. Cath MacKinnon must have left all of those. There were eight chairs around it, wooden ones with straight backs. The stove was electric and there was a small fridge. Elspeth looked inside. The milk came in a plastic jug, the eggs were in a bowl and there was a slab of butter wrapped in waxed paper. Another bowl held a white mass. It looked and smelled like it might be homemade cheese.

A large, carved wooden dresser almost filled a wall. Its shelves displayed crockery, mugs, plates, bowls. Some of them looked old but most were contemporary pottery. A door led outside to the garage at the side of the house. Inside it she found a car, a blue Volkswagen SUV. It looked in good shape. If she found the key and a licence she could maybe drive it. A path between the garage and the house led to a gate.

She stepped through it. Green grass dotted with tiny daisies stretched to the wall she had seen from the boat, then continued out to the shore. The land jutted out to the sea, a stone pier stretching into the water, and the beach swept away to the south. Far opposite her was Mull, in shades of blue. There were islands off its shore. Staffa. Iona, further south, indistinct because of the distance, then a vague shape that must be Islay. Otherwise, the distant horizon was flat. It wasn't unlike being on the prairie, especially near Manitoba's big freshwater lakes, but the sea moved differently. It had a heavier swell and the air smelled briny.

There were no other houses visible. Solitary houses were nothing new to Elspeth but prairie farmhouses were always surrounded by stands of trees, willow and spruce, to protect them from the winds. Here, there wasn't a single tree to be seen. This house stood bare and alone against the elements.

She went back inside. The kitchen had a fireplace, a screen in front of it with storks painted on it. Chinese, she thought. The fire didn't look like it had been lit in years but there was a white space heater against a wall. Elspeth pushed the big British plug into the outlet beside it and turned it on. It was cold and damp in this house. She kept her jacket on while the room warmed up.

A big enamel sink sat near a window, recessed into the stone walls of the house. The rooms were smaller that she had thought. She could see why. The outside walls of this house were at least three feet thick.

There was another door at the opposite end of the kitchen. It led to a well-equipped utility room that must once have been a pantry. It held a washer and dryer, a dishwasher, a water heater. Appliances were ranged on shelves. Others held pots and pans, canned food, including dog meat. Bottles of alcohol, gin, vodka, Bowmore whisky and a couple of other brands sat on one. There was a big bag of kibble on the floor. Wilma would not go hungry. Cleaning equipment lay at the far end. A Dyson vacuum sat beside a small freezer. Deirdre had not skimped on conveniences.

Elspeth went back out to the hallway. The dog still kept vigil on the landing, her pink tongue lolling, little furry paws poking over the top step. Elspeth chose not to disturb her. She went through another door that led into a sitting room. The walls here had been painted dark red, the trim a contrasting white gloss.

The fireplace held a large porcelain vase filled with peacock feathers, fanned out to fill the space. Above the mantel was a large painting of Deirdre when she was young, fair and long limbed, looking directly at the viewer, the corner of her mouth lifted in a sexual tease. Behind her was a stormy sea, a boat being tossed around on the waves. She lay, almost nude, on a Victorian sofa with gold and brown upholstery. The same sofa was still in the room, but now it was covered in studded dark blue velvet. Elspeth peered at the signature on the painting. MacPhail, of course, and a date: '71. Deirdre's husband had painted it more than fifty years ago, a year before he died.

She walked over to a large chest with wide, flat drawers and pulled one open. In it lay a kimono, yellow silk, with flowers and birds painted on it. Other drawers contained sari silk. Pieces of lace. Folded linen. A woven Indian rug almost covered the floor of the room. It was hand-knotted, so well made that the colours had barely faded. If Calum McFee was right, it had been made to fit this floor a hundred years ago.

The curtains at the window were of heavy silk. Framed Buddhist icons, pictures of mountain peaks with little men climbing up them, a goddess with a blue face and many arms, examples of calligraphy, hung on the walls. Elspeth didn't know much about Asian art, but these were obviously of good quality. Calum was right. She'd need to get in touch with an auction house that specialized in antique art. There must be one in Glasgow. Carved wooden cabinets ranged the walls of the house. They were full of objects. Figurines, dishes, bowls.

She ventured upstairs, past the dog, dozing now. West African masks hung on the walls of the upper landing. One of the four bedrooms had folding fans arranged above the bed, in rows of semi-circles. Most of them were hand-painted with flowers or birds.

The largest bedroom faced the sea. The bed had a purple cover, a mirror sat on top of a dresser, the wardrobe was huge. The room smelled faintly of perfume and tobacco smoke. It must have been Deirdre's bedroom. Elspeth felt like she was intruding. She glanced around then closed the door behind her. She'd sleep in a different room. The one across the landing that also looked out seawards had a bed that had been stripped. It didn't take long to discover a dresser full of folded bed linen.

The bathroom was new, a complete surprise. A shower stall equipped with a powerhead filled a corner. The sink had elegant curving taps. A large movable cupboard was stocked with toiletries and towels. A heat lamp hung from the ceiling and the towel rack had a plug attached, so it could be warmed, too. Deirdre had chosen to retain a big claw-footed bathtub, but it had been restored. The inside was pristine, the outside, sunshiny yellow. Elspeth promised herself a good soak, later.

She stood at the top of the stairs. The window facing her looked like it had been made by the same glassmaker who had built the lampshades, upstairs and down. A carpet ran down the wooden stairs, securely fastened by polished wooden rods that ran across the bottom of each riser, each held down at the end by metal clasps. Elspeth remembered seeing ones like those in her grandmother's house, forty years ago. Two narrow hand-knotted rugs ran the length of the landing, one in each direction. They met at the top of the stairs. Deirdre must that tripped on one of them when she fell. They were loose. It would be easy to catch a toe on one of those. Dangerous, Elspeth thought, especially for a woman in her eighties.

There were only eight treads down to the turn on the stairs. A large oriental vase stood in the corner. It wouldn't take far to fall and break a vertebra. Death would have been instantaneous. Elspeth reached down and patted the head of the small brown dog who now looked trustingly up at her, the one who had waited patiently beside the body until help arrived. "Good dog, Wilma," she said. Wilma rose to her feet and followed her down the rest of the stairs.

The room where Deirdre had written her books was on the main floor, opposite the dining room. It stretched the full length of the house, two rooms knocked into one with an archway dividing them.

There was nothing of Skipper MacPhail's in this room. It belonged entirely to Deirdre and it was full of books and papers. The furnishings dated back to the sixties, quite different from the dark, heavier, carved wood in the rest of the house. Tall teak shelves lined the walls at the front, a wing-backed chair with a footstool sat by an unlit fire, but there was wood ash in the grate. A dog basket with a cushion lay beside it. Wilma went straight to it and lay down again. A large ashtray sat on a small table, also containing a trace of ash. A packet of cigarettes, a lighter. A book, one by Scottish writer Denise Mina, half open, had been left upside down. Above the fireplace was a seascape in watercolour that looked like the stretch of beach out behind the house, also painted by Alasdair MacPhail.

The other end of the room was where Deirdre had worked. The writing desk was solid wood, as was a shelving unit, filled with multiple copies of Deirdre's books, many binders and notebooks, some with spiral backs. There was an ergonomic desk chair, a large filing cabinet. Elspeth pulled open the top drawer. It was almost empty. The files that were left there were old ones, relating to work. Any recent ones were gone.

The desk lay along a wall with a bulletin board above it, some notes tacked on. There were photographs, of Deirdre receiving an award, a smiling group including Calum McFee with a sign saying, *Sulla Book Festival.*

A large iMac sat on the desk. The top drawers contained the usual office paraphernalia, pens, pencils, Post-it notes, all thrown in together.

The third wall held a dresser, sixties teak again. On it was a printer and an internet router, its green lights blinking. Elspeth sat down and turned on the iMac. It whirred into life but she didn't know the password, or the code for Deirdre's Wi-Fi.

Had the police taken Deirdre's phone? There had been an autopsy and Deirdre's death had been ruled accidental. There had been no need for the investigation to go further than that.

Not having access to the internet was a problem. She searched for a notebook that might list Deirdre's passwords but found nothing.

She went back to the kitchen and found a row of hooks inside the pantry door. One held dog leashes. Another had keys. She recognized a fob to the Volkswagen and went to the garage. The car was a Tiguan, almost new, and it wasn't locked. Wilma had followed her. She hopped in and sat on the front passenger seat, obviously expecting to come along for the ride. The engine started without any problem and the tank was half full. The odometer showed that it had been driven less than 20,000 miles. Elspeth sat in the driver's seat and wiggled the gearstick. This car had manual transmission, but Elspeth knew how to drive standard. Her father had always driven one and he'd taught her how, but that had been years ago, and this stick was on the wrong side for a Canadian driver. So was the bulk of the car.

A garage door opener was hooked to the sun visor. She clicked it and the wide door behind her lifted.

She shifted the car into reverse, eased out the clutch and slowly backed it out. There must be Wi-Fi at the hotel in Tostaig, and it only was a few minutes' drive away. It was tempting to try to get there. Driving on single-track roads couldn't be too difficult. She knew she could drive for three months on her Canadian licence. She could go slow. No one would drive fast on a single-track road and she wouldn't have to remind herself to keep on the left-hand side of the road. Cath MacKinnon had driven right down the middle, on the way here. The glovebox held a copy of Deirdre's driving licence and a packet of mints, but there were no insurance papers. That was disappointing. Should she risk taking the car out? Plead ignorance if anyone stopped her?

She heard a car honk behind her and looked in the rear mirror. A silver SUV had nosed right up to the front gate. A woman got out. She had a shock of white-blonde hair that looked like it had recently been pink, wore a short skirt, leggings, boots on her feet and a black leather bomber jacket.

"Hiya!" she called out, soon as she saw Elspeth get out of the driver's seat. "I'm Annabel McQuarrie. Open the gate, will you?"

Elspeth did as she was bid. The car was driven in and parked in front of the garage.

"Glad to meet you!" The woman got out and stretched out a hand to shake Elspeth's. The dog bounded to greet her. "Hiya, Wilma," she said. Her voice was like that of some of the people Elspeth had heard in Glasgow, sharper, with a different musicality than the one Cath MacKinnon and Calum McFee used. "Cath phoned and told me that you were here. I thought I'd drop by and see if you need help with anything. How's about a cup of tea?"

7

Annabel McQuarrie knew her way around Deirdre's kitchen. She found a canister of tea bags and a jar of sugar in the back pantry. A blue teapot lay on a shelf.

"Deirdre's favourite," she said. "Good you've got the heat on. This house gets chilly."

It had been built to be heated by peat, she told Elspeth as the kettle boiled, then coal had been shipped over from the mainland. It had been banned, long since, but there was still a coal bunker out the back of the house. Deirdre had always chucked bits of driftwood in there so she could have a fire in her den but mostly she had relied on electric heaters like the one in the kitchen. She was only here in the summer, though, so it didn't matter much. Then she got stuck on Sulla, year-round. Heaters like those cost a fortune to run all winter. They'd been telling her to install a heat pump but she hadn't got round to it yet.

Annabel knew how to insure the car. "Easy," she said. "You just need to take out temporary insurance online. I'll show you how."

"I've don't have Wi-Fi," said Elspeth.

That was easily solved. There was internet at Annabel's and she also had an old, unlocked phone that Elspeth could borrow. Calum McFee was coming out on the plane on Monday. They could get him to bring a SIM card with him, then she could have the use of a U.K. phone while she was in Scotland.

But why could she not find the Wi-Fi for the house? Deirdre's passwords should all be written down in a notebook, one with a butterfly on the front, Annabel had seen it often. Deirdre had written all her passwords in it. They went through to the writing room. Annabel called it Deirdre's den.

"She had an old Rolodex. Where's that?" Annabel rifled through the shelves.

"A file drawer is empty, too." Elspeth pointed at the empty space. "I haven't found her phone, either."

"There was an iPad, as well." Annabel sat on the desk chair, her booted feet splayed. In Canada, people removed outside footwear when they entered a house. That obviously didn't happen here. "You know that your cousin was here, middle of last week? Bet he's taken them."

Iain Balfour, she said, had arrived off the ferry with his daughter last Tuesday. Annabel had come right over when she'd heard that he was here. She knew that the house didn't belong to him. Deirdre had told her that she was going to leave it to her niece in Canada. "To you, Elspeth." But Iain had said he was the executor and there were papers that he needed. Deirdre's birth certificate. Income tax returns. That explained the missing files, but why would he need her phone and iPad?

"The girl was seen driving around in Deirdre's car. We wondered if they'd take it with them but they didn't. It must belong to you too."

She clicked on the iMac. "The password's got to be something to do with Wilma," she said.

"Wilma" didn't work. Neither did "Wilma2019," the year Deirdre got the dog, but when she hit "Wilma19" the computer whirred into life.

"Bet she used names like that for everything."

Annabel was right. When they checked available Wi-Fi, "Wilmadog19" showed up. It was that easy. Setting up the car insurance was a breeze. They clicked in the information and Elspeth paid.

"You only need it for a month? That's all you're staying?"

"It's all I can afford," said Elspeth. "I won't see any of Deirdre's money for months."

"But you'll get what's coming from the books, right? Liz Fraser's in charge of all of that. She was Deirdre's agent and she's on the committee for the Book Fest. Talk to her." Annabel tapped her phone, sending Liz's contact information.

Annabel served on the book festival committee. She and her husband, Sandy, ran the café at the other side of the island. They'd made part of it into a bookstore when the festival turned out to be so successful.

"We're having a meeting while Calum's here. You should come."

They went back to the kitchen and ate some of Cath MacKinnon's scones. The home-made cheese was called crowdie, Annabel told her, great with raspberry jam. It was mild, with a slight, tart tang. The dog sat between them, expecting a share.

"You'll be selling?" Annabel asked. She and Sandy helped with house sales on the island. That was why Calum was coming over. They'd just sold an old cottage to a couple that lived in Paisley for more than the asking price and needed to get the sale finalized. "You'll get £400,000 for this house, easy," she predicted.

"You think so?" That was exactly the amount Calum McFee had suggested.

Annabel had taken off her jacket and slung it over the back of her chair. She had tattoos on her forearms. There were silver studs all up the sides of her ears.

"Definitely." She wiggled a ringed finger in the direction of upstairs. "Four bedrooms? That classy bathroom? And the place is built rock solid. The pier outside comes with it, too. There's the beach, right out there? Tell you, someone will grab it as a rental."

Half the houses on Sulla belonged to people who lived on the mainland nowadays, she explained, as summer homes. They rented them out when they weren't here. Prices had gone through the roof since the pandemic. It was too bad for the local kids. A lot of them couldn't afford to buy a house on their own island but it was great for people like her and Sandy. They owned an old house that had belonged to his family. Rented it out. It was booked solid, all summer long.

Elspeth had been right about the accent. Annabel was Glaswegian. Sandy was local and had been at college there when she met him. "We could never have lived out here without tourism," she said. "Sandy wasn't cut out to be a crofter. Farming and tending sheep's not for him, and can you see me milking cows and feeding chickens?" Not everybody here liked the changes that the summer visitors brought to the island but they suited Annabel just fine.

"It was a hard life before," she said. "The land here's mostly what we call machair. Sand and soil, too solid to dig. We used to drive on it but now we're not allowed. Fragile ecosystem, they say. Grass doesn't grow all that high. It's fine for grazing some animals but that's it. And fishing's a tough living. There's folk sit around and moan about the good old days but I'm glad they're gone."

She saw one of Deirdre's books sticking up out of Elspeth's bag, dropped near the door.

"Deirdre helped make it all happen, you know. This island is right off the beaten track. There's no direct plane to Glasgow and you've got to sail right around Mull to get here. That plane that flies in from Oban's a recent thing. There was no reason for anyone to come here until she wrote those books. Once people read them they want to come and see for themselves. Not that it's really like what she described. We're not as cute as she made us out to be." She grinned. "but on a day like this, Sulla's a bonnie place to be."

She fed the dog a piece of scone and crowdie.

"What are you going to do about Wilma?" she asked.

"I don't know. She was waiting here when Cath MacKinnon dropped me off. She'll have to go back to them."

"Lachie MacKinnon won't want her," Annabel predicted. "He kept her mother as a ratter, but Deirdre spoiled Wilma rotten. She's useless as a farm dog. We can't take her. Sandy's allergic. You'll maybe need to send her to the shelter in Oban."

Elspeth looked at the small furry head, the brown eyes gazing up at them. "She seems like a nice dog," she said. "And she was loyal to Deirdre."

Annabel was getting to her feet. "I've got to get back to the café," she said. "Things are picking up on the weekend now and tomorrow's Saturday." She shrugged into her jacket and looked at the map of the island that Cath MacKinnon had left on the table. "See there?" She pointed at a black dot on the southwest coast. "Annabel's Café and Bookshop. Come by anytime. And if you need help selling this place you be sure to talk to me and Sandy first. We'll be glad to help you out."

They walked to the door. Annabel looked at the Asian art and furnishings in the hallway. "You should start writing a list of everything that's in this house," she advised.

"Calum said a valuation person would be coming to do that," Elspeth told her.

"Do one for yourself, before he gets here. You need to know what you've got. Deirdre's insurance might have one, but your cousin could have helped himself to anything when he was here. Taken whatever he wanted and nobody would be any the wiser."

Elspeth watched her unexpected guest drive off and closed the big gate behind her. She didn't think Iain Balfour would have stolen anything. He was an orthopedic surgeon in Edinburgh. His wife was a dentist. They must be well off. And if he'd taken something small from here as a souvenir, did it matter? There was so much in this house that the thought of having to list it all was daunting. That could wait.

The dog stood at her side. "C'mon, Wilma," she said. "Let's go for a walk."

She found a leash hanging in the pantry and hooked it to the dog's collar. A well-trodden path led from a back gate down to the beach, miles of pale sand, no one else in sight. The tide was coming in, a wavy line of seaweed and debris marking how high it would reach.

Elspeth walked along firm, moist sand close to the water's edge, and let Wilma loose. Any neighbours on Sulla would know whose dog she was if she wandered off, she reasoned, but she thought Wilma would stay close. She was right. The dog sniffed along the edge of the beach but stayed nearby.

She found a piece of driftwood and threw it into the water. The dog didn't chase it. She threw another stick along the sand. The dog still preferred to sniff. Up ahead, some smooth grey rocks rose out of the sand. Elspeth walked to the biggest one and sat down.

A boat sailed by. Seagulls flew overhead. It was stunningly beautiful sitting here in the late afternoon, like something out of a tourist brochure. Blue sky, white sand, bluer water. The dog trotted over and lay down beside her. Maybe Deirdre had sat here with Wilma, in this exact spot.

Elspeth wished she could stay longer than a month, but it looked like that was all the time she would need. Annabel McQuarrie would be glad to sell the house on her behalf. She'd probably pack up all the valuable contents and ship them to an auction house too, if she was paid to do so.

Being here for the book festival would be great, but she didn't need to get involved. It was up to the committee to decide what they wanted to do with it. Someone should attend to represent the family at the memorial that was being planned, though. Iain Balfour probably had Deirdre's ashes. He could come and help scatter them, instead of her. She was scheduled to fly back to Canada in three and a half weeks, and she would be on that plane. Go back to Winnipeg and Dave. The thought made her feel tired.

She took photographs of this lovely Sulla afternoon. She'd take more when she got back to the house and send them to Dave and her mother so they could see where she was and what she was going to inherit. Show them that coming here maybe wasn't such a bad idea after all.

She gathered up some driftwood on the way back to the house. A broken wooden box lay in the sand, high above the water line, dry enough to burn nicely in Deirdre's hearth. She'd make up a bed. Have a bath in that big tub. Pour herself a glass of Deirdre's malt whisky and get another decent night's sleep.

8

Elspeth found the dog lying beside her when she woke the next morning. Wilma hadn't been there when she had gone to bed. She had nosed open the door to the room that had been Deirdre's and made herself comfortable in the middle of the bed there. She must have come through while Elspeth was sound asleep.

She went downstairs and let the dog outside. There was coffee and a filter cone in one of the dresser cupboards. Elspeth made a mugful, opened her laptop and checked to see if Dave had responded to her email. There was nothing. Winnipeg was six time zones behind Scotland. He'd be tucked up in his bed, sound asleep.

An email from Iain Balfour, however, was in her inbox.

Heard from your solicitor. Plane ticket etc. may be covered will check with mine. Keep receipts until advised. Talk? Coming to Edinburgh?

The thought of driving across Scotland was tempting. If the cost of her trip was going to be paid for, she could maybe do that. Speaking to him might hurry things along.

Zoom tomorrow? she wrote back.

She wandered into the den and opened Deirdre's desk drawers. One of them was devoted to the Sulla Book Festival and was full of bulging files. She would pass those on to Annabel and Calum. Their committee could decide what to do with them.

She went upstairs to Deirdre's bedroom. What was she to do with all of her clothes? Did Sulla have a thrift shop? Oban? Elspeth didn't want any of them herself. They were all too big, too bright for her. The wardrobe was stuffed, so were the dresser drawers.

Deirdre had liked shoes. There were racks full. She had had long, narrow feet.

A whole drawer was devoted to boxes full of jewellery. Some of it was contemporary, artisanal, big polished stones set in silver. A green pendant looked like the one Deirdre had worn when they met that day in Edinburgh, years ago. Others were made of sculpted clay or beadwork. But there were old pieces too, pearls, amber beads, golden earrings, antique filigree pendants that looked like they could have belonged to Skipper MacPhail's wife. Some of those might be of real value.

Photographs, all of Deirdre, taken at different events throughout the years, hung on the walls. A portrait and a nude, both drawn by Alasdair MacPhail, were among them. Elspeth might keep those. They were small enough to fit in her bag on the way home, if she took them out of the frames. Some items would need to be thrown out. How did you dispose of garbage on this island?

Wilma came back inside and gobbled down a bowlful of dog food. Second-day scones were okay if they were toasted but they were almost gone. There were cans in the pantry, soup and baked beans, but she could use some fresh fruit and vegetables. She would drive that blue car to Tostaig. There must be a shop there. Then she would drop by Annabel's café. She looked at the map that Cath MacKinnon had left on the table. Nothing was far away on an island this small.

Wilma followed her to the car and stood at the passenger door, looking expectant. She stood with her front paws up on the dashboard once she was inside so she could see out the windshield.

Minutes later, Elspeth was driving along the coast road to Tostaig. The sunshine was gone this morning and the sky was grey, the water darker with a green undertone. Elspeth couldn't look around very much. She needed to keep her eyes focused on the single track of road that wound its way along the shoreline. Distances might be shorter, but this was nothing like driving in Manitoba, where country roads ran long and straight. This one was full of bends and turns and the road was narrow. At least this end of the island was fairly flat. All the hills were at the northern end. She'd tackle them another day. They would require more gear shifting.

The shop was easily found. It was near a hotel, a garage across the road. A man stopped fixing a car and stood, watching, in the open doorway, as she got out, wiping his hands on an oil rag. Three men were in the shop, standing near shelves well-stocked with cases of beer and whisky bottles, talking in Gaelic, their hands thrust into the pockets of their dungarees, thick-soled rubber boots on their feet. They stopped talking as soon as she entered, and watched her, too.

She walked up and down the aisles. The shop held everything from hardware to sun tan lotion and food. More boots were lined up at the foot of a shelf. She decided to buy a pair. It would certainly rain while she was here, might later today the way that the clouds were gathering. The only ones in her size were green, and they came with substantial soles, like the ones the men wore. Those would keep her feet dry. There was nothing much on the vegetable racks.

"There'll be more coming in on the boat," a woman called over from behind a meat counter. "It's best to come here middle of the afternoon if you want a lettuce. You must be Deirdre MacPhail's niece? The one that's come from Canada?"

"I am. How did you know?"

The woman pointed to the window. "You're driving her car," she said. "And that's her dog sitting in the front seat. Will you be selling the house?"

"Eventually," said Elspeth. She asked for some lamb chops and put the few remaining apples on the shelf in her basket. One of the men was walking to the till with a half-bottle of whisky in his hand.

"How much will you be asking for it?" he asked, narrow blue eyes swivelling in her direction.

"I'm not sure. I just got here." Elspeth helped herself to some bread and a chunk of yellow cheese.

"And how long will you be staying?" asked another of the men, still standing by the liquor racks. The woman had left the meat counter and gone to work the till. She seemed to be the only person who worked here.

"It's too early to say." Elspeth had picked up enough food to get by for now. She could always have lunch at the café. She needed to get away from this inquisition. "What's the quickest way to get to Annabel McQuarrie's café?" she asked the woman as she began to unload the groceries, wishing she had brought Cath MacKinnon's map with her.

"Well," said the woman, ringing in the price of the boots. "There's a road cuts right across the middle of the island and it's faster but if you're new here and you've got the time, you're maybe best to drive around by the shore. Most visitors do. Not that there's much of a view today. We're going to get a bit of a blow in a wee while." She brought a paper map out of a drawer, the same as the one that Cath had left on the kitchen table, picked up a pen and marked a spot with a cross. "You'll find it right there."

Elspeth paid and left, all eyes on her as the door closed behind her. The man in the garage watched again as she drove away.

The road further south led past farmhouses with chickens wandering around outside. Livestock roamed everywhere, mostly sheep, some black cattle. The walls built around houses, like the one at Deirdre's, must be intended to keep animals out rather than fence them in. Elspeth had to slow down as a ewe with twin lambs wandered down the middle of the road in front of her. A sign outside a long, flat building read "Sulla Eventide Home," then she passed a church with a graveyard at the side. It looked plain and grey, a simple stone building with a small spire.

Three squat, fat houses that looked like they had sprouted out of the earth stood in a row. They had thick walls, like the Skipper's House, and were painted a spotless white. They must once have been thatched but that was long gone. Their deep black roofs reached down to the windows and they all had skylights. Elspeth recognized them as traditional blackhouses. They were featured on Sulla's tourist sites. They must be ancient but the deeply set window frames all looked new. The door of one house at the end was painted orange.

She pulled over into a passing place to let a small pickup drive by. The driver raised a hand in acknowledgement and she did the same. A campground lay up ahead, a scattering of motorhomes in it. The German couple from the boat might still be here, and she must be close to the cliffs they had talked about.

The next sign read "DB Watersport Centre." A big blue shed with a boat launch sat by a small bay. This end of the island was more populated than where Deirdre had lived. There were more houses scattered around on the green grass. She turned north onto the west side of Sulla, and the water changed. Atlantic breakers rolled in. Out there it was ocean, all the way to the coast of Canada.

Annabel's Café and Bookshop was not much further along the road, a parking lot in front of it, only one car sitting there. A wind had risen while Elspeth drove, so strong already that the car door almost slammed itself shut when she got out. The dog jumped down from her seat and trotted straight up to the front door of the café. A man with a round black cap covering his hair and an apron tied around his waist opened it.

"Hello, Wilma!" he said as the dog walked inside, tail wagging. "Come on in, you must be Elspeth." He introduced himself as Sandy McQuarrie. "Annabel's through the back. You'll be wanting to talk to her?"

Two elderly women sat at a table drinking tea and eating cake. Like the men in the shop, they had been speaking in Gaelic but they switched to English as soon as Elspeth walked inside.

"You'll be the niece that's got yourself Skipper MacPhail's house?" one of them asked as Elspeth passed by. The café was small, only eight tables. One end of the room held bookshelves, Deirdre's books prominently displayed. There was a poster advertising the Sulla Book Festival on the wall beside them. *May 16–22. Tickets available. Book your accommodation here.* "You'll be staying long?"

"Just enough to get things sorted out," Elspeth replied, noncommittal.

"And you'll be selling it?"

"I expect so." The two exchanged glances. They had the same blue-grey eyes, the colour, Elspeth imagined, of a wintery sea. Crinkly, pink skin like soft tissue paper.

"Can't think who'll want it," said one. "That's always been an unlucky house."

"Really?" Elspeth asked, intrigued.

"The men who live there all die young," the old woman remarked, matter-of fact, forking up a piece of sponge cake, sandwiched with jam. "Then their wives are left all alone for the rest of their lives, without any children to take care of them in their old age. If I were you I'd get myself back to Canada as soon as you can. You don't want that happening to you." She looked up at Elspeth, clear eyed, like she'd made the most innocent of statements, and popped the cake in her mouth.

"Come on through." Sandy MacPhail opened a door behind the counter, offering Elspeth an escape hatch. "You'll find Annabel in the kitchen." The dog walked right in ahead of her.

Annabel sat at a computer in a corner, the desk in front of her covered with papers and receipts.

"You found us! Grab yourself a seat. I've been on the phone to Calum and he'll bring you that SIM card on Monday. And Liz Fraser's going to try to come here too, so we can get things planned for Deirdre's big send-off. Can you put her up for the night while she's here?"

"She's coming all the way here for a meeting? She doesn't just do it by Zoom?"

"I think she wants to meet you in person," said Annabel.

Sandy came through. "Sorry about that," he said, then turned to his wife. "Chrissie MacPhail's through there, been putting a hex on Elspeth."

"That woman's a MacPhail?" Elspeth asked.

"Married to Norman, that was a cousin of Alasdair MacPhail's. They've got a croft not far from where you are. Don't pay any heed to what she says. She always had it in for Deirdre."

"What did she say?" asked Annabel.

"Oh, the old stuff about the house being cursed," said Sandy. "Now, what will you have? We do a decent latte and I've got a panini maker through there. We don't just serve scones and cake here."

"Sandy's right. Don't listen to Chrissie. She's just trying to stir up trouble." Annabel pulled out a chair beside Elspeth. "Folk on this island used to put it about that Alasdair's aunt Megan who lived there was a witch, just because she was Welsh and she knew things that they didn't. Then Chrissie made sure that rubbed off onto Deirdre. Most people don't believe a word of it."

"But some do?"

"It's just an old superstition. Chrissie's always had it in for the women in your family because they got that house instead of her boys. First Megan, then Deirdre."

"And she maybe thinks she can get the price down by giving the house a bad reputation," added Sandy. "Not that that's going to happen."

"Do you think the MacPhails would want to buy it back?" Elspeth asked.

"They'll never be able to afford it. Chrissie's just doing this out of spite. She's a bad old besom herself. I'd better get back and make sure she's got everything she wants or she'll be turning me into a codfish. Ham and egg with a bit of cheese do for you?" Sandy disappeared back into his café.

9

Annabel had already figured out a game plan for selling the Skipper's House. She knew it would take six months at least to free up Deirdre's estate and sell it, but she and Sandy McQuarrie could help do that when the time came. They sold for everybody around here. They would take photos and post them online. You couldn't send video from here, broadband was too slow, but you could go over to Oban and do it from there. Most houses were sold with the furniture they contained. Shipping sofas and beds to Sulla was expensive. Cookers and fridges, too. If the house was being sold as a second home or a rental, having it come fully furnished was an advantage. With a bit of luck, they could catch the end of the summer season, while lots of visitors were still around, and that was always a good thing.

Annabel had never dealt with a city art auction house before but she was game to try. She knew all about shipping goods to the mainland, though. Together, they could draw up a list of everything that needed to be done, then she and Sandy would take care of everything. Their rate was eight percent, and they would get Elspeth the best price available, no bother.

The McQuarries would do well out of the sale and it would probably be worth paying them to do the work. Elspeth didn't have much choice. She would be long gone by the time that the Skipper's House would be ready to go on the market.

They didn't know when the valuer would put in an appearance. Elspeth might need to prod Iain Balfour about that when she talked to him tomorrow and see if she could hurry things along.

Sandy carried in cappuccinos. He followed them with a panini and salad for Elspeth and kicked the door closed behind him.

"Chrissie and Donalda McFee have gone off home," he reported. "I've locked the door and put up the CLOSED sign."

"That other woman's related to Calum?" asked Elspeth.

"His mother. Calum's from here. I went to school with him." Sandy spoke with the musical cadence of an islander, the same accent that Chrissie MacPhail had managed to use earlier with more sinister effect. "You passed the blackhouses on the way here?" Sandy must have noticed that Elspeth had driven from the south end of Sulla. "Donalda has one on the end and the one in the middle belongs to Calum." The one with the orange door was owned by a university professor from Glasgow called Bernie Baxter who only came for the summer. He'd been big pals with Deirdre and was another member of the book festival committee.

"It's too bad we can't have a sale of the contents of the house when the festival's happening," said Annabel, sipping her coffee. "There's folk coming would love to take home a bit of Deirdre. You should stay for that. The book festival. Meet all the people who knew her. And be here to help scatter her ashes. Come with Liz to that meeting we're having."

Elspeth agreed that Liz Fraser could stay with her at the Skipper's House. She would attend the meeting and find out more about the festival that Deirdre had founded. Staying here until then was becoming a tempting thought. If she could have the cost of her ticket covered, she could maybe do that, but she couldn't promise anything yet. It was another thing to discuss with her cousin.

Sandy joined them at the table. Elspeth ate her way through the salad. It was surprisingly fresh. "I get a box of vegetables over from the mainland most days," he told her.

A paw gently nudged Elspeth's leg. Wilma was a scrounge but she had good manners. Elspeth fed her a piece of panini.

"There's a gale coming our way so you won't be going anywhere for a while," Annabel looked toward the window. "You can get started making that inventory of what's in the house."

This storm would blow out by tomorrow, they assured Elspeth. Calum and Liz would be able to get here in time for the meeting on Monday night. They were looking forward to having Liz here.

She was good fun to have around. The panini eaten, they walked through the café to the front door.

The wind gusted as Elspeth let Wilma into the car. She had thought she might go find the clifftops and take the dog for a walk but she wouldn't be strolling along any of those today. This side of the island caught the full force of gales blowing in off the Atlantic. The Skipper's House was on the leeward side, however. She might be able to take Wilma along the beach and stock up on more driftwood so she could keep a fire going during the upcoming storm. Sandy had told her to ignore online weather reports and check the shipping forecast instead. It was far more accurate. Listen for "Rockall, Malin, Hebrides," he had told her. Living on this island was a bit like being on a giant ship, she realized.

She drove north and soon found the road that the woman in the shop had mentioned earlier. It cut right across the centre of the island and was straighter than the one around the coast. There was small village halfway across, more like a hamlet. Balemartin, a sign said. A line of houses all looking the same ran along the roadside, modern bungalows with two or three bedrooms, unlike the houses she had seen elsewhere on Sulla. The police station stood at the end of the row.

It was beginning to rain by the time she reached the Skipper's House. That walk along the beach was not going to happen. Drops of water blown by the wind stung her face as she secured the big gate. The dog peed quickly then ran for the shelter of the house.

Elspeth retrieved the groceries and her new boots. She fumbled for the key to the door with one hand and opened it.

She noticed the smell as soon as she walked into the kitchen. It was rotten and fishy. She dropped the boots inside the door and laid the bag of groceries on the table. The dog was at the sink, sniffing.

In it lay a large, dead, stinking fish. It was long enough to almost fill the sink. Its eyes were filmed over, its fins were tattered, the skin torn, exposing raw flesh and entrails. Elspeth almost threw up at the stench.

She went to the pantry to look for rubber gloves but all she found was a box of garbage bags. She stuck her hand inside one of them and gingerly lifted the fish by the tail, then dropped it inside another black bag, tied it tight, opened the back door and threw it out into what was rapidly becoming a deluge. She would decide what to do with it later. She needed to think about this.

Had someone managed to get into the house while she was gone, so they could leave this disgusting mess as some kind of gruesome present? Did that person have a key or could they have climbed in through a window? She went to check the one above the sink. It had two framed panes of glass, top and bottom, that latched together and it was unlocked. Had it been like that when she left the house? She had never opened it but she had never looked to see if it was fastened. She walked through the house and checked all the other windows. They were all firmly latched.

She went back to the kitchen window for a closer look. The lock was circular. You turned the catch to lock it and it was loose. It might be possible to slide it around from outside, if you used a thin blade. To find out if that was possible, she would have to venture outside again. Among the coats hanging near the front door was a yellow raincoat with a hood, too big for her but waterproof. She put it on and stuffed her feet into her new boots. Then she searched through the dresser drawers and found a thin kitchen knife.

The rain teemed down, the sea had disappeared into a mass of cloud but Elspeth could hear waves crashing onto the rocks down at the pier. Wilma made it as far as the door and chose to remain inside. The plastic bag with the dead fish in it lay near the gate. Elspeth threw it further away, out onto the grass. She didn't want the smelly thing anywhere near her. She stumbled to the window through the pouring rain and pushed the blade up between the window frames to nudge the lock. Water ran up inside her sleeve but it didn't take much effort to slide it open.

She made her way back inside, kicked off the boots and shook out the raincoat, then sat down at the table. The dog padded to her side and snuggled against her leg. She rubbed the small brown ears, feeling comforted, still shaken by what she had found. Overhead, rain drummed against the slate roof.

She could call the police station, but what would she report? That someone had broken into the house and left a dead fish? She didn't even know if they had climbed in. She looked to see if it was possible to drop the carcase into the sink from the window. It was.

She didn't think she had been robbed. Her laptop lay on the table beside her, untouched, so that wasn't the motive. This looked like it had been done to scare her. To send her a message. To tell her that she didn't belong, that she wasn't welcome here.

Who knew that she was living here, and that she had gone out for a while? The three men in the store and the woman who had served her. The man in the garage opposite. Chrissie MacPhail and Donalda McFee. Who might they have talked to? Between them all, they could be related to half the residents of this island. It could have been anyone. Internet connection might not be very good here but Elspeth had little doubt that news still travelled around Sulla quite efficiently.

She didn't want to sleep in this house, knowing that anyone could climb in the window, whenever they liked. She could check into the hotel, but what would she do about Wilma? Then, she realized, whoever had done this would know that they had succeeded in forcing her out. If she found a hammer and nails she could make sure that window was firmly shut.

There were no tools in the pantry or the garage. Most likely, they were in the big shed that stood at the other side of the house. Reluctantly, she donned the yellow raincoat and rubber boots once more.

The wind snatched the front door out of her hand the minute she opened it. It slammed back against a stopper on the floor. Elspeth put her head down, dragged the door shut again and ran toward the shed. Her hood was blown off by the time she was half-way across the grass. Rain blinded her and within seconds her hair was soaked, but she staggered her way to the shed door. It was on the east side, fairly sheltered from the wind, and it was unlocked.

Inside was a workshop, an old one with old hand tools, not a power saw or electric drill in sight. Clamps were fastened at the end of benches. Planers were arranged according to size. So were screwdrivers and saws that hung on the walls. Lumber of various sizes was stacked against a wall.

Part of Elspeth's job as a stage designer was to provide theatre companies with a maquette of the set, built to scale, so they could see what the end result should look like, in miniature and to scale. She could handle tools and wood. Fixing that window so it wouldn't budge wasn't going to be difficult. She found a strip of wood and a saw, cut two small pieces and put them in her big raincoat pocket along with a jar of nails, then she lifted a hammer down off the wall and sloshed her way back to the house. Ten minutes later, the window was nailed shut.

She towelled off her wet hair and sat down again, back inside the house. Now that the window was firmly closed, she could breathe easier, but she was alone. It would help to talk to someone. The two people on Sulla that she knew could not be responsible for this were the McQuarries. She messaged Annabel to let her know what had happened. Within a minute, Annabel phoned her back. Was Elspeth all right? They could come and get her and she could stay with them, if she liked.

"I'm okay, now that the window's shut," Elspeth replied. "All the rest are closed tight. How many people knew how to get into this house when Deirdre lived here?"

"The MacKinnons always have a key, but it didn't really matter. She didn't lock her doors."

"With all the expensive things that she had in the house?" Elspeth was shocked.

"Deirdre didn't care. She had this thing about what she called 'authentic island life.' Her idea of how things should be rather than what really happens out here, but that was Deirdre. In the old days, when she first came here, nobody locked up, but now, when the island's crawling with visitors, risking it's kind of daft. In the books she wrote, no one locked their doors, so she didn't either. It's not the first time anyone's left a nasty present like that, either. Someone nailed a dead cormorant to her front door last year."

"Why would they do that?" asked Elspeth.

"Because they wanted her to go away."

"Was it the MacPhails?" Elspeth remembered how Chrissie MacPhail had told her the house was unlucky.

"Maybe. But it wasn't just them that didn't like Deirdre. Whenever there's son or daughter that has to leave because they can't afford to buy a house here, people start moaning about how all the changes here have ruined island life and sooner or later one of them decides that she was the person to blame. Sometimes they told her that to her face. It didn't work. She just dug her heels in some more and laughed in their faces. She did think that Rob MacPhail had left the cormorant. He shoots them so his mother can make soup. It's an old island delicacy. That and salted gannet."

"Who's Rob MacPhail?"

"He runs the garage. Chrissie and Norman MacPhail's younger son." Elspeth remembered the man standing at the garage door in Tostaig, glaring in her direction. "Chrissie tells folk that the Skipper's House would be his if it had come back into the family. He lives in a flat behind the garage. Good mechanic, though."

"If he shoots birds, he must have a gun."

"Well, yes. A shotgun. Lots of crofters do, in case they have to get rid of a sick animal. They're all registered. Look, nobody else is going to drop by while this wind is blowing, They'll all be staying home until the morning." Annabel reassured her. "This is just mischief. Done to annoy you. So, someone's not pleased that you're here but a rotten fish is not going to kill you. That's what Deirdre would have said."

If anything went badly wrong, Elspeth should call her or Sandy. But it wouldn't. Outside, the wind howled and rain battered the windowpanes. Nobody would be going anywhere on Sulla until this gale blew itself out.

10

The storm howled around the house for most of the night. In the morning, rain still bucketed down but the wind had dropped. Outside was a grey blur. All the heaters in the house were turned on and Elspeth was safe and warm inside. She wasn't planning to go anywhere. Wilma didn't stay outside any longer than she had to. She was happy to be inside, too. It was the perfect morning to do as Annabel had suggested and start making an inventory of the contents of the house.

That, however, was a massive task. Elspeth began at the top of the house. She took notes and photographed pieces of furniture that she thought were interesting, the cabinets, wooden chests, chairs with intricate carving on the legs and backs. There were only two or three items like that in each room. She would go through the contents of drawers and cupboards later and list them in detail.

Two rooms had carved wooden screens with painted panels. Both looked Chinese. She snapped shots of the fans on the bedroom wall, the framed Hindu and Buddhist iconography on others. The blue goddess with many arms. A red Buddha. Each of the West African masks that hung in the hallway. Captain MacPhail must have travelled through Suez and down the coast of Africa to India, then out to China and Japan to have amassed such a varied collection

Hand-knotted rugs lay throughout the house. They must all be valuable. Elspeth should record their size but she didn't have a measure. She'd go look for one in the shed, later, when it wasn't raining so hard. She stood at the top of the stairs and looked down. The stained-glass window in front of her didn't let in much light on a gloomy day like this, but when the sun shone, it would be different. She turned on the switch and a matching lampshade illuminated the place where Deirdre had died in colours of gold, red and blue.

She went into her aunt's bedroom. Again, she only listed and photographed the large, imported items of furniture. The clothes in the wardrobe were probably worth little. The jewellery was another matter and there was a lot of it. She would leave that for another day as well.

She heard the Facetime ringer on her laptop downstairs. Iain Balfour was calling, barely visible and hardly audible, but enough for her to see that he'd grown into a larger version of the boy she remembered. He'd inherited her mother's long Balfour bones, and the fair colouring that they had also shared with Deirdre. What had changed was his hair. Now he was bald and what was left was shaved to almost nothing.

This connection wasn't going to work, she barely heard him say. He'd try Messenger, on audio, instead. His voice suddenly became clearer, but his face disappeared from view. He'd been surprised to hear from her solicitor. Why hadn't she got in touch with him herself, he asked? They could talk, like now. Surely they could sort things out between themselves? Weren't they cousins, after all?

"I don't have a U.K. phone yet. I might by tomorrow. I'll let you know." She wasn't sure what to say about the lawyer question. Calum McFee had offered to help and it had seemed like a good idea, so she'd gone for it.

How were things going on Sulla?

"Blowing and raining," she replied.

"Just like always." He had no idea why Deirdre had kept that old house. Of course, it had worked to her, Elspeth's, advantage in the end. Who would have imagined that it would ever be worth what it was now? She was going to do quite nicely out of this. Better than him and his brother.

The valuer was almost done in Edinburgh. She could expect a visit on Sulla in the next week or two. A solicitor in Edinburgh was taking care of things for him. "A good lad. We played rugby at school," but it was easiest if any questions came straight to him. He'd get legal advice if it was needed.

He and his wife might keep Deirdre's flat in Edinburgh for a year or two. His daughter, Shona, was attending medical school and was ready to leave home. They could rent it to her and a couple of her friends during the school year and to visitors during the holidays. Ewan, his brother, in Australia, had said he'd be happy to sell his share of it to them.

He assumed Elspeth would sell that old house on the island, also. How was she managing with all that clutter inside it? A couple called the McQuarries might help her with that, she told him. He remembered Annabel McQuarrie.

"That's the Glaswegian with the pink hair? You think that's a good choice?" he asked.

"I haven't made up my mind. I'm checking my options. I only got here a couple of days ago," she reminded him.

"We won't have to deal with much in the way of Deirdre's belongings here in Edinburgh," he remarked. "She was renting out the flat in Bruntsfield for the past few years. All her personal things got moved to Sulla once she started living there permanently."

"But you have some of them. Files from her desk. Her phone, her iPad," Elspeth reminded him. "You were here."

"I needed to have them," he replied. "It was quite inconvenient, actually. I had to cancel two days of surgery so I could go there and back. Getting on and off Sulla isn't always easy, as I'm sure you know. The papers are needed, Elspeth." She imagined him explaining procedures to his patients in the same condescending manner. "So is all her contact information."

"But we need to know who Deirdre was talking to. The book festival is happening. Her business is still active. Her agent and her publisher might want to know what she was working on before she died."

"Ms. Fraser is welcome to get in touch with me any time," said Iain. "And she'll be able to walk you through anything to do with Deirdre's book business. You should come to Edinburgh and meet those people while you're here."

"There's a lot to do on Sulla," Elspeth reminded him. "But it's been suggested that I should stay for the book festival. That's why I'd like to get the money back for my plane fare as soon as possible. I'm going to need that extra cash to help pay my way if I'm going to stay an extra month."

"I can only cover necessary expenses, Elspeth." Iain Balfour's voice took on an unctuous tone. "You can't extend your stay indefinitely and expect the estate to cover it."

"I'm not," said Elspeth. "But being here for the memorial in her honour is important, don't you think? I'll aim to leave shortly after that. Are you going to be here for it? You have her ashes, don't you?"

He didn't think he could. His schedule was busy. Surgeries had been backed up because of the pandemic. They hadn't cleared the backlog yet and he owed it to his patients. However, if Elspeth sent him a copy of her plane ticket he would reimburse it.

"There's a train ticket too, and the ferry and an Airbnb. I had to stay overnight in Oban."

"Yes, yes, yes," he said.

"How exactly did Deirdre die?" she asked before he hung up.

"Two broken vertebrae in her neck," he said. "Severed the brain stem. She'd have gone instantly." The cremation had been a quiet affair, since so few of the family were still living in Scotland. He'd leave it to Elspeth and Deirdre's literary friends to do the honours at the book festival, he said. He sounded relieved that he didn't have to put in an appearance. Elspeth wondered if that was why he had agreed to reimburse her expenses so readily.

The downpour outside had become a drizzle and Wilma decided to venture out again. Elspeth let her out the back of the house. She could see the black garbage bag containing the fish lying out on the grass where she had thrown it. There was a green bin near the back door, and a blue one, next to a wooden box, the one Annabel McQuarrie had called a coal bunker. She could toss the bag into one of them, but how often was there a pickup? Wouldn't it stink even more? Attract flies?

The dog trotted back in and shook herself. Elspeth was sprayed with rainwater.

Now that she knew that she would have some extra cash, she could stay here as long as the end of May, when the book festival happened, but did she want to do that, if she was so unwelcome here, on Sulla? She needed to think about that.

Meantime, she should get back to the inventory, she realized. Not get distracted. It would help to get focused on that job, but she'd barely started again when a knock came to the front door. A woman opened it and stuck her head inside.

"Hallo!" she called. "I'm Jan MacLeod. Can I come in?" It wasn't really a question. She was peeling off her raincoat already. She laughed when she saw the dog. "So the MacKinnons managed to park Wilma on you, did they?"

She'd talked with Annabel McQuarrie that morning, and heard all about the dead fish. That was why she had come over, to make sure that everything was all right.

"I think so," Elspeth assured her visitor. She had nailed the window shut, but how was she supposed to get rid of the carcass? Rubbish got taken away once every three weeks, and they'd be by this Wednesday, she was told. All Elspeth had to do was leave the bin at the gate.

Jan was younger than Elspeth. She couldn't be forty yet. She had a shock of red hair, tied back with a scrunchie. Her skin was so light as to be almost translucent, dotted with freckles, and her eyes were the palest blue, her eyelashes almost pink. She'd grown up right here on Sulla, she told Elspeth as they waited for the kettle to boil, then she'd gone to Oban for high school.

"The kids from here still go there," she said. "They live in a residence during the week and come home on the plane at the weekend. I've a daughter. I call her Skye. She's going to Oban High School now. I have to put her back on the plane this afternoon. I hate it that we lose all our children so soon, just because we live out here."

"It doesn't make you want to go live on the mainland?" Elspeth asked.

"Lord, no." Jan's face brightened in an instant. "I wouldn't want to be anywhere else. I was in Glasgow for a while, mind. Went to the art school there. But four years was enough. Skye will be back, never fear."

She prattled on as Elspeth fetched mugs down off the dresser shelves. She'd never thought she would be able to make a living out here on her home island from her art, but here she was. She did stained glass. The window and the lampshades in this house were her work. She collected small stones from the beach and polished them too, then made them into jewellery.

"Some of the pieces I've seen that belonged to Deirdre are yours?" asked Elspeth.

They were, she smiled. Deirdre had spread the word about her work. That had helped during the pandemic, when Jan had depended on selling online. She had barely made it through those years but now people were coming back to Sulla for the summer and sales were improving. She had a craft shop. She opened it on the weekends right now but in the summer she sold every day.

"Tourism's booming out here. We get loads of visitors in the summertime and we have Deirdre to thank for that."

Not everybody on Sulla agreed. Lots of the older islanders went on about the old way of life as if it was a good thing, she said, echoing what Annabel had already told Elspeth, but she remembered how her grandmother was bent with hard work by the time she was sixty. Dead before she turned sixty-five.

"Her heart just gave out. It used to be so tough to make a living out here," she said. "People have always had to leave. The boys went off to sea, like Skipper MacPhail, who built this house. The girls left to find work on the mainland. Whole families took off because there was nothing for them here. The ones that came back, like Alasdair MacPhail did, were unusual and he only stayed because Deirdre wanted to. Then Sulla killed him in the end. At least that was what the old people here will tell you."

"He and Deirdre got the Skipper's House for nothing, didn't they?" asked Elspeth. "And now it's worth a lot of money. Is that why someone would have left that fish in the sink? Just because they're annoyed that I have it instead of them?"

"Could be." Jan sipped her tea. "But don't let it bother you too much. Things like that used to happen to Deirdre too. It's just badness. You know, she wrote about this island like it was some kind of paradise, where people were kind and good and funny and helpful, and sometimes they are, but they're really just like folk anywhere. Sometimes they're nice and sometimes they're not."

"Do you think it's the MacPhails that did it?" Elspeth described how suspicious Rob MacPhail had looked, watching her from the door of his garage yesterday. How Chrissie had said that the Skipper's House was unlucky.

"Rob's not the smartest. Hasn't got the imagination," Jan declared. "That family has an old grudge though, that's for certain. Chrissie could have thought up something like that and told Rob to do it. She's capable of it. My mother knows all about what happened back then." She took out her phone and checked the time. "She's over in the Eventide Home and she won't have gone for lunch yet. The minister from the kirk doesn't show up there until the afternoon on the Sabbath. How about I drive you over there? There's time to hear it from her own mouth."

11

The Sulla Eventide Home was built on a raised patch of land overlooking the sea, a single-storey building that housed only six residents. One of them was Norman MacPhail, husband of Chrissie and father to Rob and his older brother, called Young Norman, to distinguish the two of them. The name went back generations, Jan told Elspeth, like many on the islands. He had suffered a stroke. He sat in front of a TV screen in the lounge, but his eyes flickered in Elspeth's direction when they walked in. He didn't say anything. Norman couldn't speak any more.

Kate Mary MacLeod, however, had all her wits about her and, like her daughter, loved to talk. She just had trouble walking these days. Jan had shared a house with her since she'd arrived back from Glasgow sixteen years ago all by herself with a baby girl. Kate Mary liked living where she was now. She had old friends around her all day and Jan had the house to herself and Skye.

"I could never have afforded to buy it," Jan told Elspeth. "I got lucky, like you did with the Skipper's House. I'm going to inherit it."

"Let's go somewhere quieter, where no one can hear what we're saying to Elspeth," she told her mother and pushed the wheelchair down the hallway to a patio with a view of the sea. The rain had completely stopped by now. Sunbeams shafted down through patchy clouds onto a grey swell of water and seabirds could be seen flying to and from the shore. The cliffs were nearby and the kittiwakes were building their nests, the old lady informed Elspeth, pointing to a white-headed bird with black wingtips that flew overhead. No puffins yet but they'd be here soon, maybe in time for Elspeth to see them. Kate Mary was wrapped up in a blanket. Jan brought a couple of dry chairs from inside the door. It was cool out here but they were well away from prying ears.

Jan pointed to a blue blur, across the water, near the southern tip of Mull. "Over there's Iona, where the first Celtic monks came to from Ireland. Old Scottish kings are buried there. The church is still working. You should go have a look while you're here."

If Elspeth could extend her trip, she might be able to do that.

Kate Mary reached out and clasped Elspeth's hand in hers once she learned why they had come. She was soft-spoken but the look in her pale eyes was penetrating.

"She was a wild one, your aunt Deirdre," she said, "And she loved that house that she's given to you. You should keep it. Come and live with us here, on Sulla. There's no place like it in the whole world."

Kate Mary had known Deirdre for all of fifty years. She knew exactly why there was such bad blood between her and the MacPhails, and she was all too happy to tell. She took her hand back and tucked it inside the warm blanket.

"It was like this. Norman, that's sitting through there, and his dad weren't pleased when Alasdair got Skipper MacPhail's house. They didn't think Alasdair deserved it, that he hadn't worked for it. Alasdair was a painter, you know. Art was just nonsense as far as Norman was concerned. Or his father. It wasn't what men like them did. Farmers, seamen, they knew the value of a hard day's work. They said that Alasdair had gone soft, that he was useless. Not that Alasdair didn't know how to handle a boat, he did. He was a fast learner and one came with the house. He kept it moored down at that pier. That annoyed Norman and his daddy most of all. They'd have liked to have had that boat."

"But Alasdair went out in it and drowned, didn't he?" Elspeth asked.

The old lady leaned towards her. "He did that," she agreed. She spoke in the formal way of someone who has learned English as a second language. "It was a terrible thing. That happened over on the other side of the island, up where the hills are. They found the boat the next day. No sign of Alasdair. Deirdre was beside herself. She said Alasdair couldn't have fallen overboard, that he was more careful than that. And she had a point. It was a calm day when it happened. It wasn't like he got caught up in a squall. But he'd definitely gone over the side and he wasn't a good swimmer. They searched and they searched but they never found him. His body must have been washed right out to sea.

"We did have a funeral of sorts for him. It was hard to do without his body actually being there but we needed to do something. Deirdre had a bit too much to drink at it. She pointed at Norman MacPhail and said he must know what had happened. That she knew he wanted the house and the pier and the boat, but he wasn't going to get them. We shushed her up. It was just the whisky and the grief talking.

"But the very next day, we all heard that Alasdair couldn't be declared dead for years yet. We thought Deirdre would leave and go back to Edinburgh but she said that she was going to stay. The house was still hers and always would be because Alasdair had left everything to her in a will. We were surprised that he had written one. He was still a young man. Anyway, it was true. I was told that both Norman and his dad stomped out of the pub the night that somebody told them about it. The MacPhails thought that Deirdre and Alasdair would have bairns of their own and it would eventually get passed on to them, that the house would stay in the MacPhail name but that's not what happened. Now it had gone to a woman who wasn't even an islander.

"Not long after that, people started saying that Deirdre herself must have killed her husband." She turned that same piercing gaze on Elspeth, her eyes the same pale blue as her daughter's.

"They said she was responsible?" Elspeth asked, in disbelief.

"She could have been. Deirdre often went out on the boat with Alasdair. Men like Norman and his father didn't approve of her doing that. They used to say that women on boats were bad luck. And everybody knew that Deirdre and Alasdair argued a lot. We'd all heard them shouting at each other sometimes, when they'd had a few too many. So they said that Deirdre must have got into a fight with Alasdair and pushed him overboard. He wasn't a big man, you know. She was taller than he was. Then she could have swum to the shore. She was a strong swimmer, not like Alasdair. That she must have known that the house would come to her so she had got rid of him. They said that she must have made him write that will. Everybody knew that Deirdre was the boss in that household."

"Do you think that's what happened?"

"No one will ever know, will they?" The old woman smiled sweetly. "Maybe what the MacPhails said was true or maybe Deirdre was right. Norman through there," she nodded in the direction of the sitting room window, "had been out fishing that afternoon himself, with his brother. Maybe one of them got on board Alasdair's boat and that's who pushed him overboard. Who knows? Alasdair couldn't swim much at all. Once he was in the water he wouldn't have had a chance. Or maybe he just slipped and fell, all by himself, and it was all just talk.

"But that's why the MacPhails hated your aunt Deirdre and it's also why she hated them right back. She said she knew they were trying to force her out of the house but she made sure they never got it. And then she left it to you, didn't she? Made sure that the MacPhail family would never get it back. Would you sell it to them, if they came asking?"

"I don't know," said Elspeth.

"Never fear." The old lady smiled again. "They don't have that kind of money. Norman and his dad were both drinkers. All they have left is that croft that Young Norman is living on now and he and his wife have got Chrissie to put up with, as well. She lives right there next door to them." She untucked her hand and gave Elspeth's a reassuring pat. A bell rang. "Time to have my dinner," she said. They wheeled Kate Mary to the dining room and left her waiting for her soup.

Jan had time to drive Elspeth back to the Skipper's House then she needed to get home before Skye needed to be driven to the airport. She couldn't stop for lunch, but Elspeth should come by and see where she lived, any time.

"It was just a bad rumour, but stories like that stick," she said about what her mother had said. "My dad always thought the problem was the pier. The MacPhail croft is inland. That was the only mooring that the family owned. They had it to themselves most of the time that Megan MacPhail lived there, and they had the use of the boat, until Alasdair got it. Norman, the one that's in the home beside my mum now, kept another boat there, too, but it wasn't as good as the one Alasdair had. It's a fine place to have one, it's sheltered by the ness on the north side and it's away from those westerly gales that we get. Deirdre told Norman to take his boat away from there after their big falling out. He had to go pay for a mooring over at the harbour. But then she sold Alasdair's boat, too. It was a fishing boat, a fine craft, my dad said, and she let it go off the island, to someone on Islay. That caused a lot of ill feeling. It had always been a MacPhail boat so they thought she'd had no right to do that."

"What really ticked people off was that the pier was being wasted. You've seen it. It's sheltered and it's always been there. My dad thought that it was a crying shame that it wasn't being used. It wasn't just the MacPhails that thought badly of Deirdre for having done that.

"But she just shrugged it off, like she didn't care. She was fearless, you know. She could be really thrawn sometimes. Not that there was anything for her to really be afraid of. It was just people talking and being daft. There's no real crime happens here. Ask Jackie Buchanan, she's the polis around here, she'll tell you. The worst she ever has to deal with is a Saturday night drunk or a party of visitors acting stupid."

"What, exactly, is people being daft?"

They had reached Elspeth's front gate. Jan stopped the car. "I'm not really sure," she said. "Things like what happened with you and the fish. Kind of a practical joke but not really funny, if you know what I mean. Most of that kind of thing happened a long time ago, when Deirdre was just coming out here for the summer and she was writing all those books about the island. People resented that too. My mum's told me. She was telling their stories and making money off of them. So they did things to annoy her and then laughed about it. Some people thought she was making fun of them in the books so maybe they were just getting back at her. They'd swear they knew who half the people were that she was writing about. Most of it happened before I was born or when I was little. There hasn't been much of that going on lately, not since I moved back here, but Deirdre had almost stopped writing books about Sulla by then. It all quietened down.

"Then it started up again. The year before the big lockdown. You know that window I made for her? The one up above the stair landing? I built that for her because someone threw a stone through the one that was already there. There was a big party going on down at the beach one summer night. The policeman we had before Jackie Buchanan had to break it up. He thought someone from the party threw the stone because he was drunk but Deirdre wasn't so sure.

"There's another story. One night she was driving home from Annabel and Sandy's. She'd been there for dinner and she'd had some wine to drink. She drove up through Tostaig on the way home.

"She swore that someone came up behind her in the dark and forced her off the road, just before she got home. She smashed right into the end of her own wall. She was all right and she didn't want it reported because she'd had a drink, but the front corner of the car was all bashed in and the light was broken. Everybody on Sulla knew about it the next morning, of course. She'd had to leave it where it was. She couldn't drive it. Rob McQuarrie came by and told her it wasn't worth anything and he'd tow it away for parts. So she let him take it and went over to Oban. Came back with that blue Volkswagen that's still here. Not many people on Sulla have that kind of money, to be able to write off one car and go buy a brand-new one. Some folk resented it.

"Everybody said she must have driven herself off the road because she was drunk and made the whole story up. She could have been going too fast, but Annabel says Deirdre only had a couple of glasses of wine that night, and she'd had plenty to eat."

"So what do you think was going on?" asked Elspeth.

"Well." Jan turned off the engine so they could talk longer. "Have you read the Mairi MacIntosh books?"

"Just the first one. I did think she'd borrowed the story from what happened to her husband."

"Of course she did. That book was not long out. She was back to writing about Sulla again and this time she was writing as if murders happened out here. My mother said she was black affronted that she'd do that and give the island a bad name. Make folk think that that could happen here."

"Or maybe someone was worried that she'd tell a story that they didn't want heard," said Elspeth. "And now she's dead."

"No, no, no! She did die accidentally," Jan stated, no doubt in her voice. "The polis said so."

"But did they know that she thought she was being targeted? She didn't report the car crash. The policeman that was here at the time thought the stone that broke the window was thrown by a drunk at a party, nothing to do with an islander. You said so yourself. There was the dead cormorant, too. That happened not so long ago, didn't it?"

"Just last year. After the lockdown. We all thought she'd go back to Edinburgh when that was over but she decided she was going to stay here year-round instead. She told me she'd discovered that she liked winters here. Storms suited her in her old age, and she needed to live on the island so she could keep on writing about it. That was what kept her going."

"Do you think I was being warned off with that dead fish?" asked Elspeth. "Someone wanted Deirdre gone and now it's me?"

"If you're not comfortable sleeping here you can come stay in my house," Jan offered, without a moment's hesitation. "You could go right back to Canada and let the McQuarries take care of things for you once the house can be sold."

"I don't think I am going to do that," said Elspeth. She opened the car door. "I think I'll go have a word with that police constable after all and tell her what's been going on here. She should know that Deirdre was being harassed, and whoever's doing this needs to be stopped."

12

Elspeth let Wilma out when she got back to the house, got another garbage bag from the pantry and used it to double bag the fish, tied it tightly and threw it in the back of the car.

"Sorry, girl," she told the dog as she locked her back inside once more, then drove straight to the village of Balemartin and the police station. She banged on the door and rang the bell until a solid-looking woman with short hair, wearing a skirt and blouse, came out of a house next door.

"Is this something important?" the woman asked, striding down the garden path. "This is Sunday and we like to keep the Sabbath." PC Jackie Buchanan's job required her to be available 24/7, but she was protective of her family life.

"I'll be quick," Elspeth assured her. She opened the back hatch to the Tiguan and hauled out the plastic bag, then she told how she had found the dead fish in the kitchen sink.

"You came here on a Sunday to report that someone left a fish in your house?" Jackie Buchanan asked. Her accent reminded Elspeth of Annabel McQuarrie's. PC Buchanan must have come here from Glasgow or somewhere nearby. Now that Jackie was closer she could see that the skirt camouflaged shorts. Jackie was ready for business in or out of uniform, Sabbath or not.

Right now, her lips twitched like she found the fish story funny. "How long has it been lying inside that bag?"

Elspeth unfastened both the bags that enclosed it and exposed the contents. The fish lay on the driveway still inside the black plastic, rotten and smelly. It was beginning to fall apart.

"Maybe it was fresh when they left it," Jackie said, toeing the bag with a running shoe, worn with ankle socks. "People do things like that around here, you know. They go out fishing and have a good catch, then they share it around and if you're not home, they leave some for you in the sink. They don't expect to find the house locked. Not a good idea, but some of them don't think that's neighbourly. Your aunt Deirdre always left her doors open. So they found a way to get in and left it for you as a welcoming present. First year that I was here, I got home one day and there were live crabs crawling all over the kitchen counter. Someone had heard I liked them and found some in his lobster creel. Left them for me as a nice surprise."

"This fish smelled bad when I found it," said Elspeth.

"You'd been out the house for a while though, hadn't you? Maybe it had been there a few hours already. Smelled fishy enough that you thought something was wrong with it. Then it's been lying outside since then, shut up tight inside a plastic bag? Little wonder it's rotten by now."

Jackie bagged up the fish again. "I'll get rid of it for you, don't worry. Are you selling the house?" And Elspeth's complaint was dismissed, just like that.

A woman in one of the houses a couple of doors along the road walked out and waved, a gardening trowel in her hand. She stopped on her doorstep and watched.

"Probably," Elspeth answered the question. "But not until the fall."

"Doug and I might want to have a look at it," said Jackie. "How much do you want for it?"

"I don't know yet." This encounter was not going as Elspeth had intended, but if PC Buchanan wanted to buy the house, that simplified things. It could be a private sale. And if she came over to check it out, she might be more willing to listen to what Elspeth had to tell her.

"I've got someone coming to stay overnight," she said. "And hopefully I'll have a working phone by tomorrow. How about I call you and arrange a time for you to drop by and have a look?"

"Good idea. I'll tell Doug. See you then." Jackie picked up the fish in the bag and strode off around the corner of the station, holding it at arm's length. Two elementary school-aged children, a boy in shirt and tie, a younger girl in a dress, watched from the front window of her house.

The neighbour was now fussing with some flowerpots beside her front door. She stood up and stretched as Elspeth backed up the blue Tiguan and drove off, so she could get a better look.

Elspeth drove back to the house, got an enthusiastic welcome from the cooped-up dog and decided she had better take Wilma for a walk. Once more, they had the full stretch of beach entirely to themselves. The sky was pink fading to scarlet and gold, a few remaining clouds casting dark patches of purple shadow. The sea was placid, a deep blue, fading to aqua as it came closer to the edge. The tide was out, exposing an expanse of wet sand. There were whorls thrown up by underwater sea creatures. Elspeth, raised on the prairie, had no idea what caused them. Shells and small pebbles in different colours were embedded in the smooth, damp surface. There must be pieces of beach glass among them. Some rocks protruded up from the exposed seabed, covered in weed, forming pools of water. Limpets and mussels clung to their sides.

Elspeth walked along the sand, picking up sticks as she went. They were too wet to burn but she built up a pile higher up on the beach, above the water line, so they could dry, for later. Garbage was washed up as well: a wine bottle, an old shoe, lots of plastic containers and bags in various shapes and sizes, all tangled up in the band of seaweed that stretched from one length of the beach to the other. She wondered if and when it was cleaned up. Maybe she could bag some and put it out with the garbage while she walked on other days.

On an evening like this, she could understand why Deirdre had loved this place. Tourists paid good money to spend a few days here. In the middle of the summer, there would be more people on the beach but she doubted that it would ever be busy. It had to be three, four miles long. Right now, it was quiet, peaceful and stunningly beautiful and she was the only person on it. It was hard to believe that it had been battered by gale-force winds and torrential rain less than a day ago. This island, she was learning, was a place of extremes.

She turned back and looked at the pier. This was a perfect night for a swim. No one was around to see her if she took off her clothes and went into the water, but on this island you never knew who might be watching. The path from Deirdre's house was not well-trodden, but there must be other access routes to the beach. It would be just her luck if someone came by and caught her skinny-dipping. She could paddle, though. She took off shoes and socks, rolled up her pant legs and stepped into the water. It was freezing cold. Two or three steps and she changed her mind about being in the water. She walked along the moist sand barefoot, carrying her shoes.

The window at the centre of the house flashed red as it caught the light. It was the one that Jan had replaced with stained glass. As she walked back to the house Elspeth looked up at it and wondered how it could have been broken from here. There was a fifty-foot stretch of grass between the edge of the beach and the back gate, another fifty feet from it to the house. Was it possible that someone partying down on the sand could have accidentally thrown a stone all that way? The window was quite high up on the house, too. The person who threw it would have had to be as close as the wall, she thought. And why would anyone get that near to the house and throw a stone up there unless it was deliberate?

Could it have been done by a disgruntled partygoer? What reason would someone at a beach party have to come as far along as this? Unless they had gone swimming off the pier, that was a possibility. Deirdre might have yelled at them for trespassing, if they had done that. She did own that piece of land, after all. Jan had said that the police officer who lived here at the time had broken up the party. Maybe someone with a few beers inside them had blamed Deirdre for spoiling their fun and had decided to throw the stone as an act of revenge.

It was perfectly possible. There was an explanation for every one of the odd events which happened here and Deirdre had never acted as if she was in any danger from the people of Sulla or their visitors. She must have believed she was quite safe. Why else would she have chosen to stay? Elspeth was probably just as safe, too. She should worry less. Enjoy what this island had to offer.

When she got back to the house, she found an email from Dave: *Missed you. Sorry. Home tomorrow first thing. Facetime?*

That wouldn't work for her. She'd be in the meeting about the book festival around then.

Can't do. How's Tuesday? Miss you, xx, she emailed back. Then she realized that what she had written wasn't true. She had seldom thought about Dave since she got here.

There was also a message from Liz Fraser, Deirdre's agent. She had arrived in Oban and would be on the ferry tomorrow morning, then would drive straight to Deirdre's house. They could talk over lunch about Deirdre's books, prior to the meeting.

Elspeth had only the vaguest idea of what a literary agent did. Talked with publishers and negotiated contracts, for a percentage of the royalties, she assumed. Certainly Liz would know how much business Deirdre was doing. Sales from the Mairi MacIntosh books might last a little while longer, since they were new.

She scrambled a couple of Cath MacKinnon's eggs for dinner and filled the dog's food bowl, then she wandered through to Deirdre's den. There was so much to dispose of here, most of it personal.

She lifted a black notebook down from its shelf. Inside was a handwritten manuscript of one of the Sulla books. It wasn't dated but it had to be at least forty years old. Deirdre had written in longhand. Sentences were scrawled across the pages, some lines scratched out and rewritten, others with margin notes or words squeezed into the space above the ones already written. She opened another. It looked the same, different story. Each of these must hold the original draft of a manuscript.

Other notebooks were spiral-bound and were more like journals, The one Elspeth held in her hand next contained notes about what Deirdre was writing at the time, descriptions of the weather and of the sea. Of swimming in the water in the summertime. Walking on the beach.

There were lists, lots of those. What Deirdre had found embedded in the sand. Books she planned to read. A whole page about the cliff face where the birds nested and the noise they made. Notes about what she wanted to say at a book festival in Glasgow, where she'd been invited to do a reading.

This notebook was also old, written in the late 1980s, long after Alasdair MacPhail had died, when Deirdre had been churning out one Sulla book after the other, coming here every summer to write.

They had notes in them, too, whole stories written down as she must have heard them, sometimes with a description of the person who had told it, their house, or of the inside of the pub and who had been there the night she had heard it. The speakers were named. MacKinnons, McFees, McQuarries—island names. Elspeth could not see any told by a MacPhail.

Deirdre's Sulla books purported to be fiction. They carried a disclaimer that said so, but after deciphering a couple of scribbled tales, Elspeth thought she must have written them almost exactly as she had heard them. Deirdre had plundered this island for material for her books and these notebooks were the written record of her sources.

She would show the notebooks to Liz Fraser. They might be of some use, to a student, perhaps, who was interested in rural social history? But who would archive them? She counted the spines. Twenty-eight spiral-bound books contained notes. Another twenty-four were solidly bound and contained handwritten manuscripts. They weren't all novels. Some were playscripts. Those interested Elspeth. She flipped through one. It was about a family living on an island, a daughter who had left home and was visiting. The dialogue was lively and entertaining. The scenes she skimmed through weren't at all bad.

She opened Deirdre's computer. The documents contained finished manuscripts, but only a few recent ones, all Mairi MacIntosh books, going back four years. They were the ones she must have written since she had bought the iMac. Maybe she had transcribed them, or she had switched to writing directly onto the computer.

Elspeth went outside and searched in the coal bunker. She found some dry wood and sticks and used them to build a fire, then she poured herself a whisky. She had never finished the Mairi MacIntosh novel that she had started reading on the boat. This was as good a time as any. She settled into Deirdre's comfortable chair, a reading light above her shoulder, her drink on the table beside her. The dog snuggled down in her basket beside the fire, flames burned in the hearth. Deirdre must have done this herself, many times. It was a perfect way to spend what was left of the evening.

13

A red Mini Cooper rolled up in front of the Skipper's House just before noon the next day and tooted its horn.

Elspeth ran out to open the gate. Liz Fraser wound down her window. She filled the driver's seat and more. Her face was a round, pink moon, her eyes cratered in deep crevasses. A little, upturned nose sat above an equally small mouth, cushioned between pudgy cheeks and several chins. She looked Elspeth up and down. "You're Elspeth? You don't look much like your aunt."

"No," Elspeth agreed. "I don't. Everyone keeps telling me that."

The car rolled into the driveway and Liz Fraser clambered out, as wide as she was tall. She lifted a walking cane out of the passenger seat.

"Hello, dog," she said to Wilma, then turned her attention back to Elspeth.

"Provisions are in the back, and my bag." She pointed her cane in that direction. "It's open." Then she began a slow walk to the house, lurching from side to side as she went. Her light beige cotton jacket billowed in the wind over a wide skirt. She swayed like a sailboat out on the waves.

Elspeth lifted the back gate of the little car. There was a grocery bag and a box of bottles. An overnight bag. She lifted the two bags and caught up to her guest just inside the front door. Liz was looking up at the landing.

"I can't believe that Deirdre's gone," she said. Her accent was different again from the ones that Elspeth had heard so far on this trip, less musical, but the way she hit her consonants was distinctly Scottish. She sounded quite like Margaret Laird, Elspeth's mother.

"I talked to her days before she fell and she was fine. I told her those old rugs she had scattered all over the place would be the death of her. We used to joke that she'd go on forever but you never can tell, can you? Are you going to keep the place?"

"I won't get it for another six months," Elspeth said. "But then I'm going to sell it."

"You sure?" Liz Fraser's grey hair was cut so short it made her scalp seemed too small for her filled-out face. The little eyes were keen, like steel bullets. "Look at it. It's fantastic. Deirdre loved it here. This is where she did her best writing. She had plenty time to herself and that big beach to walk on. You could rent it out, you know, when you're not using it and make some money off of it."

"I live in the middle of Canada," Elspeth reminded her. "And I work on contract, for theatre companies. I've been out of work for two years. I could use the cash."

"Ach, well. That's something we need to talk about."

Elspeth left the overnight bag at the foot of the steps. They progressed to the kitchen. She laid the grocery bag on the table and went to fill the kettle.

"Don't bother with that." Liz was rooting around in the bag. "I brought cannelloni and it's time for lunch. Go get us the wine."

The box that Elspeth next lugged back from the car contained wine bottles, an assortment of red and white, brands that Elspeth did not recognize. There was gin, too, and a couple of bottles of Bowmore, Deirdre's favourite tipple. "You brought all this?" she asked, wondering how long Liz Fraser planned on staying, and how much she intended to drink while she was here.

"Always did. Deirdre usually had authors that came to the festival to stay and I expect you'll be doing the same? My contribution to the hospitality budget." She lifted the lid off a container. "Heat this up, will you?" A loaf of crusty Italian bread was placed on the table next and another container contained vegetables in a vinaigrette. Peppers, tomatoes.

Elspeth put the cannelloni in the microwave.

"I might not be able to afford to stay here that long," she said.

"Oh, you will, never fear. Let's eat and I'll tell you how." Liz waddled over to the dresser. She could fetch cutlery from a drawer but she couldn't reach high enough to lift plates down from a shelf. "Get those, will you?" she demanded. "Have you got any butter?"

Cath MacKinnon's home-made slab met with her approval. "Fine stuff," she said. She lifted a bottle of red from the box. "This'll do. Get us down some glasses, as well."

The bag also contained cheese for later— "A nice bit from Orkney and some Wensleydale"—and another container. "Pudding," said Liz Fraser. The box and grocery bag were moved to the countertop and they sat down at the table to eat.

"So, all the money from Deirdre's books goes to you and you get the house and everything in it. Deirdre gave me a copy of her will. Have you seen it?"

Elspeth had not. "Didn't think you would. I made one for you. It's in my other bag. Did you know that Deirdre was making some decent money again? You've read the Mairi MacIntosh books?"

"Just the first one," said Elspeth. "I finished it last night." Liz had cut a generous slice off the loaf and was buttering it thickly. She stopped, hauled herself up to her feet, lifted her cane from the back of the chair and limped to the door.

"Wait right there," she said. She came back and slapped a paperback and an envelope down on the table. "This one's brand new. It's not out yet." She pushed the book across to Elspeth. The rings on her fingers were embedded in flesh. "That's an advance copy. Guard it with your life. The publisher's talking about a release, middle of May, to coincide with the book festival."

Dark Waters: A Mairi MacIntosh Mystery was the title. Elspeth picked it up. The cover art was a watercolour of a fish that resembled a body swimming underwater.

"Why did she switch to writing whodunits?" Elspeth thumbed through the pages.

"Because Tartan Noir is big over here and she wanted to go to Bloody Scotland. As a writer, not just as audience."

"I saw her on YouTube, talking with Nicola Sturgeon," said Elspeth.

"Wasn't that great! It's too bad the pandemic happened. She couldn't do much more in the way of public readings after she got stuck out here, not even online. Reception's shit on this island, but I expect you know that already. She'd have been out and about again this year. Never made it though, did she?" Liz looked into the distance as she chewed, remembering. Then she swallowed and resumed talking.

"She decided to have a go at a detective story about six years ago and set it on Sulla with Mairi MacIntosh as the island's only police constable."

"I've met Jackie Buchanan. She's the policewoman working here now," Elspeth remarked.

"Good, then you know something about that. Deirdre hammered them out all through that lockdown, one after the other. She said that winters here lent themselves to writing about murder," Liz cackled, her little mouth edged in buttery grease, "And the books have taken off. They're doing great."

"But she's dead now, and this book's not out yet."

"No problem. The publisher sent me a message last week. Advance orders are selling gangbusters. It really is too bad Deirdre's gone. There was a whole bunch of book signings supposed to happen, all over the country. Live. She was going to go back to Edinburgh for the big book fest there. Eighty-two years old and nothing was stopping her. And now she's gone."

This time Liz's face puckered up, but only momentarily. She took in a breath and composed herself again.

"You're her successor as far as the business is concerned. The money comes to you but she made me her literary executor, because I know how it all works." Liz scraped the last of the vegetables onto her plate. "You'll get royalties in October."

"Not until then?" That was more than six months away, longer than Elspeth had expected. She might have to wait for that money, as well.

"Aye, but there's also the TV rights." Liz reached for the wine bottle. "Deirdre signed off on optioning the Mairi MacIntosh books the week before she died. The money for that just came in. Two thousand pounds per book for six series. That's £12,000. I've got my cut and there's a film agent had to be paid, but here's your share." The envelope slid across the table to Elspeth.

"But I don't get any money from her estate for six months," said Elspeth not daring to hope. "The will's tied up until then."

"The estate is the money she left. This came in after. It's ongoing business income. We don't have time to put everything on hold for months," announced Liz. She filled up Elspeth's glass. "There's decisions have to be made about what happens about this TV series and I'm going to have to work with you on that. Big money coming in. The work continues. Drink up!"

Elspeth opened the envelope. It contained a cheque for £8,400. Her money worries were over. This would bridge her through until she could sell The Skipper's House.

The corners of Liz's mouth lifted in a tiny smile.

"Here's how it works," she said. "Deirdre optioned the film rights to the Sulla books years ago. But those books never got filmed. That happens a lot, you know. They pay a few thousand for the option and then it doesn't happen. However, crime series are really hot on TV right now and there's a production company that thinks the Mairi MacIntosh books will make a killing. They're going full steam ahead. Getting writers together to work on scripts already. They'll be out here scouting around for places to shoot before too long. The cameras will be ready to roll, maybe by autumn. This time next year, for sure. And the minute that happens we get a mighty fat cheque, Elspeth Laird. Three percent of the production budget. So say that goes to ten million, it means three hundred thousand for us. All the work at our end's done. We just have to wait and hope nothing happens to tank the idea before then."

Liz pushed her empty plate aside. "Are you going to finish that?" Liz pointed a stubby, ringed finger at what was left of Elspeth's. "There's sticky toffee pudding for afters."

Any appetite Elspeth had had was gone. She did the math in her head. She might clear £350,000 for the house. And at least half of the TV rights after Liz and publisher took their cuts. At least £500,000. That was more than $850,000 in Canadian money. It was far more than she had ever dreamed of owning.

"Why did she leave all of this to me?" Elspeth held the cheque between both hands, like she was afraid it might blow away.

"Who else was she going to give it to? She didn't want it going to Iain Balfour and his wife." Liz got herself a bowl and filled it up with brown, syrupy pudding, then added a dollop of yellow custard. "They never appreciated her or her books. Iain Balfour's probably never read a word she wrote. I doubt he's ever read any kind of book unless it's to do with work. She was in Edinburgh every winter for most of her life and that lot never paid her any attention. They're lucky they got what they did." She stomped to the microwave, put the bowl inside and hit the timer.

"She said that she liked the little that she saw of you and that's why she left you all of this. You were all caught up in what you were doing that time you came to the Edinburgh Festival and she respected that. It was how she operated herself. She said you always had a bit of a spark in you, even when you were a wee lass. You were fun. And she thought you might be having a bit of a hard time making money in theatre and you could use a leg up. Mind you," she continued, carrying the warmed-up pudding back to the table, "when she wrote the will, she had no idea about the TV deal. That was before the price of houses soared out here, too. The flat in Edinburgh would have been worth a lot more than this place back then, so she probably did think she was divvying things up a bit more evenly than it's worked out. You just got lucky.

"Those TV shows might be a big hit," she prattled merrily on, between sticky mouthfuls. "The company that's doing them has a good reputation and if they take off, sales on Deirdre's books will go right up again. You'll be getting royalty cheques for years, yet. Maybe they'll extend the series. Even if they write new stories, they'll be based on Deirdre's characters and we'll get our cut. It's too damned bad she's dead and gone. She'd have had invitations from all over the place. New York. Australia. She'd have loved it. She might even have made it to Canada. Now—" she'd emptied the bowl in front her "—I'm going to haul myself off upstairs and have a nap before we go to this meeting."

Before she went, she handed Elspeth another envelope from her bag, one that was fatter and bigger. It contained a copy of Deirdre's will.

It said what Calum had told Elspeth. The house and all of Deirdre's property on Sulla were left to her niece, Elspeth Margaret Laird. All proceeds from her literary estate went to her as well and Elizabeth Fraser was to act as her literary executor, for a percentage of those funds. She left small bequests to Iain Balfour's two children and to both of her Australian nephews. Ten thousand pounds was to go to the Sulla Book Festival. Her property in Edinburgh and all other money remaining in her estate was to be shared equally between Iain and Ewan Balfour. Iain was to act as her executor and was to receive three percent of the value of the total estate in compensation.

It had been signed and witnessed ten years ago, when real estate values in Edinburgh had been far higher than those on little, faraway Sulla, when Deirdre's literary output had dwindled and before she had dreamed up any of the Mairi MacIntosh books. At that time, what Deirdre had planned would been an even split, between the three first cousins, Iain, Ewan and Elspeth. That made complete sense, but since then things had changed, to Elspeth's advantage. She could understand why her cousin Iain might be peeved.

14

Elspeth found it difficult to focus on what was being said during the Sulla Book Festival meeting. She wanted to think about how her financial situation had changed, to call Dave right now, to tell him that their money worries were over, that she would make up for the past two years when her income had disappeared and he had supported them both. She was looking forward to telling him that. She wouldn't owe him a single cent any more.

But talking to Dave was not going to happen for now. Liz Fraser would be staying with her until tomorrow. She could have emailed, but she wanted to speak to him. Maybe FaceTime would work; she was looking forward to seeing the expression on his face when she told him the good news.

She had to decide what to do about work, back in Canada, too. The longer she stayed in Scotland the less chance she had of signing contracts for the fall. The pressure to chase up jobs was off, but she didn't want to drop out of sight, either. She liked designing for the stage. She loved the buzz of theatre. She couldn't imagine not working, and she needed to be back home in plenty of time to get that musical theatre production designed.

"We need an artistic director to replace Deirdre," Annabel was saying. "Someone with her kind of clout."

"You think so? She planned everything and hired all the authors already. It's more of a coordinator you're after." Liz Fraser disagreed. "Don't hire anyone full time. Just get someone to help you through this year's festival. You might not want to do it any longer once this one's done, without Deirdre."

"Stop doing the festival? It has to keep going," Annabel protested. "We made half of the café into a bookstore because of it."

"So?" Liz poked at the slab of coffee cake in front of her with a fork. "People still read books. Especially when the internet's as lousy as it is out here."

Sandy McQuarrie was keeping them supplied with coffee and food, but he wasn't part of the meeting. He was working the café. Jan MacLeod sat across the table from Elspeth. Bernard Baxter — "A great pal of Deirdre's" — was on Zoom, from Glasgow, a history prof, looking the part with thinning white hair and steel-rimmed glasses, books ranged on shelves behind him. The picture on the screen came and went. "This festival must be all about Deirdre," his voice wobbled into the room. "We need to focus on that. We can decide afterwards if it's worth continuing."

"We need to get the cash that Deirdre left for the festival." Liz washed down a chunk of cake with a mouthful of latte. "It's ten grand."

"That much?" asked Jan.

"Enough to pay for a coordinator," said Liz, "and a bit more."

"I don't think you'll see that money any time soon." Calum McFee shook his head. He acted as the festival's treasurer. "Deirdre's executor is doing things by the book. But we're okay for now. Deirdre got us some good sponsors and a grant. It looks like we're going to sell out too. The ferry's booked solid, and the campground's almost full."

"How about you, Elspeth? Could you do it?" Jan looked across the table. "Everything's almost in place. I look after all the volunteers. We pay a company to put up tents. Doug Buchanan keeps an eye on that for us. Annabel looks after accommodations and Bernard manages the website. Maybe we just need someone to make sure everything happens when it should and make sure everyone gets paid."

"And keep the visiting authors happy," Liz Fraser reminded them.

"It means you'd be here on the Sunday afternoon, for Deirdre's funeral," Jan added, looking hopeful.

"Is that what it's going to be?" asked Annabel. "A funeral?"

"'Course it is," snapped Liz. "She never had one. Did you know that Elspeth's cousin sent her off to the crematorium without any of us there? Didn't let on that it was happening? Said it was just for family when I got on to him about it. We need to make sure Deirdre gets a proper send-off."

"I know what we should do!" Jan clapped her hands together. "We could put her ashes in a boat and have a torchlight procession, like they do at Up Helly Aa in Shetland. Then we walk from the festival site right along the beach to the pier beside the house and send her out on the water, on fire!"

"No." Liz squashed that suggestion. "She was clear about what she wanted. We're supposed to take her ashes out to where Alasdair MacPhail drowned, in a boat, and throw them overboard."

"It should be Elspeth that puts the ashes into the water," said Jan.

"Or my cousin Iain. Maybe he would come," said Elspeth. Her role in all of this was being decided for her too fast.

"He's still got the ashes, hasn't he?" asked Calum.

"No, he hasn't. I went and got them from him. They're in the back of my car," said Liz Fraser.

"You have them here?" Elspeth asked. "You never said."

"Wasn't the right time. But now you know, you can decide where you want to put them. They were in an ugly box when I picked them up from your cousin's house but I know a potter that makes urns so I got a nice one from him."

'You've got to stay here for this, Elspeth. Take the job," Jan insisted.

"I need to think about that. I'd like to know more about what I need to do before I take it on." Elspeth was inclined to say yes, but she needed to be sure.

"How about we get together tomorrow after you've seen Liz off on the boat and I can tell you how things stand? We could do dinner at the hotel?" Calum McFee suggested. And Elspeth agreed.

Shortly after, Liz buzzed back along the coast road in her little car, a bit too fast for Elspeth's liking. You could smack into someone on a corner driving on single-track roads that wended like these. Never see them coming.

"Where's the urn?" she asked.

"In a box on the floor behind my seat. Where are you going to put it?"

"I don't know. I don't want it where I'm going to be working. Maybe in the sitting room?"

"I gave Iain Balfour a receipt for the cost of the urn and told him I expected a refund." Liz whizzed around another bend. "Can't stand the man. Do you know that he was on the phone to me right after Deirdre was cremated, trying to find out everything about Deirdre's book deals and how much money was coming in? 'None of your business,' I told him, 'Read the will. It's clear. I'm in charge of that and all the money goes to Elspeth Laird in Canada.'

"He wanted it to go into an account that he had set up. Acted all superior, like I wouldn't understand how things work. Patronizing git. 'Not a chance,' I said. 'All I need is for you to tell me when the will has been confirmed. You've got Deirdre's bank statements up until when she died so you know how much money she had. You don't get a penny of what comes in after she's dead.

"I knew what he was sniffing after. He'd just been out here, to get Deirdre's papers and I'll bet he found out about the TV deal coming through. He wanted to lay his hands on that cash. He'd have stuck it in with the rest of Deirdre's estate then he'd have been able to split it between him and his brother and you would have been none the wiser.

"I can't stand folk like him. He's raking in the cash, his wife's doing okay too, I'll bet. Her dental practice is private. They've got more than enough but they still want more. They acted like Deirdre didn't exist for all those years and they expect to cash in now that she's gone? Over my dead body."

They reached the gate to the house just as she finished her rant.

"Are you absolutely sure that I can use the money that's coming in from Deirdre's books right away?" Elspeth asked. "It doesn't have to wait until the will's finalized?"

"'Course you can. You need it, don't you? And that money's going to come to you eventually, so what's the difference? It's my decision." Liz thumped Elspeth's arm with a pudgy fist. "Look, if the lawyers don't like it, all that will happen is I'll get my knuckles rapped. My problem, not yours. Now get out the car and open that gate, will you? And then we'll take Deirdre out of here and find a place to put her."

The lidded urn had a green and blue glaze that reminded Elspeth of the sea.

"Her bedroom window looks out the back of the house," she said. "We can put her there for now, with a view of the pier and the water."

It also meant that she didn't have to look at it. Having Deirdre's ashes so close did creep Elspeth out a bit. She needed some time to herself, too, to think about what had been said at the meeting.

She left Liz Fraser in Deirdre's den, browsing through her notebooks, and walked across the grassy path as far as the pier, Wilma sniffing along beside her. She walked to the far end. Small waves rolled up under her, the exact same shade of aqua as the urn upstairs, the water clear all the way to the bottom, only a few feet down. A school of tiny fish darted by. The sand underneath was dotted with small stones. A sailboat was coming toward her, catching the late afternoon sun, seagulls following its wake. She sat down, her legs swinging off the end of the stony pier. Wilma snuggled at her side.

Having a work contract would make her feel useful again. This one would last almost three months, would take her clear through to the end of May, just in time to go back to Canada and get back to her real job and get that theatre design done. She liked working to deadlines, having a task right in front of her nose that needed tackling. Arranging to get rid of this house and helping out with the festival would keep her busy, if she stayed on Sulla a bit longer.

The meeting with Calum McFee tomorrow would help her figure out what she should do. She realized where Liz was coming from, that she drew income from Deirdre's books as well and she would not want that money tied up for months. Maybe she was right and cash coming in after Deirdre's death could be used immediately, but Elspeth wanted to be sure that spending it was okay. She did need it if she was going to stay. She would get Calum McFee's advice on that tomorrow night too.

She walked back with the dog at her side, the house silhouetted against the blue sky, not a bush or a tree to protect it, just a single stone wall wrapped around its base. It looked bare but strong, built to withstand hurricane force winds, as it had done for generations. Rather like Deirdre herself, buffeted by local criticism but standing up to it and continuing to write the books she had set here on Sulla, regardless.

Elspeth could have all these weeks now to enjoy being here, to get to experience life on Deirdre's island, and if she took the book festival job she would be actively involved. Dispose of Deirdre's ashes. Since she had been left all this money, she owed her aunt that, she told herself.

She found Liz Fraser buried in Deirdre's wingback chair, glasses perched on the edge of her nose, a spiral notebook on her lap.

"Did you know that your aunt was receiving hate mail? Threatening ones?" Liz passed the book over.

The notebook was one of the more recent ones that Deirdre had written. It contained notes for a new Mairi MacIntosh book, one that was already entered into the computer. There were lists of author names. Elspeth recognized Ian Rankin, Val McDermid. She must have contacted them to see if they could come to the festival. Both those two must have declined, they had crosses beside them, but others were marked with a tick, the ones that must have agreed to attend. Elspeth did not recognize any of them.

There were diagrams of schedules. Drafted letters to sponsors—a distillery on Islay had been generous and wanted to have a tasting of their new island gin at the festival.

But there were diary notes, too. Sporadic ones.

Blustery day today. Hope the ferry comes in. Got to take Wilma to the vet. Dinner with Calum. Get cheques signed.

And this:

Another note through the mailbox. Says I should go back to where I belong, before anything happens to me. The entry wasn't dated, but she had started the notebook around Hogmanay of 2019, New Year's Eve in Scotland. Elspeth's father had celebrated that day all his life. Deirdre had been invited to a New Year's party at the McQuarries' and wrote that she was looking forward to it. This message must have been delivered since January of that year.

"There's more than one?" asked Elspeth.

"Look here." Liz had marked another page.

On my windshield this time. "Don't go driving by yourself in the dark." Someone must have dropped by last night after I'd gone to bed. Left the gate wide open and the cows got in. Cach all over my front grass this morning.

"Did she ever say anything? About being scared, living here alone?" Elspeth asked.

"Not a word to me." Liz frowned up at her. "I don't suppose she kept these messages anywhere?"

"I've seen nothing. She must have got rid of them. Maybe she burned them."

"Or someone's removed them," said Liz. "What's the cop out here like?"

"Not very interested." Elspeth explained about the dead fish. "She didn't take it seriously. She acted like it was a prank. Everybody I've told about it has said it's probably someone that doesn't like me being here, letting me know that they want me gone.

"The police can't have seen notes like these. They did an autopsy on Deirdre and declared it was an accidental death. I don't think they ever considered it might have been something else."

"We should check for more," said Liz.

They hauled all the spiral notebooks through to the kitchen table. By the time it was dark out, they knew that there had been incidents when Deirdre had first lived here, when the Sulla books had been at their most popular, annoying ones but not life threatening. Then there had been years when nothing had happened. The notes with the threats Liz had just found were more recent.

Liz slapped the last notebook in front of her shut. "We need to find out if the police knew about these. Let's see what PC Buchanan's got to say about this. First thing tomorrow."

15

Liz Fraser was not going to catch the ferry back to Oban next morning. It sailed just after 11:00 am and PC Jackie Buchanan was not available until noon.

"I'll stay," she announced. "I want to hear what she says." She took her place at the kitchen table and said she'd be on the phone with someone called Inga, from her office in Edinburgh, for most of the morning.

The relevant pages from Deirdre's notebooks had been copied. They showed:

Late summer 2019, the stone through the window.

In October, the note on the windshield.

The same winter, the incident with the car on the way back from dinner at the McQuarries'.

There was nothing else for the next year and a half. "Lockdown," Liz Fraser said. There were two other notes:

May 2022. The cormorant on the front door. A note had been attached to one of its feet that said, *"Haven't forgotten you're still here,"* with a smiley face.

A pile of cow dung had been left on her front doorstep shortly afterwards and another note pushed through the letterbox. *"I'm watching you. Won't be long now."*

Then there was nothing until the day that Deirdre had fallen down the stairs.

"We don't want the police confiscating any of those." Liz had copied the relevant pages and stacked the notebooks back on their shelves for now. She intended to transport them to her house in Edinburgh for safekeeping once the book festival was over. "Once they've got them there's no telling when we'll get them back. Those'll need to be archived when all this is done. Somebody might want to write a thesis about Deirdre's writing," she said, "or commission a biography."

That solved the problem of what Elspeth should do with the notebooks, but she wasn't sure that Liz was right about keeping them from the police. The more evidence they collected, the better. Meantime, she left her in the house, loaded Wilma into the car and went to find the MacKinnon farm. Liz had gobbled through her supply of eggs and butter. Elspeth needed more supplies.

She drove along a road that cut across the island just north of the Skipper's House, hills on the northern side. She still hadn't explored that end of Sulla. It looked pretty and she was used to gear-shifting the car by now. She'd save it for an afternoon after Liz Fraser was gone.

A well-maintained croft house stood in a field, a smaller house beside it, both enclosed by the inevitable walls to keep beasts out. She slowed down so she could look. There was a barn, big enough to house cattle, and several outhouses. This farm looked substantial, well maintained. A man in work clothes walked out of the barn. He must be Norman MacPhail, son of Chrissie, the one they called Young Norman, and brother to Rob. He looked her way but didn't wave. He must know who she was, driving this distinctive blue car. Elspeth checked the time on the dashboard. She had left Deirdre's house two, three minutes ago. The MacPhails were closer neighbours than she had realized.

The MacKinnon farm was almost at the Atlantic shore. It only had one house and a barn. It was rundown in comparison with the MacPhails, and smaller. Cows and sheep were grazing nearby and fat brown chickens pecked at the ground outside. A collie and a brown terrier that resembled Wilma got up from the barn door. All three dogs sniffed at one another, but Wilma followed Elspeth into the house as soon as the door was opened. She had become a house dog and assumed she had permission. The other two stayed outside.

Cath MacKinnon was making small pancakes on a black iron griddle. "Drop scones," she said, "We like to eat them instead of bread. What's this I've been hearing about a dead fish?"

Her husband, Lachie, walked in the door, a lean, wiry man in dungarees and rubber boots. Elspeth recognized him. He was one of the men whom she had seen in the shop at Tostaig. He kicked off his boots. He'd been told all about it in the pub, he laughed, like it was a joke. "Somebody said you've nailed the window shut, too." He sat down at a worn, well-scrubbed wooden table and lifted a knitted cover off a big, brown teapot.

Elspeth declined a cup and the pancakes with jam. How could the islanders know that she had hammered nails into the window frame, unless someone had been by and tried to open it, she wondered, but she didn't ask. She needed more eggs and milk, she said. And butter. She had a house guest.

Cath opened the door of a fridge and took out a big enamel jug of milk, then a bowl of crowdie.

"Are you going to get the McQuarries to sell and go off back to Canada soon?" she asked.

"Not yet." Cath deserved a straight answer. It maybe didn't matter if Lachie repeated everything Elspeth said in the pub that evening, she told herself. "I've been asked to help with the book festival. There'll be a memorial for Deirdre. I'd like to be here when that happens."

"And what's going to happen to all those lovely things in the house? Will you be selling those?" Cath had put a plate of warm pancakes in front of Lachie. He spread one with butter and jam, then spooned a dollop of soft white cheese on top. Wilma the dog moved closer.

"I can't sell the house or anything that's in it for six months because the will is tied up until then," she informed them both.

"So you're going to be staying that long?" Lachie asked.

"I don't think so." Elspeth watched him nod his head as he chewed, absorbing that fact. His face was weathered from hours spent outside but he also had the red veining around his nose of a habitual drinker. The dog sat at his side, waiting, but she wasn't going to get a bite.

"Once the book festival's over I'll be gone. You wouldn't like to have Wilma back?" she asked. "I can't keep her."

Lachie shook his head. “Nice dog,” he said, “but that writer woman spoiled her. Turned her into a pet. She’s useless now.”

“But if I had to go to Oban and stay overnight or go to Edinburgh for a couple of days? Could I leave her with you? I’d pay for her board and bring dog food.”

“We could manage that.” Cath called Wilma over and fed her half a pancake. She obviously liked the dog more than her husband did. “And I can come by and take care of the house for you if you need to be away for longer.”

Elspeth drove back to the house shortly after, food in the trunk of the car and another small mission accomplished.

A police car stopped on the road outside the Skipper’s House at exactly noon. Elspeth offered to open the gate and move the blue car forward to make room for it in the driveway.

“No bother,” said Jackie Buchanan, in uniform, dressed for business. “There’s room for folk to squeeze by.”

“This is the window?” She walked over to it, soon as she’d said hello to Liz Fraser, and shook the casement. She measured the distance from it to the sink and photographed it, from the outside as well.

“I’ll need a statement from you,” she told Elspeth. She didn’t say if she’d photographed the rotten fish before she trashed it and Elspeth wasn’t going to ask. This visit wasn’t going to be about the recent break-in any more. It was about the threats made to her aunt.

Jackie stood at the kitchen table and read the copied pages from Deirdre’s notebooks.

“I heard about the stone through the window,” she said, “but I was never told any of the rest of this.” She pulled out a chair and sat down. Liz was already seated opposite. Elspeth joined them.

“You know that a lot of practical joking happens on islands like these,” Jackie told them. “It’s almost a tradition. Maybe it went on because TV reception used to be pathetic and it gave everybody something to talk about, and a bit of a laugh.

“But it was also a way of getting back at people. Doug and I know all about it. It happened to us when we got here. We were outsiders from Glasgow. My predecessor was from the Isle of Harris and he fit right in. They didn’t mess around with me because I was the polis but Doug got more than his fair share. His boats would get moved during the night. Bits of equipment would go missing and we'd find them hanging off a fencepost at a road end the next day."

"Did anyone leave shit on your doorstep?' asked Liz.

"No, nothing like that, but you should have heard the row that happened when Doug proposed giving the local school kids swimming lessons. There's people here still think you shouldn't do that. If the Good Lord wanted you to swim he'd have given you fins, and if the sea's going to get you, she will, they say. Some islander phoned my boss and tried to get me transferred because of that. Fat chance. It didn't happen and we're staying."

"Deirdre got threats and then she died, though," said Elspeth.

"Of natural causes," Jackie insisted. "But this is all interesting. You know, I liked your aunt. She used to stop by and talk to me when she needed to find out about how things worked in Police Scotland for those new books she was writing. I said I'd tell her as long as the constable she wrote about wasn't like me.

"Tell you what. I'll take what you've got here to my boss. See if he thinks it needs to go to the Fiscal for another look."

"The who?" asked Elspeth.

"The Procurator Fiscal. That's who decides if a crime's taken place in Scotland and if it should be investigated," Liz explained, from the other side of the table.

"Don't expect much to change," said Jackie. "I saw Deirdre's body, and the rug that she tripped over. The post-mortem showed she broke her neck. It all makes sense that it was an accident. But you know what? I'll go have a blether with Young Norman MacPhail. He can see your house from his back field. Maybe he noticed a car outside here that day when you were out visiting the McQuarries and that fish was dropped off."

"The MacPhails are the family most likely to have done this," Elspeth objected. "They've had it in for Deirdre from the start."

"Which means they had fifty years to get rid of her. Why wait this long? And leaving a dead fish to annoy you isn't going to get them the house back." Jackie folded the printed copies into a wad and stuffed them in a shirt pocket. "Now, since I'm here, how's about we go for a wee look around. I wouldn't mind a walk down to the pier, too. Do you mind if I take some pictures so I can show them to Doug?"

She took her phone out of her pocket and opened the pantry door.

"Well, will you look at this," she said admiringly.

It took more than an hour for her to go through the house. She was impressed by the bathroom as well. "Too bad she didn't get a downstairs loo put in while she was at it, and I don't like that yellow bathtub. But we can change that.

"You know what." She took a paper notepad out of another shirt pocket, laid it on top of the cistern and wrote down a name and phone number. "If you're worried, I'll get Doug to come over here and put deadbolts on the doors. You never know who Deirdre might have given a spare key to. He'll check the window catches for you as well, and mend that one where you hammered in those nails."

The house that she and Doug lived in came with her job, she added as they walked outside. If they bought, they could rent the Skipper's House out until they were ready to move in. She took snaps of the pier. Doug ran the local watersport centre and it was exactly what he needed for his work. If they did buy, he would like to move his business here, eventually. Elspeth should let her know what price she was asking, soon as she had decided.

"So much for that," Liz Fraser muttered once Jackie had driven away. "She's just going to go through the motions as far as Deirdre's death's concerned. She's far more interested in buying the house. But I'll be happier leaving you here on your tod if I know you can lock the place up properly. I'm not leaving until her husband's come by and seen to that."

Meantime, she was going to get back to work. She'd go pick up fish and chips at the hotel tonight and Elspeth could go have dinner with Calum McFee all by herself.

16

Tostaig Hotel stood near the harbour, with ample parking space outside. It looked much like the Skipper's House but was three times wider, stone built, upstairs and down, with additions. The kitchen was on the ground floor. A room had been converted into an office with a hatch into the hallway and another into a residents' lounge. The predominant colours were cream and brown. The furnishings were basic, the pictures on the walls snapshots of life on Sulla, long ago, sepia, fading with age. Long dead islanders stared out from the walls: fishermen, crofters in the fields or digging peat, children outside the school with their teacher. One of them must be of Megan MacPhail, the Skipper's wife, the one for whom he had brought home all his treasures.

The bar was tacked onto one side of the building, the restaurant onto the other. It had a row of windows with a view of the harbour, but not on a March evening like this, overcast, with rain beginning to drizzle down. A light shone out by the harbour wall and another lit up the parking lot, but otherwise it was pitch dark outside.

The restaurant was empty. A blonde woman with braided hair wrapped around her head, wearing a white apron, poked her head around a door that led to the kitchen.

"If you're looking for Calum, you'll find him in the bar," she said. She looked and sounded like she might be Scandinavian.

Calum beckoned Elspeth inside when she opened the door. "We can order here and have a drink first," he told her. A group of men leaned against the bar. One of them straightened up when he saw her. Elspeth recognized the dark-haired man who had watched her from the garage door. He must be Rob MacPhail. He downed what was left of his beer and put the glass firmly on the bar top.

"I'll be off then, Donnie," he said and walked past Elspeth as if she didn't exist.

Lachlan MacKinnon was another, still wearing his dungarees and black wellie boots.

"Fancy meeting you again," he said. "Second time today." Another drinker was Colin, the harbourmaster. He seemed friendly enough.

The blonde woman came through a back door behind the bar with menus, simple single-page ones. Her name was Frieda. She was Norwegian and was married to Donald MacPherson, the barman. They owned the hotel.

"I bought fresh shrimp off a boat today and the lamb's local," she told them.

Calum had a half pint of pale ale in front of him. Elspeth opted for lime soda. She might have a glass of wine later but she'd have to drive home along that narrow, winding road in the dark and it looked like it would be raining by then.

"Jackie Buchanan was at your house earlier, just after you'd visited us?" asked Lachie MacKinnon.

"She wanted to see around," she said.

"Are Doug and her interested in buying?" Donnie asked, curious.

"She was just looking."

"So what was she doing visiting Norman MacPhail right after?" Lachie propped an elbow on the bar, pleased to show what he knew.

Elspeth shrugged. She wasn't going to say.

"Maybe we should go through to the dining room." Calum McFee picked up their glasses. He led the way to the door. "'Night, boys," he said. They heard Lachie MacKinnon laugh as it shut behind them.

Calum led her to a table near the restaurant window but close enough to the kitchen that Frieda didn't have to walk far.

"You sure she won't hear everything we say and relay it right back next door?" Elspeth hesitated.

"Frieda won't do that," he said. "She's got her head screwed on. So's Donnie. He just pours men like Lachie their booze and lets them talk. What was Jackie Buchanan doing at your house, though?"

"She and Doug really might be interested in buying it." Elspeth took her place opposite him. The rain was coming down heavier. It streamed down the window beside them. "I could maybe do a private sale if they offer. Or I could leave all that to Annabel. What do you think?"

"I'd go with Annabel if I was you," he advised. "She'll get you the best price and you'll be gone back to Canada long before you can make the sale. She'll take care of all those antiques that are in the house too. Annabel knows how these things work and you need someone you can trust if you're going to be that far away. She's sold several houses out here for non-residents and she'll do a good job. It's worth paying her to do it."

Frieda appeared with plates of shrimp, plenty of them, in the shell, with a tangy dipping sauce on the side and some fresh salad.

"Frieda's a good cook," he said. "This hotel looks plain but don't let that fool you. This dining room will be packed all summer long."

"And there might be filming happening as well, later in the year," she told him.

"That might happen? For the Mairi MacIntosh books? I know they paid Deirdre for the rights to film the Sulla books years ago but nothing ever came of it."

"It sounds like it's for real this time," Elspeth told him, cracking the shell off a shrimp. "Liz says they'll be shooting by this time next year."

Frieda brought a bottle of wine and uncorked it. They waited for her to fill their glasses and disappear through the door once more.

"Filming might go on for several seasons," Elspeth continued. "They want to do a six-episode series based on the first book and then they're hoping to follow that with all the others. You might have filming happening here for years if that happens. This could go international."

"And that means you will have money coming in, regularly?" he asked.

"I could use a lawyer here." She drank some wine, a French burgundy chosen to go with the lamb. She smiled. "Will you help me?"

She liked this big, comfortable man and was easy in his company. Deirdre had entrusted her affairs to Calum and he was here, right on the spot, every couple of weeks or so. Perhaps he could be her eyes and ears on what was happening on Sulla when she was back home, in Canada, at the other side of the globe.

"So." He grinned back at her. "What needs immediate attention?"

She told him about the cheque that Liz had given her. How it had come in after Deirdre's death and Liz had said she could go ahead and cash it.

"She might be right," he said. "Let me check."

The shrimps were all eaten. Lamb arrived at their table, with roast potatoes and fresh green beans. Lemony carrots.

"That's the problem," she told. "I need enough money to tide me through until the end of May if I'm going to stay that long, and I just don't have it. I'm waiting for a cheque from my cousin, to cover my fare here, but I don't know when I'll get it. I've been unemployed these past two years, since the theatres closed and work dried up. I'm low on cash. If I can't use the money from Liz's cheque I don't think I can stay."

"I can solve that one." He cut up a slice of meat. "Deirdre used to get £10,000 for being the director of the book fest, just so it was on the books as a real job." Elspeth remembered that was the exact amount her aunt had left to the festival. "She donated it all right back. We can do the same with you, if you take on the book festival job. Half the work's been done already so I can only pay £5,000 but I can transfer it to you as soon as you sign on, then you'll have some money to see you through. We can wait until you sell the Skipper's House and then you pay it back, so it won't really cost us, if that's okay with you. The festival's all run by volunteers, but that's the main job. If you come by my house tomorrow I'll get a letter of agreement for the job drafted up. You can think about any other things you want me to look into while you're at it. Anything to do with Deirdre's will and the house sale."

That was enough to pay for an extra couple of months in Scotland.

"Liz didn't catch the boat today?" he remarked. "She's still at the house?"

"How did you know that?" She was surprised he knew.

"Because Lachie MacKinnon said so back in the bar before you walked in." He grinned again.

"Lachie knew?'

"The island likes to know who's here and who's not. He'll have seen the car outside your house. And Colin the Harbour knows who's driven on or off the boat. They talk all the time."

"Liz will be leaving once I get the locks to the house changed." Elspeth told him about the dead fish and why Liz had stayed, about the entries they had found in Deirdre's notebooks and how they had reported them to Jackie Buchanan.

"Jackie's going to find out if the case into Deirdre's death should be reopened," she said. "But she sounds doubtful. Is it true that people have pranked each other out here for years?"

"Perfectly true." He topped up her wineglass. "You don't want to be around at Halloween. They play all kinds of tricks then. The adults, not the kids." He put down the wine bottle. "There's a lot of gossip happens here, too. You don't want to pay too much attention to it.

"I was here when Deirdre died. I talked to the detective inspector that was sent over to find out what happened. They took it seriously. I saw where she fell. The body was gone by then, but the rug was just where it had been left, all puckered up. It did look like she'd slipped and fallen. Nobody out here was surprised when they said it was an accident."

"So I shouldn't be worried because someone left me a dead fish?" she asked.

"Some people just have an odd sense of humour," he replied, "but if you want to deadbolt the doors and get the window catches double checked, go right ahead."

He went through to the bar to settle the bill. This dinner was on him. She could treat him to a curry in Oban before she left to go back home, he told her.

"You'll be okay, driving in this?" He met her at the front door. Rain was sheeting down by now and a wind had risen. She'd be fine, she said, and bolted through the downpour to the blue Volkswagen, glad that it was parked right outside the hotel. She hung onto the car door, the wind pushing against it. Once she got inside, it slammed shut behind her.

Elspeth didn't drive often in rain like this. Snow and ice didn't faze her, she was used to those. Winnipeg winters lasted five to six months. The ground stayed frozen October to March most years. Downpours in the summer often came as thunderstorms that passed in minutes. You could swing over to the side of the road and wait it out. There was nothing as relentless as this, and roads here didn't come with shoulders that you could pull onto if you had a problem.

She turned the heat on full blast, chilled by the wetness, and sat for a moment, listening to the wind howl, the rain batter the side of the car, the wipers swishing back and forth, then she set off.

Driving on this wet night was like being on a prairie highway in a snowstorm, visibility reduced to almost zero, when you kept your eyes focused on the small patch of road that you could see ahead, maintained your speed and kept on going. The rain streaked white in the headlights, blinding her, not unlike snow blown almost horizontal by the wind. There, the similarity ended. Prairie roads ran straight and flat, this one did not. It wound its way around the shoreline. At times there was only fifty feet or so of grass between it and the place where the land fell away to sand or rocks. Then there was the heaving mass of the sea. She tried not to think about that. At least she did not have far to go, she reminded herself. It was only a four- or five-mile drive until she reached the Skipper's House, according to the car's GPS. About six kilometres, she told herself.

She turned on the radio. All she got was static.

She became aware of headlights flashing across her rear-view mirror as a car swerved around the bends in the road behind her. It was closing in on her, the driver more confident in these conditions than she was. There should be a passing place fairly soon, where she could pull over and let it through. She slowed down even more, afraid she would miss the sign for it in the dark. She wasn't even sure if she would see it.

The car behind her was closing in fast. The light in her mirror was almost constant now, dazzling her. Still the rain teemed down. She looked in the mirror again. The car was right behind her, too close for comfort, forcing her to drive with more speed than she wanted in this downpour. She took a corner then another bend, grasping the steering wheel, trying to stay on the slick road. Then she remembered that Annabel had said that the ground here was firm enough to hold a car. She swerved onto the grass, her tires skidding on the wet surface. The car slid sideways, then stopped as the other vehicle roared off along the road. She couldn't see the kind or the make in the downpour, far less read the registration plate.

Her heart was beating fast. The wipers still swept back and forth. The wind gusted and raindrops hammered against her side of the car. She could hear waves crashing, close enough to be heard. Her fingers were shaking.

She took several deep breaths. The ground, the machair, was firm enough to hold the car, as Annabel had said it would. She hadn't driven in far enough to cause much damage to it. Slowly, she turned the wheels and drove back onto the road. She reached the passing place shortly after. Minutes later she saw lights glimmering in the wet darkness, from the windows of the Skipper's House. By the time she had opened the gate, garaged the car and gone back to close it, she was drenched.

"You look like a drowned rat," said Liz Fraser, safe and warm inside. "How was your night?"

17

The rainstorm had blown over to Mull and the mainland by morning. Clouds loomed over the land to the east, barely visible though the mist, but sunlight shafted down onto the little Isle of Sulla and the seabirds were flying again.

Liz had sent Elspeth off to have a hot bath last night after she got home. By the time she had come downstairs, wrapped in a terry robe that reached her ankles and could have fastened around her twice, there had been a hot whisky toddy and a blazing fire waiting for her.

They'd talked about whether she should tell Jackie Buchanan that someone had run her off the road. The rain battered against the windowpanes but she was safe inside, sipping warm, honeyed whisky with a small dog at her feet.

She had no idea who had been driving the other car. It could have been an impatient driver, eager to get home, frustrated at her slow speed. Someone who knew she could pull over onto the machair any time and make way, that they didn't need to wait for a passing place. She had not been in any real danger, she said, trying to convince herself that what had happened had not been serious.

"Still." Liz disagreed. "They should have waited. Stopped to make sure you were all right. They must have known it was you. Who else has a car that looks like that out here on Sulla? You couldn't see them in the rain but they had you in their headlights. Maybe they knew that you didn't know much about driving here, on a rainy night. I think someone decided to give you a right scare. Someone had a go at you."

It was just as well that Elspeth was getting the locks changed. Anybody could have borrowed that key Deirdre kept in the coal bunker and have had a copy made, she said next morning, in bright sunshine once more.

"What key in the coal bunker?" asked Elspeth.

They went outside to look. The grass smelled wet and green, the little daisies scattered over it just beginning to open up. There was a small hook inside the wooden bunker, near the top in the corner. It was empty.

"She always left one there." Liz propped the lid up with one arm. "Never locked her doors when she was living here. Said you needed to be able to trust your neighbours." She snorted in disbelief. "But she did lock up whenever she went away and that was her spare." She let go of the lid and let it crash down.

"That settles it," she said. "I'm not budging until all the locks on this house are changed. I wonder how long that's going to take." She huffed off into the house to let Inga in Edinburgh know about her change of plan.

Elspeth walked down onto the beach, the dog trotting at her side. Waves were crashing against the rocky shore at the other side of the pier but the island felt clean, washed by the rain. Her phone pinged. Jackie Buchanan had texted. *Doug can pick up deadbolts & install at your house later pm today. OK?*

The locks were going to get fixed before nightfall. Liz could catch today's boat after all, if she hurried. Elspeth raced back to the house to tell her.

"No," she declared. "Tomorrow will do. I want to make sure everything's okay before I leave."

Elspeth decided to get to work. She wanted to access the files in the big iMac and in Deirdre's desk drawer, the ones about the Sulla Book Festival. If she was going to take on that job she might as well get started.

"You still want to do that?" asked Liz. "Are you sure it's a good idea?" She was frying up eggs, three of them, all for herself, with fried bread. "We're not sure that Deirdre died accidentally. Someone doesn't like you being here either. If it was me I'd be on that plane back to Canada, soon as I could. Get Annabel to sell the house. You don't need to be here. The book festival will muddle through without you."

"I've been in Scotland more than a week already," Elspeth responded. "I need to be in Glasgow twelve days from now if I'm going to use my plane ticket and there's so much happening here. Running the book festival gets me involved and I'll be able to help plan Deirdre's memorial. That's a good thing, isn't it? Don't you think I owe it to her?"

Liz slowly nodded her head in agreement. Elspeth left her sitting at the kitchen table, the dog staying close since there was still food on the table, and went to Deirdre's den.

The incident last night in the car had shaken Elspeth more than she was letting on. She had felt physically threatened. Liz was right. She could go straight home, be back in Winnipeg, thirteen days from now. Wait six months until she could use the cash that Liz had given her, with more to come her way afterwards, plus the money from the house sale whenever that happened. But once she was there, what would she do? Those were going to be long, empty months with only one work contract. She'd be dependent on Dave for a long time yet.

Here, there was an interesting job, hers for the taking. New people to meet and talk to. Decisions to be made. The door swung open and the dog padded in.

"And how do I find you a good home so soon, Wilma?" she asked. The terrier's long brown tail batted back and forth as she heard her name.

Was she in any danger? Liz seemed determined to make the goings-on here on Sulla into a big drama, but Calum McFee agreed with the police. He thought Deirdre's death had been an accident. And if someone had wanted to kill Elspeth last night, they could have forced her off the road on a bend, close to rocks or the edge of the sea. They hadn't. She'd gone off on a bare stretch, with nothing in her way. She had been perfectly safe. Maybe it was true that someone had just been in a hurry, frustrated because she was driving so slowly.

She wanted to talk to Dave about it. It was just past nine in the morning, the middle of the night in Canada. He would be asleep. She'd like to speak to her mother as well. She emailed both of them. Almost immediately, Margaret called back on Messenger. Her face popped up on the screen. She was often awake at three a.m., she said. She had just made herself some tea.

Her mother was agreeably surprised to hear how much Deirdre's island home was worth and that the items she had dismissed as junk were now valuable antiques. Elspeth swung the monitor round so she could see the rest of Deirdre's den.

"It didn't look like that, last time I was there," she said. "She must have had a wall knocked down. It was pokey inside, because of those thick walls, like being in a rabbit hole. That island's such a bleak, lonely place, basically just a rock in the middle of the Atlantic, isn't it? Not a tree in sight. I don't know how she could stand living there."

"It's a tourist trap now," Elspeth told her. "And it is beautiful on a sunny day. When were you last here?"

"Just after Alasdair McPhail went missing." Margaret had come to Sulla to keep her sister company. She had still been living in Scotland at the time. That was long ago, before Elspeth had been born. It hadn't stopped raining when she was there. Rumours had been flying around among the islanders about what might have happened to Alasdair. It hadn't been a good time.

"I've been told that," said Elspeth. "I ran into Chrissie MacPhail who's married to Alasdair's cousin, Norman. She tried to tell me that the house is cursed." She laughed, making a joke of it.

Her mother frowned at her from the screen. She didn't seem to think it was funny. "Maybe it is," she said.

"Since when did you turn superstitious?" Elspeth asked, surprised. Margaret was a scientist, a realist.

"I'm not," her mother snapped back at her. "It's just that nothing good ever seems to happen there. You'll be home soon, though."

"I might not." Elspeth explained about the Sulla Book Festival and how they planned to honour Deirdre at it. How she'd been asked to help manage the festival in Deirdre's place.

"I think I'm going to do it," she said. She told her mother about the plan to film Deirdre's latest books for TV. "You'll maybe be able to see Sulla on Netflix in a couple of years," and she was going to make a lot of money if they were successful.

"Well, imagine that," said her mother, her face and voice fading then returning.

"They want to take Deirdre's ashes out on a boat and put them in the sea near where Alasdair drowned. Why don't you come over, Mom?" Elspeth continued. "You could do the honour and Deirdre's friends here would love to meet you. You'd be able to see how much Deirdre accomplished and how much people appreciated her."

"Honour her?" Margaret's voice turned scathing. "Appreciated? She deserves none of it. Let me tell you, Elspeth, Chrissie MacPhail was right. Nobody's ever been happy in that horrible, cold house. An old aunt of Alasdair's was holed up in it for years, surrounded by all those relics of her past life, stuck there all by herself in the middle of nowhere. Alasdair hated the place. He wanted to leave, he told me so, but Deirdre was having none of that.

"'Why would we', she said. They had free lodging and she was writing about the island already. She'd go off foraging for stories. She had a little tape recorder she used. Then she'd shut herself away for hours, writing them down. Alasdair's relatives kept telling him he should help with the sheep or the fishing, and he wasn't interested. He wanted to get back to Edinburgh. Funny, isn't it, that the first thing Deirdre did when she had some real money of her own was buy that flat there, exactly where he had wanted to go, after he was dead and gone? Deirdre could be so perverse at times."

"I liked her," Elspeth interjected. "I didn't see much of her but I thought she was interesting. And fun to be with. Look what she's left me!"

"Oh, she could be entertaining when she wanted to be." Margaret's face cleared on the screen again. "But she had a wicked tongue in her head and she certainly knew how to use it. A nasty temper, too, when things didn't go her way.

"That's what happened. When Alasdair died." She leaned closer, her face wobbling again, her voice coming and going. Elspeth had to listen hard so she could catch everything she was saying. "I've never told this to a soul," her mother hissed. "But maybe you should know. You don't tell anyone. You hear me?"

Elspeth nodded in agreement.

"It's why I left that island and never went back. Why I won't come to this funeral that you're arranging."

"What happened?" Elspeth listened. She'd never heard her mother speak like this.

"Deirdre was on the boat with Alasdair the day he disappeared. She told everyone afterwards that he'd gone out alone but that wasn't true. She lied about that." Margaret whistled through her teeth as she drew in a breath. "They got into an argument when they were out on the water, round on the Atlantic side of the island, where it's hilly and there's nobody else around. About him wanting to leave. She was determined to stay. They were stuck out there in the boat, yelling at each other, and she stood up, she was so angry. He did, too, and she shoved him instead. He went right over the side. She was as big as him, you know. Maybe stronger.

"She could have helped him get back on board but she didn't. She fired up the outboard and left him there. She said they weren't far off shore, but he wasn't the swimmer she was. She must have known he might not make it because she cut the motor as soon as she got to the next bay, jumped into the water and swam to the beach. She got back onshore but he didn't.

"And you know what? I think she was glad to be rid of him. 'Alasdair had become a bit of a bore,' she said one night, in that bleak, windswept house that you're living in. She'd had a few whiskies or she wouldn't have said. She knew he had the deeds to the house, that he had left everything to her. If the body didn't show up she'd need to wait until he was declared dead but that was okay. She could stay on Sulla as long as she liked and carry on writing about it. 'This island's going to be the making of me,' she told me. And she was right. She got the house, and she stayed and wrote more books. But it's tainted," she said, her face clear and steady on the screen once more. "So is all that money you've inherited. Ill-gotten gains, all of it.

"I only saw her when I had to after that. Your granny insisted I should go for a visit when we were in Edinburgh, but that's all I ever did. Last time I saw her was when we buried Granny Balfour and closed up the house in Carnoustie. I never went back after that. I never wanted to see Deirdre again."

"I've kept her secret all these years," she said, "But it shouldn't die with me. Someone else should know the truth. And now you do. Go ahead and have your ceremony for her, if you must. Throw her ashes overboard and let her sink. Then sell the house. Get rid of everything that belonged to her. I don't want to see any of it. But don't ever tell a soul what I've told you today. Promise. It's our family secret and that is where it stays."

"I promise," said Elspeth.

18

That afternoon, Elspeth pulled the blue Tiguan up outside the row of three blackhouses on the other side of Sulla. Calum McFee's was the one in the middle. The inside had been renovated to match the outside.

"Take a walk through and have a look," Calum told her. A sleek, tubular wood stove replaced the original stone fireplace. The kitchen was neat and compact with stainless steel appliances and granite countertops. The washroom had an efficient shower stall and there was a bedroom big enough to hold a double bed but not much more.

"Just enough room for me," he said. "My grandparents raised four weans here, can you imagine?"

A glass conservatory had been added onto the back. It held wicker furniture but no flowers. "Don't have time to water them." Two tall cupboards stood against the main wall. One held fishing equipment, the other was a locked gun cabinet. There was a pair of shotguns inside, she was told.

"My dad's." He noticed Elspeth raise an eyebrow. "He liked to go shooting birds."

The walls, inside as well as out, were painted white. There were photos on them, old ones of boats and fishermen. One showed a much younger Calum holding up a dead salmon, proud of himself. He must have been a schoolboy or a student at the time it was taken.

They sat in his little living room, just room for a sofa and armchairs beside a coffee table at one end, a sideboard at the other, a small table and chairs. He had drafted a description for the job of interim book festival coordinator. The contract would end at the end of May, and would pay a fee of £5,000. The agreement didn't say she had to donate it back but she understood that was expected.

He passed it to her to read. She signed and he clicked on his laptop. Minutes later, the money had been transferred into her Canadian bank account She could afford to stay on Sulla, to do the book fest job and to be present at the memorial for Deirdre. He'd get in touch with Iain Balfour or his solicitor and get an update on where things stood with the will. Find out when that valuer was going to get to Sulla.

There was a loud knock at the door. It opened and a woman in a Shetland knit sweater with an intricate coloured yoke and slacks walked in. She had white hair tied back in a bun and wore glasses.

"My mother," said Calum. "She's been wanting to meet you." Elspeth recognized the woman who had been having tea with Chrissie MacPhail at Annabel's café the previous Friday.

Donalda McFee had to be about Deirdre's age, in her late seventies, maybe eighty. Calum must have inherited his large frame from her. She carried herself erect and held a plate in her hand. Scones again, but these ones had raisins.

"Haven't you put the kettle on yet, Calum," she said, her voice one that Elspeth now recognized as that of a native Gaelic speaker. Calum must speak both languages too, Elspeth realized. That would be useful in an island legal practice like his.

"So very sorry that your aunt died the way she did." Donalda settled into a comfortable armchair. "But it would have been a quick death. A merciful way to go. Certainly better than mouldering away in the Eventide Home along the road. I hear that there's to be a memorial for her and that you'll be staying for it?"

"Yes," Elspeth replied. "I'm going to help to run the book festival while I'm here as well."

Calum McFee brought through three mugs on a tray, a milk jug and sugar bowl, a plate with a pat of butter.

"Now that's a good thing," said Donalda. "I do enjoy the book festival. I volunteer on the Friday, when you have the Gaelic authors."

"Can I ask you for help with that? I don't know the language," said Elspeth.

"Neither did your aunt. She never learned a word of it." Donalda McFee looked seriously at her over the tops of gold-rimmed glasses, then she smiled. "Of course. Glad to. Have a scone. They just came out the oven."

They were warm. Butter melted into them. Donalda revealed that she knew that the Buchanans were interested in buying Deirdre's house and that Annabel would probably handle the sale. If she had heard about the dead fish episode as well, she didn't say.

"Tell Annabel she should have a sale here on Sulla before she sends all those nice things the Skipper brought back to Megan MacPhail off the island. There's people like me wouldn't mind having one or two of those pieces."

"Really, Mother?" Calum laid down his mug, "Don't you think you've got enough in that wee house of yours? Where would you put them?"

"Oh, I'll find a spot, never fear," said his mother. "There's a painted screen with cranes flying on it that I always liked. Have you seen it?" Elspeth knew the one she meant. It was in the corner of an upstairs bedroom. The old lady could have it when the time came to get rid of everything.

"Would you like to come and see my house?" Donalda asked. "I've kept it in the traditional style. Not like this one."

Donalda led Elspeth next door. The big stone fireplace, built to burn peat, remained functional, a box of logs beside it now. "I get the wood shipped in and Calum stacks it outside in my shed," she said. "But there's talk of us cutting peat again. I would like that." The kitchen had a table in the middle, a dresser like the one in Deirdre's house but smaller, and an Aga.

"I had that put in thirty years ago. It still works fine."

Two wedding photos hung on a wall, one of Donalda on her wedding day, in a sixties calf-length flared wedding dress with a short veil, her husband, Calum's father, as tall as she but lankier, in a suit that looked too large for him, taken outdoors, the sea behind them. The other had been taken on the steps of a church and showed a younger Calum, his bride also decked out in white.

"That's Gillian," said Donalda. "A city girl. She couldn't stand living out here, not even in Oban. She went off back to Glasgow. Teaches mathematics at a secondary school there. She's married to someone else now." So Calum McFee was divorced.

The little house was full of books. Shelving reached floor to ceiling in every room, making each room even smaller than it was.

"I've got all of Deirdre's books, of course," she said. But she also had shelves of poetry, mainly Scottish. Novels too. A whole wall was dedicated to Gaelic writers. There were history books, biographies, atlases, dictionaries. She'd never gone to university, like her son, she told Elspeth, but she liked to think of herself as well read.

She lifted a photograph from a shelf. It had been taken on a beach, many years ago, a black and white snapshot. There was Deirdre, in shorts, her hair tied back in a pony tail, her long legs stretched out on the sand. She held a beer bottle and was squinting in the bright sunlight. Alasdair MacPhail sat behind her on a rock, his head thrown back, laughing.

"There's me." Donalda pointed. She'd had long, dark hair in those days. She was wearing a cotton dress, a belt cinching her waist. "I was seventeen, and that's Murdo, Calum's father." There was the same man that Elspeth had seen in the wedding photograph, when he was a gawky teenager. "We weren't married yet."

Another woman was closer to Deirdre and Alasdair in age. She was pretty, in a floral sundress, smiling for the camera.

"That's Chrissie MacPhail. Her husband, Norman, took the picture. They'd just got married. That was taken the first summer that your aunt came to Sulla. We had a picnic. I thought you might like to have that, so that you'd know that we did have some happy times. We were all good friends, until Alasdair died and things went wrong.

"I never blamed your aunt for anything," she said. "I never believed the things some people said about her afterwards. I'm glad she stayed and wrote down our stories so they wouldn't be forgotten. I told her a few myself sitting by the fire here. She had a little tape recorder. You don't know what happened to the tapes, do you?"

Elspeth hadn't seen any. She said she'd look.

"We wouldn't have a book festival if Deirdre hadn't started it," said Donalda. "It's a wonderful thing, all those writers coming here and bringing their books with them. I get all stocked up for a winter's reading. I don't know what I'd do without it."

They walked back outside. The blue Tiguan was parked in Calum's driveway, behind an older model Peugeot that Calum drove when he was on Sulla.

"You'll be selling that?" Donalda asked. "That old thing I'm driving's getting past its best." A Ford Fiesta sat in her own driveway, showing signs of rust. "Maybe I'll buy it from you, when it's time for you to go."

Elspeth went back to Calum's cottage to collect the paperwork. They looked out the window. Donalda was walking around the Tiguan, peering in the windows, getting a good look at it.

"She's still driving?" Elspeth said.

"She'll never stop," he replied. "She's getting deaf but her eyesight's still fine."

"That's quite the collection of books she's got there."

"You're telling me." He laughed his big, deep laugh. "She should have had an education but she had to stay in Sulla and look after her mother. Cancer, and my mother was the only daughter. She never got to stay on in school and she's been making up for it ever since."

Elspeth turned in the doorway. "Did you see anyone follow me from the hotel last night?" she asked.

He shook his head. He'd gone back into the bar after she had gone. Lachie MacKinnon had left already but Colin the Harbour was still there and they'd had a chat. Then he'd gone home, in the opposite direction from Elspeth.

She told him what had happened.

"Strange," he said. "You think it was deliberate?"

"Or someone was impatient. I was going slow. I wasn't sure of myself on that narrow road in the rain."

"Yes, but you don't force someone off the road in weather like that. Anybody local would have known that the passing place was coming up."

"It's just like what happened to Deirdre, isn't it? When she smashed into her wall?"

"That was years ago, before the lockdown, and we all thought she'd made that story up." He leaned against the door jamb. "That she'd hit the wall herself and said that to save face, because she was embarrassed and she'd probably had something to drink. Are you sure you want to stay on Sulla? I don't think you're in any great danger. But you don't want to be living in that house all by yourself if you're afraid. You can leave, you know. The book festival will happen whether you're here or not and Annabel and I can take care of the house sale for you when the time comes."

"No," she said. "Doug Buchanan's at the house right now, putting deadbolts on the doors and making sure that the windows fasten properly. Liz is staying until tomorrow. I'll be fine."

She drove off. She'd put the photograph that Donalda McFee had given her into the brown envelope that held the book festival contract. It lay on the seat beside her.

Deirdre and Alasdair MacPhail had been happy that day at the beach. So had Chrissie MacPhail and her husband Norman, Alasdair's cousin. She remembered the grim-faced old woman who had confronted her at the café. She'd never have recognized her as the bright, attractive girl she had been fifty years ago.

By the time she got back to the Skipper's House, Doug Buchanan had been and gone. He'd left a receipt for the hardware on the kitchen counter with the new keys but hadn't charged anything for his time.

"He does like what he saw of this place," Liz reported. "Had a good look while he was here. Spent ages down at the pier. Took measurements. That's okay, isn't it? I said he could. He went into the shed too. It looked like he was checking to make sure it was sound. Said he wished he'd brought a lock for that, too and did you want one put on?" It might be a good idea, but what would anyone want to do with old hand tools?

Wilma was out in the yard, sniffing around.

"I might go to Oban tomorrow," said Elspeth. "I could go to a bank and find out if I can deposit that cheque you gave me. I might as well put it in my account for now. And I've been paid for the book festival job so I can stock up on groceries. I could go over on the boat with you. I'll see if the MacKinnons can take the dog."

"Och, leave her here with me." Liz joined her at the window. "I can stay another day. I kind of like it here on my own. I'm getting all kinds of work done with nobody to interrupt me. I can see why Deirdre thought this was a great place to live and write."

Elspeth booked her car on the ferry for the next day, and the Airbnb she had booked before was available. She'd leave the money for the TV rights untouched until she was sure she could spend it. It would take ages for it to clear the banking system anyway. Once that happened she could access it. Meantime, she could spend some of the book festival cash. She could go to a real supermarket and buy some fresh fruit and vegetables, away from prying eyes and awkward questions.

19

The bank in Oban was pleased to deposit the cheque for optioning the film rights to Elspeth's Canadian account. It would be a couple of weeks before she could access it, but that was fine. Calum might know if she could spend some of it by then. She could maybe do some sightseeing before she headed back across the Atlantic. Why not, if she could afford to? Once she had filled the trunk of the car with enough groceries to last for weeks and a box of fresh food, she found herself with time on her hands. She could start playing tourist right now.

She drove south, following the coastline. The road cut over from the seashore to the edge of Loch Fyne. She found herself in a small, pretty town called Ardrishaig then followed a road that wove between hillsides and loch water to Tarbert. There, she ate fish and chips, looking at the picturesque fishing harbour. Google Maps showed that the road went back across a peninsula to the Atlantic once more. She was on the Mull of Kintyre, with the islands of Islay and Jura offshore, and it was tempting to explore further, but she needed to get back to Oban before nightfall. Maybe the next time she visited the mainland, she could do that. Take a boat over to that historical isle called Iona.

She rose bright and early the next morning, ready to catch the ferry. The boat trip was familiar this time. She met a family from France and was able to practise her French. A gaggle of students from Surrey were backpacking their way through the Hebrides. It was a beautiful morning, the sea calm and sparkly blue, the coastline clearly visible. Beaches, treed hillsides, small bays. The tourists oohed and aahed as they passed the brightly painted houses of Tobermory.

Elspeth stretched out her legs and dozed for a while on the deck once they reached open water, accompanied by the throb of the engine and the gentle swell of the waves, seagulls screeching in the wake of the boat. A couple of the students were throwing food scraps to them. The birds swooped down, each one trying to be the first to grab them.

When they approached Sulla, Elspeth went to look, just as she had before, eager to see her house from the water, the beach and the road to Tostaig. A family also stood watching, speaking Gaelic. They must be islanders. She smiled in their direction but they didn't smile back. Colin the Harbourmaster, who she now knew was called Colin the Harbour on Sulla, waved, however, as she drove off the ferry, making her feel as if she was coming home. Donnie, it seemed, was Donnie the Hotel and Rob McQuarrie was Rob the Garage.

"We've all got the same surnames out here so it helps sort us out," Calum had told her. He was known locally as Calum the Law.

Minutes later, she was outside the Skipper's House, surprised to see the gate standing open. Some sheep had wandered inside the wall and were munching the grass in front of the house.

The door to the garage was closed. She parked in front of it, went to the back of the Tiguan and opened the hatch, then she heard a dog bark. It sounded like Wilma. She looked around to see if the dog had wandered off outside the wall, but she could see no sign of her. She lifted a box of groceries out of the car and made for the back door then she heard the bark again. It was definitely coming from outside the house.

"Wilma?" she called. The responding bark sounded like it came from the shed at the opposite side of the house. She put down the box and walked past the grazing sheep. When she opened the door, Wilma squirmed against her legs, tail wagging, then noticed the sheep. She barked at them but didn't chase them. They paid no attention to her. Elspeth laughed, but she did wonder why the dog was there. Had Liz taken a dislike to her? But why shut her in the shed and leave the gate wide open? She could have just put her out into the yard, and closed it. She shooed the sheep out onto the road, Wilma getting in the way, and fastened the gate.

The back door that led into the kitchen was unlocked. She opened it and walked in. Liz Fraser lay on her back on the linoleum flooring, between the sink and the table, her big body mountainous, with a river of blood running down the side. The handle of a knife stuck up out of her chest and more blood had pooled around her.

Wilma made straight for the body. Elspeth dropped the box of groceries, grabbed the dog's collar and pulled her back. Liz was wearing the same clothes that she had worn when Elspeth had left yesterday. She must have been lying here overnight. The blood had congealed. Her grey eyes stared at the ceiling, the little mouth hung open.

Elspeth backed out the door, dragging the terrier with her. She closed it behind her with her other hand and reached into her pocket for her phone, then realized that she was beginning to shake. She let go of the dog and slid down onto the doorstep, her back against the door.

Jackie Buchanan's contact number was entered into her phone. She fumbled, glad she only had to press the right button.

"You've got to come right now, Jackie," she whispered, hardly able to speak, soon as she heard the voice on the other end. "Someone's been here and killed Liz Fraser."

Jackie Buchanan arrived in less than five minutes, siren blaring.

"Go sit in your car," she told Elspeth, soon as she arrived, "And take that dog with you." Elspeth watched Jackie take latex gloves from the trunk of her police car, put them on and bustle back off into the house. Her teeth had stopped chattering but she still couldn't get that image of Liz's big, round body and all that blood out of her mind. This all seemed unreal, like something out of a movie. She rubbed the dog's warm head for comfort then realized that Wilma must have been locked in the shed all night too. She must be hungry and thirsty.

Jackie emerged, phone to her ear. "My husband, Doug, will meet you there, sir," Elspeth heard her say. Then she came to the car and climbed into the passenger seat.

She fired a barrage of questions at Elspeth. That was Liz Fraser, who had been here a couple of days ago when Doug dropped by? Why was she still here? Hadn't she planned to leave? Where had Elspeth been? When did she get back? Had she touched anything inside or outside the house?

Elspeth found herself babbling, about how she'd gone to Oban and never thought that Liz would be in any danger, how she should have known better, how Liz had worked with Deirdre for years and now they were both dead and the dog was hungry and she hadn't fed her. The doctor was on his way, said Jackie. "You'll need to stay somewhere else for now." She called Annabel McQuarrie. "I need some help here," Elspeth heard her say.

Dr. Thomson was in his sixties and semi-retired. Serving Sulla was a part-time job. He had the avuncular manner of an old-fashioned country doctor and he wasn't going to be told what to do by Constable Buchanan.

"She isn't going anywhere, Jackie," he called to her as Jackie hurried off to fetch him a protective suit so he could go inspect the body. He opened the driver's door to Elspeth's car and hunkered down beside her.

"How're you doing, my dear?" he asked Elspeth. Then he fished into a pocket and produced a tube of mint candies. "Suck on one of these," he instructed. He had a small dispensary back at his house. He'd get some pills for Elspeth soon as he was done here. Just something to help her calm down after this shock.

Booking Elspeth into the hotel was an option but Jackie thought the beds there might be needed for the police. A helicopter was bringing over DI Alexander from Oban and there would be a Major Investigation Team arriving with him, she explained. SOCOs. Scene of Crime Officers. She didn't often get to use those words, working on quiet little Sulla.

Annabel drove up minutes later. She loaded Elspeth and the dog into her own car.

"Let's get you away from here," she said, getting a good look at what was going on at the same time.

Jackie would check in later with Elspeth, she said, and get a statement. The DI might want to talk to her, too. She disappeared off inside the house.

"They'll take the body to Oban," Annabel predicted. A helicopter whirred overhead as they approached the café. All of Sulla would know within minutes that something serious had happened at the Skipper's House.

Sandy McQuarrie put a large, sweetened latte and a chocolate croissant in front of Elspeth. Wilma the dog got a bowl of water. She wolfed down a hamburger.

Jan called, wondering what was going on. "Who? Liz? I'll be there right away." She, Annabel and Sandy had known Liz Fraser for years. Liz had come out to Sulla to visit Deirdre almost every summer and they'd got to know her better since the book festival had started. "Why on earth would anyone want to kill her?"

"Everything that's been happening at your house has to be connected." Jan plopped herself down at Annabel's table beside Elspeth once she arrived. "You have to tell the police all about it. Everything that you know."

"But maybe it's got nothing to do with the Skipper's House after all," said Elspeth. All the sugar she'd consumed had helped steady her nerves. "Liz had nothing to do with it, not with selling it, or who inherited it. She and Deirdre's connection was through her books. This has got to be something to do with what Deirdre was writing."

"The new ones? The whodunits? Why those? It's not like she's going to write any more of them," said Sandy.

Cath MacKinnon showed up next. She had driven by the house and stopped to find out what was going on. The ambulance was outside but Dr. Thomson had already left. Doug Buchanan had fetched a detective inspector from the airport and a policewoman in plain clothes. They were all fussing about in big white boiler suits with hoods now, masks on, too, and she hadn't been able to get near. Doug Buchanan had just been leaving as well. He'd told her that more police were coming over on a boat, bringing cars.

"There's never been anything like this happen on Sulla that I remember," she said.

"Not since Alasdair MacPhail went overboard and drowned." Jan sat back and folded her arms. "Maybe Chrissie MacPhail is right and that old house is doomed."

"It's never been a happy house," Cath agreed. "Although Deirdre seemed to like it well enough. Can I have one of those nice coffees too?" she asked Sandy, and took a third seat at the table. "Are you going to need me to look after Wilma?" she asked Elspeth.

Annabel was leaning against a kitchen counter, on the phone, talking to Calum McFee.

"Calum says that Bernie Baxter might let you stay at his house," she told them. "He won't be there for a month yet, so you could have it to yourself and Donalda's got a key."

"She can't stay by herself," Jan protested. "Skye's back at school in Oban. I've got a spare bed."

These were Deirdre's friends, and now they were rallying around Elspeth. They had all known Liz. They were shocked by her death, too, and doing their best to help.

Annabel was now talking to Jackie Buchanan. Elspeth would need things from the house, she told her, like clothes and her laptop. She hung up, rolling her eyes.

"She says you can't have anything for now. That it's a crime scene. Jackie can be a right officious wee madam when she likes." Her phone went back in her pocket. "She's figured out that if you were in Oban overnight you'll have enough stuff in the car to tide you over. It'll depend on the detective that's in charge to decide if you can get things from the house but that won't be until tomorrow. She'd going to be by to see you later."

It occurred to Elspeth that these friends were also the only people on this island who had known who Liz was. Who else would have known that Elspeth had gone to Oban, was staying overnight and that Liz was alone in the house? Could she really trust them, friendly and helpful as they were? But then she remembered that Colin the Harbour kept track of who arrived and who left the island. He would have known that Elspeth had caught the ferry and that Liz's Mini was still here. Colin went to the pub and talked. Anyone on the island might know.

If Bernie's house was available, she said, she thought she'd like to go there. Calum would be right next door, for now. And Donalda. She wouldn't really be alone. And Cath wouldn't need to take Wilma home with her. She'd like to have the dog with her, for company.

Dr. Thomson's car rolled up outside. He wouldn't stay, he said, but he handed Elspeth a bottle of sedatives.

"Take one right now," he insisted. It was a terrible business, he agreed as Annabel filled a glass of water at the sink and they all watched Elspeth swallow.

"How long had Liz been dead?" Elspeth asked.

"A while."

"Since yesterday?"

He expected so. He saw the frustration in their eyes as he avoided answering and relented.

"I can't tell for sure. Rigor mortis has set in so she's been dead more than eight hours, maybe as long as twenty-four. I can tell you she died right away. She wouldn't have suffered."

But how long had Liz known that she was about to die? That whoever was with her at the time had intended to kill her? They all sat in silence after the good doctor left.

Calum called back. He'd talked to Bernie. Elspeth could have his house for now. It was almost the end of the university term and he'd have to be in Glasgow for most of April. Calum and Donalda could go over to the Skipper's House and bring over Elspeth's car. He knew DI Alexander and wouldn't mind saying hello. What else did she need?

He and Donalda showed up an hour later. They'd managed to retrieve the Tiguan and the box of groceries that Elspeth had left at the door to the house, but that was all for now.

"Come along, Elspeth," said Donalda, "and we'll get you moved in."

20

Bernie Baxter's house had been renovated at the same time as Calum's, by Mike Nicolson, the local contractor. The design was similar, but here primary colours and comfort prevailed, armchairs you could bury yourself in, bright paintings on some walls, others, like Donalda's, covered in bookshelves.

Finally Elspeth was alone. She flopped down into one of the armchairs. Liz Fraser had been murdered, no doubt about that. Deirdre had been targeted, perhaps killed as well. She herself had been harassed. She regretted having signed that agreement with the book festival. Maybe she could withdraw from the job, given the circumstances, and change her flight back to an earlier date. Get away from this place. Go back to Winnipeg and to boring but safe reality. Leave the police to figure out what was going on here.

Her iPad was in her overnight bag. Bernie's house didn't have an internet connection but Calum's did and his house was close enough for her to piggyback on his Wi-Fi. She texted him and got the passcode, then she emailed Dave, in Canada. *Must talk, ASAP. What time?* Then she wondered what to do with herself

She could use some fresh air. She leashed up the dog, crossed the road and walked onto the machair. It stretched, flat and green, all the way to the seashore. Huge breakers rolled in from the west. Home was over there, a long way away. The sky had turned grey, the water was charcoal tinged with green, as dark as her mood.

A path led along the shoreline, to the cliffs at the southwest corner of Sulla. The wind caught at her clothes and blew her hair as she walked. Seabirds were flying in to nest on rocky ledges and spray splashed up against rocks. A sign, put up for birdwatchers, said that this place was called *Creagan Geala*, the English translation below it: The White Rocks. It was an appropriate name. The cliff face was plastered with bird droppings. She looked to see if there were any puffins, she would recognize those. There were plenty of seabirds but not one brightly coloured bill. They mustn't have arrived to nest yet.

Elspeth walked back to the cottage, windblown but feeling fresher for the exercise, and found a box lying on the doorstep. Cath MacKinnon must have dropped by with eggs and milk and butter. She'd left a long hank of rope as well, so Wilma could be tied up outside. This house had no wall around it to keep a dog from wandering off. She was grateful. Cath was thoughtful and considerate, but Elspeth was glad she hadn't stayed to talk.

A hallstand stood in the entrance to Bernie Baxter's house. It held walking sticks and a couple of large umbrellas and had a tall wooden back with hooks and a mirror. Elspeth caught sight of herself, blown hair, cheeks rosy from walking outside. She was surprised to see how healthy she looked. Bright-eyed and very much alive.

Jackie Buchanan's car drew up outside and a tall man in street clothes got out the passenger side. As soon as Elspeth opened the front door, Jackie turned the car and drove off back the way she had come.

"Hello!" The man stretched out a hand. "I'm DI Fergus Alexander. May I come in?"

He was tall enough that his head almost touched the ceiling. "Bonnie wee house," he remarked conversationally, looking around the living room. "I like what they've done to it. This won't take long. I just need to ask you a few questions. PC Buchanan will come and get me soon as we're done."

He didn't need coffee or tea, he assured her and lowered his lengthy body into an armchair. His feet, in polished brogues, were planted firmly on the ground so his trousered knees stuck up in front of him. He smiled at Elspeth over the tops of them, like this was a normal, everyday visit, nothing to do with murder.

"Now then," he said, by the sound of him another man who'd grown up in the Highlands and Islands. He laced long fingers together. Elspeth faced him, feeling very small in comparison. DI Alexander wore a moustache above fleshy lips. Sandy hair with a touch of ginger, combed over from a side parting. His jacket was tweedy and his tie was tartan, in soft greens and blues.

"Who, exactly, is that woman that's lying dead on your auntie's kitchen floor?" he asked, still smiling.

Elspeth explained how Liz Fraser had been Deirdre's literary agent and her friend, here on business, to meet with Elspeth and the book festival committee. How Liz had stayed an extra day while she, Elspeth, had gone off to Oban.

Did Ms. Fraser have any relatives that Elspeth knew of? She didn't, but Liz's assistant in Edinburgh would know. She asked if the Inspector wanted Inga Hansen's email and took out her phone to look for it.

Fergus Alexander pulled a black-covered notepad from his pocket and uncapped a fountain pen. Elspeth watched him write down the information in neat small handwriting. He laid the pad down on the arm of the chair, screwed the cap back on and laid his pen carefully on top.

"So you were away the whole night?" he asked.

She had left on yesterday's ferry and returned this morning.

"And you will have receipts for all of that?" She wasn't sure where she had put the ferry ticket. Maybe it was in the car.

"Colin the Harbour saw me when I drove off the boat," she said, surprised to find herself suddenly put on the defensive.

"We'll check. And you'll get that receipt to us, soon as you find it?" He still smiled.

"I visited the Bank of Scotland in Oban," she said to him. "I did a transaction with a teller. You can check with them if you like." She wasn't going to let him think of her as a possible suspect. "Look, there's things you should know about what's been going on here. My aunt Deirdre was being threatened by someone and now she's dead. Someone tried to force me off the road two days ago. Now Liz Fraser has been murdered. There's something wrong going on here."

"Deirdre MacPhail's death was ruled an accident. I investigated it myself." DI Alexander spoke evenly. His smile didn't fade. He folded his hands together above his bony knees.

"And on the face of it, it looked like it might have been, but maybe you were supposed to think that," Elspeth countered.

"Come along now. She was eighty-two. Had a gammy hip. Tripped on a rug and fell down the stairs." He looked as if he would like to laugh.

"But there were things that never got reported to the police. She was being harassed, long before that happened."

She rattled through the list. The stone thrown through the window. The dead cormorant nailed to the door. Threatening notes. Poop left on her doorstep, and how, like Elspeth, Deirdre had been driven off the road, into a wall. "That could have killed her," she said.

"But it didn't," said Fergus Alexander, not convinced. His eyebrows, sandy brown to match his hair, rose questioningly above green-grey eyes that still looked amused. "Deirdre MacPhail made up stories," he reminded Elspeth. "She was good at it, wasn't she? I've read a couple of her books myself. Your auntie had an active imagination."

"She wasn't making all that up. She kept journals, with notes." Elspeth protested. "And she did report the broken window to the police."

"I remember that," he said patiently. "It was investigated. Probably just some tomfoolery down on the beach, a party that got out of hand. Some visitors just don't know how to behave and they had been drinking. But nothing else was reported. If her car was all smashed up, why didn't she say?"

The answer was that Deirdre had been drinking that night and hadn't chosen to tell. Elspeth wasn't sure how she should reply to that.

"And anyhow," he continued, taking up his notebook and pen once more. "It's the death of Elizabeth Fraser that concerns both of us right now. Do you know of anyone here on Sulla that would have wanted to kill her?" He uncapped the pen, ready to take notes.

"No, I don't," said Elspeth. "I thought at first that it was to do with the house but now I wonder if it's something to do with Deirdre's books. That's the only connection Liz Fraser had to the people who live here. That and the book festival."

"Who did she pal around with while she was here?"

Elspeth reeled off the names of the members of the festival committee, feeling uncomfortable as she watched him write them all down. These were all people who were being kind to her.

"There are lots of people on this island that were pleased that Deirdre wrote the books," she added. "They made this island popular for tourists. But other people don't like how they've changed life here. They hated Deirdre for writing them. Only that's not new. It's been going on for a long time. There were accusations aimed at her years ago when her husband died and she inherited the Skipper's House but it all stopped, eventually. It started up again just after Deirdre started writing murder mysteries five or six years ago and now it looks like there's going to be a TV series, filmed here on Sulla. Liz was helping to make that happen."

That link was obvious, now that she thought about it. Filming was the most recent development in Deirdre's career and if the Mairi MacIntosh TV series was successful, it could spread the island's fame worldwide.

"You're basically saying that half the people who live here had a good reason to kill that woman?" Fergus Alexander appeared skeptical.

"And I'm the most likely target next." Elspeth sat forward on the edge of her chair, eager to convince. "I'm the person who will benefit the most from the TV series. I'm in danger here. I need to get back to Canada."

"We can't have you doing that." Fergus Alexander recapped his pen. "Everything you've just told me is very interesting and I'll certainly take that all into account, but I'm going to need you to stay here for the time being."

"You cannot be serious," Elspeth protested. "I'm not a suspect. I was in Canada when Deirdre died and I spent last night in Oban. I've told you everything I know. Why can't I leave?"

"Because," DI Alexander explained, as if he was addressing a child, "we know that your aunt fell downstairs all by herself. It was ruled an accidental death and that case is closed. This death is the only murder I am investigating. I'm assuming that Elizabeth Fraser was in charge of what happened to any money that comes in now from those books, but most of it goes to you?"

Elspeth nodded.

"So she was managing those accounts and I presume she was being paid for that? Receiving a percentage? So maybe you had a falling out about that? With her gone, you'll get more money, won't you?" Elspeth listened to him and felt her mouth fall open. "There's no saying that you couldn't have killed Ms. Fraser before you got on the ferry yesterday. That body's been lying there for quite some time. Did you get into an argument? Take a knife out of a drawer and stab her with it?"

"You think I killed her?" Elspeth was astonished. She scrambled to think through all the reasons that showed she could not be the murderer. "The dog was locked in the shed outside. Why would I do that?" She could hear how lame that excuse was as soon as the words came out of her mouth.

"To keep it from getting at the body? You knew it would lie there for a day." DI Alexander dismissed her suggestion.

"I wasn't here when Liz died. You need to listen to me. I'm not your murderer! I'm more likely to be the next victim."

"You'll be fine." His fleshy lips stretched into a smile once more as he tucked the pen away and reached into another capacious pocket for his phone. "You've got Calum McFee and his mother right next door to keep an eye on you. The McQuarries live along the road, too, and they're a capable pair. I'm going to be staying at the hotel for a day or two, with a whole forensic team. There's never been this many police on Sulla before. Tell you what. I'll get Jackie Buchanan to stop by and make sure you're all right once a day. She'll check up on how you are doing."

That way, he would make sure that the police knew where she was, Elspeth realized. He called Jackie to come and pick him up.

"Come over to the Skipper's House tomorrow," he said, "and I'll make sure that my folk let you pick up what you need. Just your own things, mind. Nothing that belonged to your aunt." He looked at Wilma, lying on her back with her legs in the air. "Nice dog, that. I'm quite partial to a wee terrier, myself."

Going back to the Skipper's House was the last thing Elspeth wanted to do. Or spending any more time in the company of DI Alexander. She watched him drive away. So did Donalda McFee. She came right over to Elspeth's front door.

"That's Fergus Alexander, isn't it?" she asked.

"He thinks I murdered Liz Fraser!" Elspeth wailed and burst into tears.

21

Donalda found a box of Kleenex and also a crystal decanter full of single malt whisky in Bernie Baxter's sideboard.

"Blow your nose," she instructed Elspeth, "and sit yourself down." She poured a couple of generous measures into glasses, crystal to match the decanter, and handed one to Elspeth. The whisky was smooth, but neat and strong.

"I need some water in this," Elspeth said.

"That's from the distillery in Oban. Fine stuff. Bernie always gets the best." Donalda, ever the traditionalist, made it clear that she did not approve of diluting good whisky but she did fetch a small jug of water to oblige. Then she sat down as well.

"You were in Oban yesterday, weren't you? How can Fergus think you could have been here and stabbed Liz Fraser?"

Elspeth had had enough time to get her breath back.

"He thinks I killed her before I left. Liz died yesterday. The body's been lying there all night."

"But why would he think you'd want to do that?"

"For money," said Elspeth. "You know that Liz is Deirdre's literary executor? I get any cash that comes from the books now that she's dead, but Liz manages the business and she gets a cut."

"There can't be that much more that will come in now that she's dead, will there? Deirdre isn't going to be writing any more books. It'll just be royalties, from the books that are left, won't it?"

"It could be way more," Elspeth told her. "Did you know that they're going to start filming the Mairi MacIntosh books for TV?"

"Deirdre did say something about it. But that's happened before. They were going to film the Sulla books and nothing ever came of it."

"It looks like it's really going to happen this time. There'll be film crews here by the spring, at the latest, Liz said. Deirdre signed off on the deal just before she died. That's going to pay lots and Liz would have got a percentage. But it's not enough for me to want to kill her! I'm going to get way more money than I ever expected, what with the house and everything in it and now the filming. This makes no sense! What is that man thinking?"

"Fergus has always been a bit of an odd duck," said Donalda. "His family was Wee Free." It was cool inside the little house. She got up and turned on an electric heater. The bars on it soon glowed red.

"Wee Free?" asked Elspeth.

"Strict Presbyterians. Old Testament, observe the Sabbath. Real Bible-thumpers. There's a kirk here like that. No dancing or any real singing." Donalda sipped her neat whisky. "Some of them still only sing psalms and paraphrases, unaccompanied. A man called a precentor leads the singing. Sings out the first line and then they all join in. Some people think it sounds interesting but it's an acquired taste. Fergus has a fine voice, you know. His mammy was sure that was what he would do when he grew up. Be a precentor. He was allowed to sing at the Mod when he was growing up. That's the Scottish Gaelic festival that happens every year in some part of the Highlands. I still go when I can. I saw Fergus often when he was a wee lad, standing up there in his kilt. He won all the prizes, year after year. The Alexanders didn't believe in singing for the sake of it. They only let him do it because he was singing Gaelic and they wanted to support the culture.

"He went to Oban High School, same year as Calum. They boarded together in the hostel. The music teacher thought that he should go on to Music College in Glasgow and get proper training but the family was having none of that. All the Alexander men join the police. His dad was an inspector before him and his grandad too, so that's where Fergus was going, whether he liked it or not. His mother would have had him out of school and into the police cadets when he was sixteen if she'd had her way, I was told, but the headmaster at the school insisted Fergus should stay on and write his Highers. Scottish school leaving exams," she explained. "He did well, too. Fergus was a smart boy. He could have gone to university, like my Calum." She smiled, proud of her son.

"And he's still, what did you call it, a 'Wee Free'?"

"I don't think so. He maybe leads the singing now and then but he's not a fanatic. He belongs to a choir in Oban. I heard him sing the *Messiah* the year before we got locked down. And he's in a group that used to put on musicals before the pandemic. I heard that they're starting up again. Gilbert and Sullivan. Old Mrs. Alexander must be turning in her grave." The thought made Donalda laugh, and she wasn't done yet. Elspeth was glad to listen. The story was a distraction, maybe intentionally so.

"He met a girl from Ballachulish and they've lived in a nice house in Ardrishaig for years now. Calum says his wife was worried sick when Police Scotland amalgamated their divisions a few years back. They thought he might get transferred to Glasgow and she certainly didn't want to have to move there. But Fergus got to stay in Argyll. He's done well, I suppose. He's made detective inspector and he'll be able to retire with a big police pension in a few years' time, while he's still quite young. It's a quiet job out here compared to some places. I expect he's hoping to get this all cleared up soon as he can, then he can get back to his singing."

"But he can't pin this on me!" Elspeth complained. "If someone killed Deirdre, then Liz, isn't it likely to be me next? I told him, but he doesn't seem to want to take that seriously. He talks down to me like I'm a preschooler. He says I have to stay here. I want to go home to Canada, but I can't leave." She felt herself tear up again and wiped her eyes.

"Of course he's not going to let you go," said Donalda, matter-of-factly. "You're too close to what's happened. Not that I think you did it, but he's going to have to be sure about that. We need you here too, to make sure the book festival happens and that we say goodbye to Deirdre properly. Don't you worry. We'll all keep an eye on you. But what's this about Deirdre? You think she was killed, too? She fell down the stairs, didn't she? Wasn't that an accident?"

Elspeth drank the last of her whisky. Her glass was refilled, right away. Donalda added a splash of water for her this time, without being asked.

"There's all these notebooks that she kept in the house, scribbles really, like a cross between a journal and a to-do list. Notes about what she was writing. It looks like she wrote down everything daily. I haven't read them all. But in some of them she writes about how someone was harassing her. She got notes telling her she needed to watch out, there was the dead bird left hanging on her door, the car crash. The police don't know about any of that. They only know that someone threw a stone through her window five years ago. They take everything at face value. They say that some drunk partygoer on the beach threw the stone. She fell and broke her neck. They didn't investigate that any further either. But I wonder if she wasn't alone that night. Maybe someone pushed her and made it look as if she tripped on a rug."

"Where are these notebooks now?" Donalda sipped her whisky, listening.

"They're in the house. I told the inspector about them but he didn't seem to think much about them."

"Well, he wouldn't. Fergus Alexander isn't going to take kindly to being told he's made a mistake. He's been in charge around here forever. What he says goes." Donalda was interrupted by a loud banging on the front door.

"Are you home?" Jackie Buchanan stepped in without being asked and walked through to the living room. Wilma the dog went to greet her. "I've been told to drop by and check up on you, Elspeth Laird."

"You'll have a dram?" Donalda raised her glass. "You're off work now?"

"Best not," said Jackie, "but I wouldn't mind a cup of tea."

"Right you are." Donalda got up to go fill the kettle. "What's going on over at the Skipper's House?" she asked as she walked past Jackie. "Have they taken the body away yet?"

"Flew it out by air ambulance. There's a bunch of SOCOs busy fingerprinting everything. They're going to want yours," Jackie told Elspeth, turning an upright chair from the table around so she could sit and face her. "You're supposed to drop by tomorrow, right? They'll probably do it then."

"Will DI Alexander be there?" asked Elspeth. She did not want to come face to face with the inspector again.

"He comes and goes," said Jackie. "Dishes out orders then takes off to go talk to people. He's been over at the MacKinnons already, and the MacPhails."

"Doesn't he know that they might have something to do with all the bad things that were happening to Deirdre?" Elspeth asked.

"I think he's more interested in finding out if anyone was hanging around your house yesterday."

Donalda came back with a mug of tea for Jackie. "Elspeth says Fergus thinks she did it," she said. "Knifed Lizzie then took off in the boat to Oban. Then pretended it was all a big surprise when she got back here and found the body."

"You?" Jackie looked at Elspeth. "I hadn't heard about that. He just said that you were staying over here for now so you'd be out of his way."

"Elspeth wants to get herself off back to Canada, in case somebody's out to get her next," Donalda continued to explain.

"Can't say I blame you. Why does Fergus think that you would want to kill that woman that was visiting you?"

"I didn't do it!" Elspeth protested. "I left on the ferry the day before. He says I could have killed Liz before I went."

"There'll be a post-mortem," said Jackie. "If you had done it she'd have been lying there more than twenty-four hours before you got back here and found the body. So if they find out she died later than that, you'll be in the clear. I wouldn't worry if I was you." At least the local police constable didn't think Elspeth was the killer.

"He doesn't believe that Deirdre could have been pushed down the stairs when she died, either. And maybe she wasn't but he should have checked that out at the time," Elspeth told her.

"Did you tell him that?" Jackie raised an eyebrow and suppressed a smile. "He won't like that. DI Alexander is never wrong."

"It could be me next, but he isn't taking that seriously either."

"Maybe he is," said Jackie. "That's maybe why I have to stop by every day and make sure you're okay. But don't fash yourself. We'll take good care to make sure that you're safe. And here you are, in Bernie's house, where Donalda can watch out for you. Calum too, when he's around. The SOCOs will be finished at the Skipper's House soon enough, but you don't want to be staying there all by yourself now this has happened."

"I need to get in! My laptop's still there." said Elspeth. Her laptop was lying on the desk in Deirdre's den, beside the big iMac.

"All the computer stuff's being sent off to Glasgow." Jackie reached for her phone. "I'd better give them a bell." She went into the hallway to make the call and went out the front door, away from listening ears. "Calum's just driven up," she called back to them. "I'll tell him we're all here."

"Jackie's a good policewoman," Donalda said.

"You sure about that?" Elspeth asked. "She didn't pay much attention when I told her about finding a dead fish that someone left in the house."

"I heard, but don't worry. Jackie notices everything but she doesn't make a fuss about it. She knows that her main job is to keep the peace out here and she does a good job of that."

Jackie came back. "Just as well I called them. They had your computer all bagged up and ready to go. One of them will check it out tonight and then they'll decide if you can have it back. She's going to call you later and get your password."

Calum McFee followed her into the house. "You'll be having one?" His mother tapped a finger to the decanter.

"Best not. I said I'd have dinner with Fergus Alexander tonight," he said. "Can't have him thinking I've been drinking and driving."

"That house is going to be in a bit of a state by the time they're done," Jackie told Elspeth "I'll make sure it's cleaned up before you move back in. How long can you stay here?"

"For four weeks," Elspeth told her.

"That's good. We might have this all sorted out soon," she said. "Then you'll be able to move back in, no bother." She would drop by each evening for now, on the way home from work and she gave Elspeth the number for her mobile. She was to call her if anything at all happened that seemed odd, or if anything scared her. Donalda could make sure Elspeth was okay every morning?

"I can do that," Donalda replied.

Calum was booked onto the plane the next day. He had to get back to his office in Oban.

He would bring as much work as he could over to Sulla while all this was happening, he said, so he'd be around here, right next door, as soon as he could. Elspeth felt more at ease, as if a strong, protective wall had been placed around her.

She checked her email when they had gone. Dave had messaged.

Weekend is best. Saturday?

She desperately wanted to talk to him before then. She couldn't get back to Winnipeg right now. She was stuck here, with a police inspector who had her on his list of suspects. Did she want to tell him about that? She knew what he'd say. That she needed to calm down, not overthink this. And maybe he was right. The whole idea was stupid, wasn't it? There was no way she'd be accused of killing Liz. And there was nothing Dave could do to help her, from so far away. She would just have to stay put and wait this situation out.

22

The police presence was evident at the Skipper's House when Elspeth arrived the next morning. Liz's car was still in the garage but two other vehicles filled the driveway. One was white with blue and yellow markings, POLICE written boldly down the side. The other was an unmarked Kia. Elspeth pulled onto the grassy verge near the gate and watched a small woman in white protective gear walk out of the house to meet her. There was no sign of DI Fergus Alexander.

DS Julie Lawson brought disposable clothing to Elspeth and watched while she put it on. Soon they were both completely covered, head to toe. Elspeth got a chance to see a round, dark-eyed face before it was masked. Straight eyebrows, firm mouth. DS Lawson worked with DI Alexander, out of Oban, she said. He'd told her what needed to be done. She needed fingerprints, first. Then she would walk through the house with Elspeth, to the office on the ground floor and upstairs to the bedroom where she had been sleeping. The bathroom. She didn't need to go into any other rooms, did she?

"Isn't that car you're driving the one that belonged to Deirdre MacPhail?" she asked, noticing the blue Tiguan. "Isn't it part of her estate?"

"It is," Elspeth agreed, "but I've been told I can drive it for now and it has been left to me. I've covered the insurance." She showed the documentation on her phone. The policewoman squinted at it.

"What about my computer?" Elspeth asked. Julie Lawson had phoned her last night and said she could have it back.

Elspeth was glad that she didn't need to go into the kitchen. Liz's body would be gone but there would still be blood. Important forensic evidence, she imagined. The police would be measuring how it spattered to help them determine where Liz and her assailant had been at the time of the attack. She felt slightly sick at the thought and her proximity to it.

She did want to get dog food, though, and Wilma's food bowls. The choice at the shop in Tostaig was limited and she wasn't sure that Bernie Baxter would approve of her feeding a dog out of his soup bowls.

The detective sergeant sighed. Nothing that belonged in the house was supposed to go but she didn't think a bag of dry dogfood and a few cans out of the pantry would be important to the case. She called through to the kitchen. Elspeth caught a glimpse of a white-suited man with a camera. He would put them aside for her, she was told.

They went upstairs. DS Lawson had been in the Skipper's House before, after Deirdre had died. "This house is like a museum," she said as they reached the upper landing. "I couldn't stand living in a place like this. All of this old furniture must trap dust. How does anyone keep it clean?"

The house had been dust-free when Elspeth had first arrived. She didn't think that Deirdre was the type to fuss over housekeeping. It must have been professionally cleaned, after her body, too, had been removed and taken off to Glasgow for the autopsy.

Elspeth's carry-on case was still in the bedroom. She had only taken a light overnight bag to Oban with her, one she had found in the bottom of Deirdre's wardrobe. She was still wearing the clothes she had left in two days before. The DS listed every item she planned to take with her. She would have to sign for it all, and DI Alexander had asked DS Lawson to take down a statement from Elspeth, about where she had been, yesterday and the day before. He also wanted all of her receipts.

Elspeth had found as many as she could. A grocery bill from a shop in Oban, and one for petrol. She had a paper note from the bank saying she had deposited a cheque in sterling to her Canadian account. She had a phone record of an Airbnb payment. She had no proof of her drive down to Tarbert.

"Maybe we can go in here and I'll write down everything you can tell us, starting from when you left this house, two days ago, right through until when you came back here and found Ms. Fraser's body," the policewoman said, opening the door into Deirdre's den.

There was more evidence of police action inside the room. Fingerprint powder was everywhere. Deirdre's iMac was gone.

"I need access to my aunt's work files," Elspeth said. "I'm filling in for her, managing the Sulla Book Festival, and it's coming up in a couple of months. I need to work on that. I know you have to keep the computer but Deirdre kept track of things on paper. Her work files are all in the bottom right-hand drawer of her desk."

They looked. The files were still there, but Elspeth couldn't take them. The book festival was a point of connection between Sulla and Liz Fraser so any paperwork related to that was staying where the police could get at them.

"Everything you need to know will be in the computer," Elspeth argued in frustration. "All the paper files will just be duplication." But DS Lawson was not going to budge.

"We'll be out of here in a few days," she said. "You'll be able to get back in after that. You'll have to wait until then."

Then Elspeth noticed the empty shelf, other side of the room, where Deirdre's spiral notebooks had been. She and Liz had taken them through to the kitchen, stacked them on the table. Had they still been there, when she found the body? She couldn't remember seeing them.

Julie Lawson said she'd go look. She came right back.

"There's nothing there," she reported.

"None of them? There were more than twenty of them. Deirdre used them as journals. She kept notes of everything that was going on in her life. They were here when I left to go to Oban. Whoever killed Liz must have taken them!"

"I need you to wait in the hallway." DS Lawson stood up and led her out of the room. She went into the kitchen and Elspeth heard her ask the constable to drive Elspeth and her belongings back to the house where she was staying.

"We're going to have to examine that vehicle you're driving after all. If everything's all right, we'll get it back to you later," she informed Elspeth when she re-emerged.

"But why?" Being without a car on Sulla was going to be a problem. "I took the car with me to Oban. You've seen the ferry tickets." Then it dawned on Elspeth that DS Lawson must think that she, herself, could have taken the notebooks, had perhaps disposed of them in Oban. They would be checking the car for fibres, as proof. Elspeth was indeed a suspect.

"I can't manage on this island without a car," she complained.

"You'll have to. It'll need to go to the mainland so we can have a proper look at it. Maybe you can rent something for now."

They wouldn't find a thing to incriminate her in the Tiguan. Elspeth knew she didn't need to worry about that, but this was inconvenient. Maybe she could catch the plane to Oban this afternoon and bring a rental back on the next day's ferry, as long as the police didn't expect her to remain stuck on the island for now.

They did. "We don't want you leaving Sulla. Someone can put a car on the boat for you and you can pick it up at this end," DS Lawson informed her, but she was able to offer some help. She knew a garage in Oban that had rentals and wrote down a name for Elspeth.

A young constable drove her back to Bernie Baxter's house in the police car with the name emblazoned on the side. He offered to stop at the shop in Tostaig in case she needed anything, but she said she'd be okay. She could just imagine the questions she'd be asked at the checkout, while a police car waited for her outside the door to transport her back to Bernie Baxter's house. The policeman insisted on carrying the dog food and her bag to the front door for her. Calum McFee walked over to Bernie's. They watched the police car disappear around the bend.

"Did they confiscate Deirdre's nice blue Volkswagen?" he asked. "Why would they want to do that?" She told him.

"They won't find a thing," she said, "but now I don't have a car, unless I can get a rental sent over from Oban."

Not to worry, she could borrow his while he was off the island, he said, if she didn't mind driving around in the old Peugeot. Maybe the police would check the Volkswagen right away and she'd get it back, before his next visit. And Bernie had a bike in the shed behind his house. She could have a shot on that.

Wilma had come with him and was bouncing around Elspeth's feet. "She was barking when you left, so I took her over to my house for company," he said. He would need a lift to the airport, middle of the afternoon, if she was going to borrow his car. Could she drive him over? Meantime he had some work to finish up. He'd see her in a couple of hours.

Elspeth carried in the bags and closed the door behind her.

"I can give you some real dog food now," she said to the dog and filled the bowl with kibble.

Calum had eaten with Fergus Alexander last night. He hadn't seemed surprised that Elspeth and the car she was driving were under investigation. Had he learned from the DI that Elspeth was a suspect in this murder case, or had his mother already told him? If they had discussed that, in the middle of the hotel dining room, wouldn't the kitchen have heard? That news would be irresistible. The whole island would know by the time this day was over.

But Calum was as friendly as ever. He was lending her his car and he was still acting as her lawyer. She'd maybe find out what he knew on the way to the airport. It would take less than ten minutes to drive there. Not much time to talk.

In the meantime, she wasn't sure what to do with herself. She couldn't work on the book festival without knowing what was already planned. She could call Annabel or Jan but she'd rather meet with them face to face and she had no transportation.

She sat down at a small table in Bernie's kitchen and thought.

She knew that she wasn't responsible for Liz Fraser's death but someone on Sulla was. Whoever had vandalized Deirdre's house, broken in when she herself was living there and had forced both of them off the road, hadn't been out to kill. It was more like they wanted to convince Deirdre, then herself, to leave the island. Just gone, not dead. Her presence in the house was annoying someone.

Killing Liz couldn't have been about that. And why were the notebooks gone? They had mentioned the threatening notes that had been left for Deirdre. Had there been anything else incriminating in them? And who else would have known about them?

The antagonism against Deirdre had started when she inherited the house then had petered out. It had begun again five years ago. What was happening then? The book festival had just got going and was bringing more visitors to Sulla.

The first Mairi MacIntosh book had just been published, as well. It described a murder, and this island prided itself on being relatively crime free. Did someone think that those books tainted the island's reputation? If so, it was ironic that a serious crime investigation was now happening for real.

When had filming on Sulla first been mentioned? And to whom? She didn't know, but Calum would.

She went through to the living room and looked through the sideboard drawers. She found stationery in one and a lined writing pad. She would write lists, to help her figure this out.

Who might Liz Fraser have invited into the house?.

The MacPhails. It was possible that Chrissie would have been asked inside. They were neighbours. So was Young Norman, Rob MacPhail's older brother, the one who still farmed the croft.

The MacKinnons. Cath MacKinnon was harmless, she was sure of that, but was Lachie? He seemed feckless, drank too much, but he might be impulsive enough to do something stupid in the heat of the moment.

Annabel and Sandy McQuarrie. They were helpful. Eager to sell the house for her, and everything in it. The sooner that happened, the sooner they got paid. Could Liz have said anything to them that would have put a stop to that? Or delayed it?

If that was true, shouldn't she add Jackie Buchanan and her husband, Doug, to the list? They wanted to buy the house. She should find out whether that was still the case, now that there had been another unexpected death there. She wrote down their names, too. Then she ran a line through them. If she started suspecting the local police, she must be getting paranoid, she told herself.

Elspeth could think of no reason at all for Jan MacLeod to benefit from Liz's death, or Calum McFee. But Jan had access to past history through her own mother. Donalda knew things, too, from way back. Both Calum and Jan would have heard old stories, growing up. Maybe one of them knew something that they shouldn't.

Donnie MacPherson and his partner, Frieda, must have met Liz often enough while they were working at the hotel. There could be a reason for one of them to dislike her. Liz had come to Sulla often over the years. She must have met many of the four hundred or so permanent residents.

Elspeth didn't know half the people who lived on Sulla. It could be any of them. What she was doing was futile. She scrunched up the sheet of paper in frustration and tossed it into a garbage can.

Many of the people she had listed seemed kind and considerate. She needed to work alongside them and she needed their help if she was going to live in this isolated place for the next three months. But could she trust any of them?

She needed to ask questions. The more actual facts that she found out, the better. Things might become clearer if she got the right answers.

23

Calum McFee had other matters to discuss on the short car ride to the airport, so Elspeth's questions remained unanswered.

"If you look at the will, it says that Deirdre's agent will continue to manage her literary affairs, receiving her usual percentage. The rest of the money goes to you, as beneficiary, but you can decide to appoint another agent, at your own discretion. So you can replace Liz."

"I should talk to her assistant, Inga, in Edinburgh," Elspeth said.

"Do that, soon as you get home," he advised her. "And call, don't send a message. We need to know. We don't want your cousin, Iain Balfour, sticking his nose into this. He just might try to absorb the royalties that are due to you into the estate so he'll get a cut, and if the film cameras start rolling over here by September, he could try to claim that, too."

"Is he entitled to do that?" Elspeth was in the driver's seat, trying to get used to the gearshift on Calum's old car and a soft clutch.

"Nah. But he might think he can get away with it since you're going to be back in Canada before long and I'm just a teuchter solicitor that wouldn't know better. He's the type that might chance it."

"A teuchter?" She found it hard to pronounce the word.

"We slag southerners off by calling them sassenach and they call us teuchters in return," he laughed. "It kind of means country folk that don't know much."

Elspeth turned at a sign that said ISLE OF SULLA AIRPORT, with an arrow pointing to a low building, just big enough for a couple of offices and a waiting area. A small yellow prop plane sat out on the single runway and a handful of cars were parked at the door.

"Find out if Iain's already spoken to Liz Fraser's assistant and if he has, let me know, right away." Calum rubbed Wilma's furry brown head as he picked up his bag from the back seat. Then he stuck his head inside the front passenger door once more.

"Don't worry yourself about what Fergus is saying," he said. "He just likes to get people riled. It might be a week before the post-mortem results show up but they'll show when Liz died and I expect that was long after you left the house to go and catch the ferry."

"So you're sure I didn't do it?" Elspeth tried to make a joke of it.

"You've no reason to kill her, have you?" he said. "Plus I don't think that you're the murdering kind," he added and a wide grin spread across his face.

He strode off to the airport building. The dog had hopped over into the vacated front seat. Elspeth stroked her fur and watched him go. She wondered what his story was, why he lived here alone next to his mother when he wasn't working in Oban. There had been no mention of a second wife or children. He must have a social life on the mainland. Why else would he be going back there, right before the weekend? She wouldn't mind knowing a bit more about him, now that he was her neighbour as well as her lawyer. There had been something mildly flirtatious about that last comment. He was kind of attractive, in a big, furry way. Comfortable. Like a friendly Newfoundland dog a friend of hers had once owned.

Was he right about her cousin, Iain Balfour? Was Iain greedy enough to grab as much as he could of Deirdre's money from her? One thing was for sure. Iain couldn't be involved in any way in Liz's murder. He was far away in Edinburgh.

She drove straight back to Bernie's house and called Liz Fraser's assistant.

Inga Hansen was not in the office; she was home, deeply saddened by the news of Liz's sudden death. She wasn't Liz's employee, she told Elspeth. They were partners, at work and in life. She'd only answered this call because she needed to know what had happened on Sulla.

Elspeth told her as best she could, downplaying the gory details.

"It must have been quick," she said, trying to soften the news. "It doesn't look like she suffered. I think someone must have stopped by to visit and they got into an argument. The knife was probably one that was in the kitchen and it looked like it went straight into her heart. She'd have died straight away." She wasn't sure that was entirely true but it did mesh with what she had seen and it did seem to console Inga a little. She replied, sounding a little less miserable.

"The police have been here, asking questions," she told Elspeth. "They wanted to know all about Liz's relationship with Deirdre and what she was doing staying on Sulla with you."

"There's a big investigation going on here too," said Elspeth. "They're being very thorough."

Inga was designated as Liz's next-of-kin. "She has relatives in Fife but she didn't get along with them. She hasn't spoken to any of them in years. They didn't approve of our lifestyle." She had been told there would be a post-mortem and she couldn't arrange a funeral until the body was released. "We have many friends," she said. "They're all shocked about this and they'll want to be there. Lots of them were friends of Deirdre's, too. You should come and meet them."

Asking her what would happen to Deirdre's business so soon after this bereavement seemed inappropriate, but Inga brought the subject up herself. She could take Liz's place, if that was what Elspeth wanted, she said. She and Liz had co-owned the business. She knew Deirdre's publisher and the film company's plans were progressing quickly. She would have to get back to work soon.

"They're thinking they can do six episodes per book. That's very good news, so there will be several years of filming if everything goes according to plan. They've got a writing team working on the scripts already and someone's going to be sent to Sulla soon, to scout out suitable sites where they might shoot scenes. There's been some mention of using Deirdre's old house. You might want to hold off on selling the place. They'll pay you well for that, and they might be shooting soon. By September." She was going to take the weekend off work but she'd be back in the office on Monday. Why didn't Elspeth come to Edinburgh for a visit? They could meet in person. She'd introduce her to Deirdre's publisher, too. "We all have a share in this," she said. The invitation was attractive but Elspeth couldn't go.

"I have to stay on Sulla for now and help with the book festival." She didn't mention that DI Alexander had forbidden her to leave the island. "Maybe you can come here for that, instead?" That was a possibility. Inga could take Liz's place on the festival committee. They needed the connections to the book industry that she could provide.

Inga had heard nothing from Iain Balfour but she knew that Liz hadn't liked him. "She said she thought he was a bit cocky." The news about Liz's death was just getting out now, so he might know already. If he called, she would let him know that business was carrying on as usual. She seemed glad about that. Deirdre's file was obviously one she did not want to lose. They could keep in touch regularly by Zoom for now, if Elspeth wanted.

Elspeth hung up, relieved at how smoothly that had gone. A text from Annabel McQuarrie dinged on her phone

Come here for dinner? Police have been. Will ask Jan too.

Wilma had found a tennis ball and was dropping it at Elspeth's feet then looking pointedly up at her. She didn't fetch sticks but obviously a ball was a different matter. Elspeth had no idea where it had come from but she had no intention of throwing it around inside Bernie Baxter's house.

"Come on, girl," she said. "We'll go outside," but before she reached the door she heard a car pull up. She glanced out the window. Chrissie MacPhail was paying a visit.

"I'm not coming in." Chrissie stood outside the door, ignoring the fact that she hadn't been invited. "I'll say what I have to say right here and then I'll be gone."

She was taller than Elspeth, not fat but solid, sturdy legs firmly planted in sensible shoes, her wispy white hair cut short. She wore a quilted vest over a thin, woolly sweater and a tweed skirt and looked nothing like the curly-haired, smiling girl that Elspeth had seen in the photo, the one taken sixty years ago on a beach with Alasdair and Deirdre MacPhail, when they were all young and happy.

"I don't know what you've been saying to the police about me and my boys. We've had that inspector over at the house asking all kinds of questions about where we were around the time that woman got herself killed. Wanting to know why we coveted that old place that Deirdre MacPhail was living in, like we ever did. I've told you, and I told him, I never wanted it. Why would I want to stay in that godforsaken spot when we have a fine croft house of our own and good grazing land as well? And a nice wee house right next door for me to move into now that I'm on my own, so I can leave Young Norman and his wife the big house to raise their own bairns in? I'm better off where I am. Rob, too. He needs to be close to his work.

"I haven't set foot inside the Skipper's House in years and I don't want to. And I never had anything to do with that woman that's died now. Certainly I've seen her before, in the pub with Deirdre MacPhail now and then, but I never spoke to her, nor her to me, neither. I never had anything to do with her. Not me or my lads."

The corners of her mouth curved downwards. When she clamped it shut, she looked lipless.

"That inspector's been over at Rob's garage half the morning, too, stopping him getting on with his work. All kinds of folk driving by and seeing what's going on. It'll be all over Sulla that Rob's been questioned. Just as well my man Norman's in no state to know what's going on. He'd have a few words to say about this, I can tell you. I'm not having my neighbours thinking ill of me or my sons, either, because the likes of you is telling lies about us. You're just as bad as that old auntie of yours. She was always trouble, too.

"Why don't you get back on a plane and go back where you belong? Leave us to get on with our lives, bothering nobody, just like it was before?"

"I can't go back until the book festival's over." Elspeth was finally able to get a word in. "I've said I'll take Deirdre's place running it. And there will be a memorial for her."

"That's more nonsense too." Chrissie MacPhail glowered at her, undaunted. "That book festival just brings more people that don't belong over here on the boat. Why aren't you burying Deirdre in Edinburgh or wherever it was she came from?"

"Because she wanted her ashes to go into the water, near where she lost her husband," Elspeth retorted, hoping that would silence Chrissie MacPhail but the old woman barely stopped for breath.

"She was a heathen, just like him." She spat out her contempt. "Can't have a respectable burial, like ordinary folk. Bad rubbish, the pair of them. You, too. You keep your mouth shut about me and my family or it'll be the worse for you. Badness just gets more badness." And she turned right round and walked away back to her car.

Elspeth blinked. She almost wanted to laugh, what Chrissie MacPhail had said was so absurd. But she had also just been threatened, the same way that Deirdre had in those notes she had written about. Chrissie drove off, but Elspeth felt very alone, here by herself with only one small dog for company. Calum was gone and there was no sign of Donalda. She needed some friendly faces around her. She took Wilma with her and set off in Calum's old Peugeot to Annabel's, an hour too early for dinner.

Donalda McFee was in the café sitting at one of the tables having tea with Kate Mary MacLeod. Her walker was parked behind her chair. "Kate Mary needs to get out of an afternoon," said Donalda. "What's the matter with you? You look like you've seen a ghost."

Elspeth blurted out the story of Chrissie MacPhail's visit.

"Bad old witch," said Annabel. "Doesn't she know that DI Alexander's been talking to everybody?"

"Aye," Sandy called over from behind the counter. "He's been here, too. Makes us all feel like we're on his list."

"Chrissie's a proud soul." Donalda poured what was left in a teapot into her cup and Kate Mary's. "She had a tough go of it with Norman. He was always tight with the money."

Kate Mary nodded her head in agreement.

"Chrissie was stuck out there on the croft with those two wee lads until Donalda here taught her to drive," she said. "Chrissie used to say that Deirdre was a spoiled woman but I think she was jealous of how Deirdre was able to live her life on her own terms. Rob's a bit like his old man, not in looks but in spirit. A good mechanic, mind. Young Norman's much nicer."

"And Chrissie bosses him around because of it," added Donalda.

Elspeth's phone beeped. She had a text from Jackie Buchanan.

At your house, checking in. Where are you?

Elspeth had forgotten that Jackie would stop by on the way from work to make sure that she was all right. She went outside to call her back and apologize.

"You need to tell me if you're going to be out," Jackie's voice rang out from the phone. "But I've got good news for you. The SOCOs will be done in the house by the time the boat leaves tomorrow. I'll get it all cleaned up by teatime and you can move right back in again whenever you want."

Elspeth shuddered at the thought. She would prefer to stay where she was for as long as she could.

24

Jan MacLeod arrived at the café just in time to give her mother a peck on the cheek. Donalda and Kate Mary were finally leaving. Sandy went out to help load Kate Mary's walker into the back of the little Fiesta.

"Did all three of them grow up together? Donalda and Kate Mary and Chrissie MacPhail?" Elspeth stood by the window, watching the two old friends drive off.

"They're closer than that. Chrissie was a McFee before she married Norman MacPhail." Jan waved to her mother through the glass. "And my mum's dad was his cousin. We're all one big, happy family here on Sulla."

"If Chrissie was a McFee and Donalda married one, they're not really related, are they?" Elspeth found it hard to imagine those two coming from the same gene pool.

"No," said Jan, counting out relationships on her fingers. "But Calum McFee's a second cousin to Rob and Norman MacPhail."

"Calum never got married again?"

"Why're you asking?" Annabel called from the back counter where she was helping Sandy clean up. They both looked in Elspeth's direction, interested.

"Nothing like that!" Elspeth protested. "I've got my own guy, back home in Canada. I just wondered."

Sandy had returned and was opening the fridge. He took out a couple of salad containers.

"It's a fine night for a barbecue," he said, "We don't get many of those, this time of the year. I've got some lamb chops I can do on the grill. Otherwise, it's going to be what's left on the shelves here." At short notice, that sounded fine.

They moved through the house to a patio, out at the back. It sat on a bay, facing the wide expanse of the Atlantic. For once, there was little wind and the sun shone brightly on the slowly swelling sea.

"Look, we've got visitors." Jan pointed. A cluster of grey heads poked out of the water near some rocks. The seals watched them as they looked back. "Sometimes they keep an eye on people," she said. "We used to have a neighbour played his pipes to them of a summer evening and they'd all come close to listen."

"Calum has been married twice." Annabel opened a bottle of white wine and finally answered Elspeth's question. "First to some girl he met when they were students in Glasgow. She's a teacher now, over there."

"Then there was Simone," Jan added to the story. "French. Very chic! She wore the best clothes. But she didn't like living here one little bit and he wasn't happy in France. He wanted to practise law here, at least that's what he told us."

"They lasted a few years, though." Annabel passed Elspeth a glass. "Had two wee girls. They used to bring them here in the summertime. Calum got that blackhouse from an uncle years ago. It was their summer home. Simone always complained it was far too small for them. And Sulla was too cold and windy. She never wanted to have much to do with us."

"She acted like she thought we were peasants." Sandy broiled lamb on the grill. He'd added a burger for the dog and had Wilma's undivided attention. "Calum's paying for his daughters' education. One of them's studying in Paris. He came back to Oban for a quiet life, he says."

"And that works for us," his wife added. "Having to work with a solicitor off-island was a real pain."

They loaded up their plates. Potato salad. Carrot and beet slaw.

"Sorry we're out of greens," said Sandy. "I've got a boxful coming in on the boat tomorrow."

"Jackie Buchanan says the police are going to be leaving on it," Elspeth told them.

They settled onto folding chairs, ones that could be put away quickly on windy days. But this wasn't one of those. The air was almost still, the sea gently shifting, silver and bluey green all the way to the horizon.

"Is DI Alexander going with them?" asked Annabel. "He came here at lunchtime today, when we had customers. We told him he'd have to wait. Wasn't pleased about that. He wanted to know where we were the past couple of days and how well we knew Liz Fraser."

"It sounds like he asked the MacPhails exactly the same thing," said Elspeth.

"Aye, but it's the attitude." Sandy had cut up the hamburger for the dog and put it in a bowl. "He looks at you like you're a fly he'd like to swat." He put the bowl down and watched the contents disappear. "Too bad I'm allergic," he said. "I'd like a wee terrier like that just fine."

Finding a new home for Wilma was still an unsolved problem.

"Fergus is a bonnie singer, though. He sang at my cousin's wedding." Jan was the only one of them who had not been questioned by DI Alexander.

"Maybe he'll drop by and talk to you tomorrow," said Annabel, "before he catches the boat."

"Jackie Buchanan says I can go back into the Skipper's House but I don't want to," Elspeth told them. "I'd rather stay where I am for now."

"Do that then," they all agreed. Bernie Baxter wouldn't be back on the island for three or four weeks yet. They were sure that he wouldn't mind.

They had planned to talk about the book festival but this evening had become too mellow for work. Elspeth could go over to the house and pick up Deirdre's files tomorrow. She'd check through them and get back to them with questions.

"See if you can find the authors' contracts," said Annabel. "That's the main thing." Jan had taken down notes of all their meetings. She would send copies to Elspeth, no bother.

"I'd go over to the house with you tomorrow but it's a Saturday, and I need to get the shop open." Jan screwed up her nose. "What kind of mess is it going to be in?"

"Jackie said she'd make sure it's all cleaned up." Elspeth sipped the cold wine. "I'll be all right. And I won't stay there for long. Just enough to pick up the files."

It was comforting, being here on a warm evening. She relaxed. Soon Sandy was clearing up their plates and talking about pie. Maybe some coffee? Annabel knew who Jackie would get to do the cleaning job, a local girl called Kimmy, a bit slow but she was a good worker. Kimmy would get that place all shined up. The only thing was she'd tell anybody who wanted to listen all about how much blood she'd had to wash off the floor.

They all looked out west. The sky had turned pink and gold, the sea reflecting it back. The seals were gone.

"Did you know that Liz had a partner in Edinburgh called Inga? They worked together? She's devastated," Elspeth said.

That led quite naturally into a conversation about Liz Fraser. They didn't know her all that well, they said. She came and stayed with Deirdre some summers, before the pandemic. Liz had been brought onto the book festival committee because she knew authors and other people in publishing but it was usually Deirdre she'd talked to. She'd attended a couple of festivals before the pandemic had locked them down but she had mainly hung around with the writers when that was happening. This was the first time Liz had been on Sulla in the past couple of years.

They had absolutely no idea why anyone would want her dead.

"Someone here must have killed her, though." Annabel put a plate of half-eaten rhubarb pie down on the patio table. "And she must have known whoever it was well enough to let them into the house."

"But that could be anybody. Liz used to hang around the pub of an evening with Deirdre. She'd have met a lot of the people who live here. And she'd have no reason not to welcome anybody in." Jan frowned. That was how things were done on Sulla. Everyone here knew everyone else and they often popped into one other's houses unannounced. Someone could have walked right into the Skipper's House.

But what would have led Liz into an argument, one serious enough to make someone want to kill her? Her only connection to the island was through the book festival.

"And Deirdre's books," said Elspeth. "Was anybody annoyed because she'd started writing murder mysteries, set here? Sulla prides itself on being almost crime free, doesn't it?"

Could be, they agreed, but everybody knew that those stories were all made up.

"Not like the Sulla books that she first wrote. There's a fair bit of truth in those," Sandy commented in a quiet voice.

"How about the filming?" Elspeth asked.

"What filming?"

"That's really going to happen?"

"Here? On Sulla?"

All three of them looked surprised.

"There was some talk, years ago, but nothing ever came of it," Sandy said. "Is that on again?"

"Not those ones," Elspeth told them. "They've moved on from there. It's the Mairi MacIntosh books that they're interested in now. Deirdre signed off on a TV series not long before she died and Liz said they're going to go ahead, without her. They're eager to get started. Inga just told me that they'll be sending a location scout out here real soon."

"Wow!" Jan's face lit up. "That's great! Maybe they'll be looking for extras. I wouldn't mind doing that. Skye would too."

"Do you know when they might start shooting?" asked Annabel.

"Inga thinks it might be as soon as September. She says they're working on the scripts right now."

"Fantastic!" Jan enthused some more. "A TV series will put us right on the map. Look what happened to Shetland after they shot that series there."

"Do we want that?" Sandy McQuarrie sounded less keen. "Aren't we full up with tourists already? We're a little island, where would we put more visitors? And what if more people want to buy a house and make it into a summer home? Prices are high enough already."

"Don't you want that to happen?" asked Elspeth.

"We've reached capacity." Food and drinks lay untouched as Sandy explained. "All the accommodation for this year's booked solid already. The hotel, the Airbnbs, the campground. There's nothing available from now until October. If those police had arrived a couple of weeks later, they'd never have found rooms at the hotel. All the spots on the ferry for caravans and the like are taken. People that want to come over for the book festival have to book months in advance."

"But isn't that a good thing? It might not last forever. It'll be a while before the TV series comes out. It will help keep Sulla popular," said Elspeth.

"That's true," he replied. "We're making more money off of this tourist boom than my mum or dad ever dreamed of, and it's a lot easier than trying to grow food here or keeping sheep and a few cows. But it's hard on the island. All those cars tear up the road surfaces. There's people go out sailing and get into trouble. We've got no lifeboat. We have to go out and do our best with the boats we have until rescue crews can get here from Oban.

"Doug Buchanan and Colin the Harbour have had to rescue someone off a skerry now and then. You know the cliffs? They get swarmed with birdwatchers. Some of them climb down and get stuck on the rockface, and of course they scare the birds away. It's really stupid. The beaches, too. You should see the rubbish that gets left behind, and that all has to get cleaned up. Most of our visitors are good folk." He raised a hand and rubbed his head. Without his cap, she could see that his hair was red. "But some of them act like idiots. It's great to see everybody enjoying themselves but they spoil what they come to see, if you know what I mean."

Annabel was listening closely, thinking about what he was saying.

"Still," she said. "If film crews are coming here, we need to be ready for them. Know what?" she turned to Elspeth, "The Skipper's House would be a great location. Deirdre's own home? They're going to love it. Don't sell it right away. We can still get all the antiques out of there and over to Glasgow for auction, but leave some furniture so it looks lived in. And that picture of Deirdre over the mantel, leave that too.

"A film crew's going to pay good money so they can use that house and you'll make a mint off it as a rental once it's famous. I could manage it for you. We'd both do well off of it. You don't want to be selling right now, after this murder's happened there, anyway. That's going to bring the price right down."

"It's always the money with you, Annabel." Sandy got to his feet and went to get more coffee. It wasn't said disparagingly. He spoke with a hint of admiration and a smile on his face.

"I'll bet Jackie and Doug Buchanan are going to make a low offer for the place." Annabel grinned back at her husband. "That's why she'll have wee Kimmy scrubbing the house clean again."

"That's right!" Jan agreed with her. "And it's why Doug's been over putting on new locks."

"Come to think of it, he'll have met Liz Fraser." Annabel flung back her head and laughed. "Maybe it was Doug that did it!"

And they hooted with laughter at the suggestion.

"He's been telling Colin the Harbour all about his plans for your place." Jan added to the joke. "How he can put a boathouse up at the pier. Offer swimming lessons. Lifeguarding, stuff like that. He really wants it."

The laughter petered out. None of them believed that was true, but it was a sobering thought.

"There's lots of folks around here wouldn't mind owning that pier. It's one of the most sheltered moorings on the island," Sandy reasoned. "It could be any one of them."

"I can't sell for months yet," Elspeth reminded them. "We'll maybe know a lot more by then."

It was getting dark, the sun sinking into the sea, the sky streaked with scarlet and purple, a narrow band of deep blue marking the spot where the Isle of Tiree lay, far over the horizon to the northwest, a ribbon of cloud above it. Way over to the south there was a faint blue outline of land. Northern Ireland, she was told.

"This weather's going to change," Sandy predicted. "We're in for another blow by morning. Let's just hope it doesn't stop the ferry from landing and taking DI Alexander and his crew back to the mainland."

It was getting cooler outside. They carried in the plates and glasses. Jan helped Sandy fold the chairs and stash them into a shed, so they wouldn't get blown away once the wind got up.

Elspeth drove back to the row of blackhouses, the dog at her side. The sea was a bright, luminous blue by now. Lights shone from Calum and Donalda's windows. If Deirdre had spent her summers like this, Elspeth understood why she had chosen to keep the house on Sulla and come back each year. Why she had chosen to remain, during the pandemic lockdown and after. On a night like this, Sulla was idyllic.

25

The next morning the island's mood had changed once more. Wind gusted in from the west, sending waves crashing against the shoreline. Dark clouds scurried across the sky, bringing sudden squalls of rain with them. Elspeth sat in the little blackhouse all morning, reading through minutes from the book festival and financial statements that Jan had emailed her while raindrops battered skylights that had been set into the steep roof. There might not be much for her to do right now with regard to managing the festival. The authors had all been contracted. Four of them had been invited to stay in the Skipper's House. Elspeth would be back there by then. She could play host.

Jan looked after marketing and it was all under control. A company handled ticket sales and some events were sold out already. Annabel was taking care of accommodations, Doug Buchanan had venues in hand; tents and equipment rentals were booked. There was only the event to commemorate Deirdre that needed to be planned and added to the schedule.

She was not going to have to work hard for her fee. She definitely would not keep it. She'd use the money right now, while she needed it, but donate it back, just as Deirdre had done, once the house was sold.

She waited until lunchtime then called Dave online. He got up early, even on a Saturday. He was meeting someone for breakfast then he had to supervise soccer practice, was busy, he said, but the news of Liz Fraser's death made him pause.

"Do you need to get away from there? Come home right now?" he asked.

"I can't. The police won't let me leave the island. I'm on their list of suspects." She tried to make light of it. She described DI Alexander's theory and how absurd it was.

"So you're okay?" he asked. "You're not really going to be arrested?"

"No way!" she assured him. "But I'm glad to be out of that old house. I've got good neighbours where I am now, so I'm not so isolated. There's one or two people I think I can trust and the local policewoman checks up on me. I should be in the clear with the police once they know exactly when Liz Fraser died. I'll be fine, and I promised I'd stay here until the book fest."

"Well," he said. "You can change your mind about that. Let me know." He didn't have any more time to talk. He was running late and was due at the restaurant already. The one he named had been a favourite of theirs in pre-pandemic days.

"Who are you meeting there?" she asked, but he'd already switched off the connection. She was puzzled. Hurrying off to Saturday breakfasts was something new in Dave's life.

She had not had time to tell him about the money she'd get from filming, either. She wished they'd had longer to talk but that would have to wait. Meantime it was early afternoon on Sulla. The ferry would have arrived. The police should have cleared out of Deirdre's house by now and she could go and pick up the paper folders that were there.

Wilma lay on a chair beside her, seemingly asleep, but one eye watched every move she made. "Hey, Wilma. Let's go out," she said.

She remembered to hang onto the car door so it wouldn't blow back as Wilma hopped up into the front seat. The wind was behind her as she drove the road that crossed the island. Two cars were parked outside the police station as she passed through the village of Balemartin, one a squad car, one unmarked. DI Alexander or another person from his team must be staying to continue the investigation.

The ferry had made it in. Cars waited to board at the harbour, another police car among them, so some of the MIT were leaving. Colin the Harbour noticed the Peugeot drive by and raised a hand in greeting. Rob the Garage was talking to him. He glanced in Elspeth's direction, then turned his head away.

A sudden deluge of rain swamped the windshield. Calum McFee's wipers made hard work of clearing it. Through gaps in the streaming water, she glimpsed cars pulled in at the hotel and visitors running for cover. Another two cars were parked outside the Harbour Guest House and the OPEN sign was up at Jan MacLeod's craft shop The tourist season was getting underway, in spite of the weather.

The rain stopped as abruptly as it had started, but a car loaded with luggage and children crawled its way along the coast road in front of her, all the way past the Skipper's House. Elspeth didn't mind if they dawdled. She was not looking forward to going back inside. She watched the family in the car stare and point at the police tape as they drove by. It was still looped around the wall but the gate stood open.

There were no police cars there, but a small white van stood in the driveway and Elspeth saw Liz's red Mini, still parked in the garage when she looked inside. It had not been hauled off to the mainland for examination, unlike Deirdre's Tiguan, the one that Elspeth had been driving. Elspeth left the Peugeot out at the roadside. She closed the gate and left Wilma to explore the yard while she went inside.

Kimmy MacLeod had not finished cleaning. The kitchen smelled of bleach and not a trace of blood remained. The dresser gleamed. So did the sink and counters. She was vacuuming the sitting room rug when Elspeth walked in.

"Great machine, this," she said, turning off the Dyson. "Does a grand job." She spotted Wilma outside the window. "Don't you be letting that wee dog come in here and mess up my clean floors, now." Kimmy was short but round, no more than twenty years old, an apron tied over jeans and a tee, fair hair fastened back with a scrunchy, stray strands tucked into a hairband as well.

"Would you like a cup of tea?" she suggested, with smiley eyes and a big grin. "I'm almost done in here but I've still the big room next door to do."

"Don't worry about it," said Elspeth. "I need to get some work done through there. I can clean it up myself."

"Are you sure? It's a terrible mess with all that white powder the police have been using."

Elspeth went to look. The flat surfaces had, indeed, been fingerprinted. She could see marks all over them. Some of those were her own, others belonged to Deirdre. She pressed a finger onto one that looked the same size as hers. It fit exactly. Other prints were larger. Her aunt had had bigger hands than her. There was a large, empty space where the computer had been.

Another empty space showed where Deirdre's missing notebooks had been kept. The ones containing the manuscripts had been examined but were still there. She checked the drawers in the file cabinet. They looked exactly as they had been last time she looked.

She went in search of a cardboard box so she could carry the files she wanted back to Bernie Baxter's house. Kimmy was in the kitchen filling a teapot. Teacups had been set out and a plate with wrapped biscuits.

"Tunnock's wafers," said Kimmy proudly. "Deirdre kept them in a tin on the back shelf, specially for me."

"You clean here often?" asked Elspeth. Kimmy did. Deirdre had had her in once a week, regular. Paid her well, she hinted.

"What's happened to her wee Chinese men?" she asked.

"Wee Chinese men?"

"The ones she kept in the sideboard with the dragons on it, up the stairs. The green and white ones. Come on and I'll show you." She waddled off out the kitchen door. She stopped on the landing on the way up.

"This is where Deirdre died," she said, in a theatrical whisper. "At least there wasn't a lot of blood, like there was in the kitchen." That had been a real mess. But Kimmy sometimes helped when her dad killed a sheep. She was used to the sight of blood.

The sideboard she had mentioned was a large Chinese cabinet at the far end of the landing. She opened it up. Two glass jugs sat on a shelf.

"Those never used to be there." Kimmy pointed at them. "There were all these teeny wee people instead, Chinese folk carrying baskets, one of them was pushing a barrow. There were birds and beasties too. A donkey and a dog. A cat, but it was the wee men I liked the best." A pottery bowl rested on the shelf underneath. "That shouldn't be there, either. There were green statues as well. Like the big ones below." The bottom shelf was deeper. It held three pieces of jade, one a dragon. Elspeth lifted it out. It was heavy for its size, smooth and shiny.

"How many were there of these?" she asked.

"Lots. Those two shelves were full, the rest just weren't so big. Deirdre kept them inside the sideboard because she said they were hard to dust but I got to take them out once a year and wash them all. Those jugs have been put there to make it look like they were never here. Somebody's took them." She turned innocent blue eyes to meet Elspeth's. "There was all that blood in the kitchen, where that lady died. Maybe somebody came here to steal them and she saw them doing it and that's how she got stabbed. Do you think we should phone Jackie Buchanan and tell her?"

"Maybe we should," Elspeth agreed. If the missing jade pieces were good quality, they would have been valuable. She wasn't sure if the smaller pieces had been here when she first arrived at the house. She had glanced inside the cabinets but there had been so much for her to take in, it was all a bit of a blur. It would be worth knowing if anything else was missing.

"Let's go drink that tea." She led Kimmy back down to the kitchen, "And you can tell me if you've noticed anything else that's different in this house before we talk to Jackie. When where you last here?"

"Just before Deirdre fell down the stairs." Kimmy pulled herself up onto a kitchen chair. Her feet didn't quite reach the floor. She sugared her tea and reached for a caramel wafer. "I haven't been back since," she said. "The police mustn't have made a big mess then like they did this time."

"When did you last see the figurines in the cupboard?" Elspeth asked. Kimmy wasn't sure. She didn't always look. Sometimes Deirdre had just wanted her to do a quick dust around; it was only on days that she polished that she stayed longer, and she spring cleaned once a year.

"How about we go for a walk through the house when we've finished our tea," said Elspeth, "and you can tell me if you notice anything else that's been taken?"

"Is that going to take long?" Kimmy hesitated. "The police said I'd be done here by two o'clock. The boat's in and I told my mum I'd go get messages at the shop on the way home. I've got a list."

"I'll pay you for the extra time," Elspeth told her. "And you can phone your mother and tell her if you're going to be later."

"All the bananas will be gone. My mum said to be sure to get there in time. She likes bananas." Kimmy's bottom lip stuck out, a stubborn look.

"How about I talk to her and tell her you were doing an important job for me?" That was enough to reassure her. So was a promise that she'd be paid extra for overtime.

They started at the top of the house. A trap door in the ceiling led into the roof, with a pull-down ladder. "I've never gone up there," said Kimmy. "I don't like heights. My cousin's Mike Nicolson. He built that bathroom for Deirdre. Isn't it grand? He told my dad what it cost. He said she paid thousands and thousands of pounds for it. The water tank's up there. Mike'll know what else."

They walked through the top floor, room by room. Kimmy shook her head when they went into Deirdre's room. "It was always messy like this." She pointed at the clutter on the dressing table. She didn't know if anything was missing from there. The urn sat on a chest at the window. Elspeth was about to explain what it was when they heard Wilma barking outside. They left the bedroom and went to a front window to look.

A car had stopped out on the road. The passenger door opened. An elderly man got out. He leaned on a cane and stood, looking directly at the house, the wind catching at a light jacket he was wearing and at his pant legs and his white hair. He wasn't tall, was thin, and sported a beard. Elspeth stared at him. She had no idea who he was but something about him was familiar. He waited at the wall, fingering the police tape, then grasped the stones along the top as the wind buffeted him. A young woman had been driving. She was taller than the man, had long, dark hair and was casually dressed, as was he. She walked toward him and Elspeth saw him point up at the house, explaining something to her. She pushed her hair away from her face then took his arm to support him as they made their way slowly to the gate. Wilma had stopped barking and gone to welcome them, tail wagging.

Elspeth ran downstairs and stepped outside. The wind blew against her, bringing some raindrops with it as she walked across the grass.

"Can I help you? Are you looking for someone?" she asked.

The man leaned against the stone gatepost as the young woman opened the gate. He eyed Elspeth up and down, then walked through. Elspeth grabbed Wilma before she ran out the gate. The man was more interested in the house than in speaking to her.

"It hasn't changed much," he said to the young woman. She reached for his arm again. Elspeth shut the gate behind them. "What's the police tape about?" he asked.

A gust of rain caught them. They couldn't talk out here.

"We'd best go inside before we get soaked," Elspeth said. The wind blew her words away. Kimmy MacLeod was standing inside the front door, holding it open. Wilma raced inside as it began to pour and Elspeth followed. She grabbed an umbrella from the hallstand then ran back out to shelter the pair as they made their slow progress across the wet grass. The wind pushed against the fabric of the umbrella as she held it over their heads.

"Welcome to Sulla," the man commented ironically to the woman. His accent was North American, like Elspeth's. They got inside the house. Elspeth shook raindrops off the umbrella and Kimmy closed the door behind them. Wilma shook herself and sprayed them with water. The couple were standing in the middle of the hallway, looking around them.

"She didn't change much. All the old stuff's still here," the man said to the woman. "See all these?" He raised his cane and pointed to the cabinets, the Chinese watercolours on the walls. "Your great-uncle brought those all back from Asia on a boat, so he could give them to your great-aunt Megan. She was the love of his life. Next to his ship." And he laughed. He had crinkly eyes, deep set into the lines on his face.

Elspeth realized where she had seen him before, a younger version of him, in a photograph, when his hair was as dark as that of the girl beside him. Then he had been leaning against a rock on a beach, Deirdre MacPhail at his side.

"You're Alasdair MacPhail," she blurted in surprise.

"I am indeed," said the man. "And this is my house. Who are you and what are you doing here?"

"Elspeth Laird. Deirdre MacPhail's niece." Elspeth stared at him. "She left this house to me. You're supposed to be dead."

26

Alasdair MacPhail had flown into Glasgow from Calgary, Alberta, two days ago, his granddaughter, Ainslie Goertzen, with him. He'd read a report of Deirdre's death in the *Guardian* online, booked the flights and come to claim his house back before anyone else laid their hands on it.

"Sounds like it's just as well I did," he said as he pushed the door to the living room open with his cane. His granddaughter looked at Elspeth and shrugged an apology before she followed him into the room. Kimmy MacLeod still stood at the front door, gawking.

"We'll need to finish this job later," Elspeth told her. There were a couple of £20 bills in her wallet. She stuffed them into Kimmy's hand, gave her the umbrella and opened the door. "If you hurry, you might still get some bananas for your mother at the shop," she said.

"I need to take off my pinny." But Kimmy wasted no time getting out of her apron and stuffing the bills into her pocket. She popped up the umbrella and ran to her van. Elspeth wondered who she would talk to first, at the shop.

She closed the door behind her and went back to the living room. Alasdair MacPhail had found a seat in the middle of the big blue sofa, the one that Deirdre had lain on when he had painted her, now reupholstered. He pointed up at the picture with his cane.

"See her?" he addressed his audience of two. "That's Deirdre. I painted that." He turned his attention to Elspeth. "I don't want it, so you can keep it. It's three weeks since she died. How did it happen and how come the police are still around?"

"They say she tripped on a rug and fell down the stairs." Elspeth sat on the arm of a chair beside the fireplace so she could face him.

"They *say* she tripped?"

"It was ruled an accidental death," Elspeth told him. "But someone else just died here. Deirdre had a literary agent called Liz Fraser. She'd come to visit for a few days. I went to Oban on the ferry earlier this week, stayed overnight and when I got back, I found her lying on the kitchen floor. Someone had stabbed her. The police have just left. That's why the tape's still up."

"That's not good." Alasdair MacPhail propped his cane between his knees and placed both hands on top, looking like some old Scottish chieftain. "You hear that, Ainslie? A murder's going to bring the value of this old place down." His granddaughter was wandering around the room, looking at the other pictures and the objects displayed on every surface. "Do they know who did it?"

"Not any idea." Elspeth had no intention of telling him that the local CID had her on their list of suspects. She had questions of her own to ask him. "You didn't die, like they thought you did?"

"Who me? No way!" He laughed, a rough cackle, then started to cough. He reached inside his jacket and brought out a tissue to wipe his mouth.

"You disappeared," Elspeth persisted. "They searched for you. You were declared dead after seven years."

"I guess they didn't look hard enough." He took a pack of cigarettes from his pocket. "I was in Halifax by then, in Canada. Long gone and far away. You're Canadian, too?"

"From Winnipeg. I'm Elspeth. My mother was Deirdre's sister. We emigrated when I was two."

"Really? You're Maggie Balfour's kid?" He looked her up and down as he lifted a cigarette from the pack. "I'd never have known it. You don't look like her, do you? Pass me that ashtray, would you?" He pointed at a large pottery dish that lay on the mantel. His granddaughter picked up a smaller dish from the top of a sideboard and placed it on an end table for him instead.

"That's four today already, Gramps," she reminded him.

"Hasn't killed me yet." He winked at her and lit up. "So Deirdre thought the house belonged to her and she's gone and left it to you?" he asked. "Sorry, but I'm going to have to disappoint you. It was never hers to give. You know, it wasn't worth much when I left here, but that's all changed. Ainslie found out how much houses out here are going for these days. Imagine that! Who'd have thought this old place would be worth a lot now." He coughed again then continued. "I didn't want to live here then, and I don't now, but what I'll get for it is going to pay for Ainslie to go to grad school and a few things beside. So that's why I'm back. To make sure I get what's mine. Are you staying here?"

"Not for now." Elspeth struggled to hide her dismay at this news. "I moved out while the police were here."

"That's fine then. We can stay here, Ainslie. Who's in charge of the will?"

"My cousin Iain. He's in Edinburgh."

"Great," he said, puffing on his cigarette. "We'll take a trip and go see him. You'll like Edinburgh, Ainslie, and I need to talk to him. I'm the surviving spouse so I should get most of everything that Deirdre left. He and I will need to have a bit of a blether and you can go see the castle."

"We really should call ahead, Gramps." Ainslie had picked up a Chinese bowl and was turning it over in her hands.

"Ach, no. It'll be a surprise," said her grandfather.

"This has got to be worth something." Ainslie held up the bowl.

"Do you like it?" Alasdair turned his head to look. "This house used to be full of stuff like that. It looks like it still is. It all belongs to us now, girl. Take your pick, and we'll get it shipped home for you." He stubbed out the cigarette and noticed a look of consternation on Elspeth's face.

"It's like this, Elspeth," he explained. "I was still legally married to Deirdre. There was never a divorce. Ainslie's gran and I lived common-law. I got this house from my aunt Megan when she died. It and all the things my uncle Rob bought for her when he was out sailing the seven seas. It has always been mine. I just let Deirdre stay on here, rent-free."

Elspeth had no idea what to say but thoughts were racing through her head. She wished Calum McFee was still on the island. Would he know what happened in a situation like this? Would she lose the house and all its valuable contents?

Ainslie had moved over to the window. The rain outside had stopped for a while.

"There's a man just getting out of a car," she said.

Elspeth joined her to look. The gate was wide open and a nondescript silver sedan was parked in the driveway, where Kimmy MacLeod's van had been.

"That's Detective Inspector Fergus Alexander," Elspeth told them. "He's investigating Liz Fraser's death." She went to open the front door.

The DI took off his coat, still damp from the rain, and handed it to her.

"What's all this about a ghost come back to haunt us?" he said, in his best jokey manner.

"In the living room." Elspeth hung the coat on a hook by the door then followed him. By the time she made it inside, Fergus was standing in front of the fireplace, between the old man on the sofa and the painting of Deirdre MacPhail on the wall behind him.

"There's a lassie in the shop telling everybody there that you are Alasdair MacPhail. But how can that be? You fell off a boat and drowned more than fifty years ago." Fergus Alexander maintained his jocular tone but his look was stern. He stood, feet apart, hands behind his back.

"Looks like I didn't." The old man leaned back against the blue cushions and grinned up at him. "The police sure got that wrong, back then, too." He still spoke with a hint of Scots if you listened closely.

"Where have you been?" DI Alexander looked down at him.

"Let's see." Alasdair MacPhail held up a hand and counted, finger by finger. "Edinburgh first. That's where I was when your folk started looking for me. I wasn't all that far away, was I? Then London. I had some pals from art school that were working there. Halifax, Nova Scotia, a couple of years after that. I got myself a good job there, teaching at an art school, then I moved to Alberta. An art college in Calgary hired me. It's a university now and they made me professor emeritus when I retired. They still call me Professor MacPhail."

Fergus Alexander refused to be impressed. "If you washed up on this island all those years ago, then left without telling anyone, someone must have helped you," he said.

"More than one. Good friends of mine. Said they'd never tell and they didn't. Maybe what we did was stupid but we were young, back then. I just wanted to be shot of this place, and Deirdre. Now I'm back, no harm done, right?"

"They're saying at the shop in Tostaig that this house used to belong to you."

"And it still does." Alasdair stretched an arm along the back of the sofa. The other still grasped the cane in front of him. "That's why I'm here."

"You're telling me that you owned this place, walked away and never came home, let people think you were dead. Left a grieving widow to think you had drowned..."

"Grieving widow be damned." Alasdair's voice cut in, suddenly annoyed. He grasped his cane with both hands and pointed it up at the picture of Deirdre again. It missed the police inspector by inches, close enough that he stepped sideways. The old man hauled himself up onto his feet.

"That's her." He leaned on the cane again and pointed with his free hand. "The woman I married. The one that almost killed me. She was on the boat with me that day. Pushed me overboard then she fired up the engine and roared off. Left me floundering there, way off shore. Knew fine that I was never a great swimmer. She left me to drown and she didn't give a damn."

The inspector's face swivelled round so they were almost nose to nose.

"But you didn't drown. And you didn't report what she'd done."

"No, I didn't. Look at her. Fine-looking woman, wasn't she? Bigger than me and stronger. She was never someone you'd want to mess with. Deirdre always had to have her own way. I'm telling you, if she hadn't got me that time she'd have done it another day. And if I'd come and told you, what would you have done about it? Nothing, right? 'Please, constable, my big, strong wife's trying to kill me'? You'd have laughed in my face."

"You could have left her." Fergus Alexander folded his arms and took a step back.

"Which is what I did," Alasdair MacPhail responded. He flopped back down onto the sofa, exasperated, and reached for the cigarette pack again.

"Gramps..." his granddaughter protested.

"Don't say it, Ainslie, I need a smoke." He took out another cigarette and lit up.

"Well, then." Fergus Alexander looked down at Alasdair MacPhail once more. "That's your story. How am I supposed to believe it? There's nobody can corroborate what you're saying."

"Yes, there is." Elspeth had watched and listened from just inside the door. "Deirdre MacPhail told my mother exactly the same, herself, not long after it happened, and my mother told me. It was exactly as my uncle says. He and Deirdre went out on the boat together and got into an argument, about how he wanted to leave Sulla and go back to Edinburgh but Deirdre was determined to stay. They got so mad at each other that they stood up in the boat and Deirdre pushed him. He fell over the side." She moved closer. Smoke wafted up above the old white head, between her and Fergus Alexander.

"My aunt drove off and left him there, just like he says, but when she reached the next bay, she got in closer to the shore, cut the motor and jumped overboard herself. She let the boat drift and swam to a beach. They were close to the north end of the island, on the Atlantic side, where fewer people live so hardly anyone would have seen her. She knew Alasdair might drown and she left him there. Deirdre deliberately covered up the fact that she had been out on the boat with him. And when he didn't show up and you all assumed he was dead, she pretended she knew nothing about it.

"My mother's in Winnipeg. You can get in touch with her and ask her yourself."

Her uncle stubbed out his cigarette and turned on the sofa so he could see her.

"Elspeth Balfour," he said, "Come around here beside me and let me give you a hug."

Elspeth stayed where she was. She wasn't ready for that yet. "I'm a Laird, not a Balfour," she reminded him. She did feel uneasy. Her mother had sworn her to secrecy, but now the truth needed to come out. Ainslie, standing at the window, gave her a thumbs-up. Alasdair MacPhail picked up the cigarette stub he had just discarded and hauled himself to his feet again. He held it up in front of DI Alexander's nose.

"Here you go," he said. "That's got my DNA all over it and this island's full of my relatives. You'll have no bother proving who I am."

27

Word that Alasdair MacPhail had returned from the dead spread like a virus through Sulla. The first contingent of long-lost relatives rolled up to the door just as DI Alexander was checking where Alasdair had been these past two days.

"Where do you think? I got off a plane in Glasgow," he said. "Ainslie's got the tickets." He hobbled over to the window. "Is that Chrissie out there, that married my cousin Norman?"

He wrapped his arms around her, soon as she came inside. Chrissie MacPhail greeted him in Gaelic and they laughed. It transformed her face. For a second, Elspeth could glimpse the girl she once had been. Her son, Rob the Garage, was outside, ripping down police tape and piling it up by the gate. Wilma scurried back and forth, greeting more visitors. They brought whisky and food, cake and sandwiches mainly, so they could eat and dance and mingle. The MacPhails of Sulla had decided that a celebration was in order and Alasdair was related to half the island.

Ainslie was greeted warmly. Her name might be Goertzen but she had MacPhail blood in her. Fergus Alexander was barely acknowledged. He made for the door. People glanced Elspeth's way then acted like she didn't exist. She was thinking about leaving herself when her uncle seized her arm and held it high. "See this lass?" he announced to all of his clan, gathered in the living room. "She's a good one. Told the truth about me and Deirdre to that detective inspector that's just leaving and got me off the hook. You be nice to her."

Someone passed Elspeth a whisky glass. She noticed DI Alexander through the window, sloping off toward his car, shrugging his arms into his raincoat as he went, Wilma trotting at his heels. He glanced back at the house as reached the car door. He would be back, for sure. She should have told him about the missing jade, but that would have to wait. She called the dog in and shut her in Deirdre's den, out of the way.

Everyone wanted to hear Alasdair MacPhail's story—what had really happened that Saturday afternoon long ago?—and he was happy to tell.

"She drove the boat off and left you?"

Alasdair MacPhail shrugged. "That was Deirdre for you," he said. He didn't tell the rest of the story, but there were dark mutterings, about how the boat had been found adrift and how Deirdre had never let on she had been with him that day, out on the water. He wasn't telling who had found him, either, half dead on the shore, the people who had taken him in and helped him get off the Isle of Sulla without anyone knowing. He got some sideways looks. Why had he chosen to disappear from Sulla and let them all believe he had drowned? But most of his relatives were up for a party. They were here to have a good time and celebrate.

He had done well in Canada, he told them. Lived in Cochrane, near Calgary, right next to the Rockies. He was a retired university prof and he still got asked to teach sometimes. He painted, too.

A second wave of visitors arrived, Donalda McFee among them. She was enveloped in a hug, just like Chrissie before her. "Good to see you, Nalda," Elspeth heard him say. She heard them talk about going to the Eventide Home the next day to see Kate Mary. He could visit his cousin, Norman, too, while he was there.

"He can't talk anymore and he's in a wheelchair," Donalda warned him.

"Is that right? I used to be scared of him. Remember how he beat me up when we were kids? But look at us now, Nalda. The last ones left standing. You, me and Chrissie."

Chrissie was in the kitchen, organizing food as more bowls and plates arrived. Someone had brought in wood and fires were lit, in the living room and Deirdre's den. Wilma got loose again.

"Get that beast out of the kitchen," Elspeth heard Chrissie MacPhail say. The dog was sniffing at the table leg where Liz Fraser's body had lain. There was no sign of blood, but Wilma could detect the smell.

No one in the house mentioned the murder in Elspeth's hearing but she could see a couple of women at the kitchen sink looking at the floor and whispering in one another's ears. Rob MacPhail poured himself a glass of whisky and glared in her direction. He said nothing to her, as usual.

This wasn't her party. She put down her glass, leashed up the dog and got her coat, waved goodbye to her newfound uncle, closed the door behind her and walked into the drizzle outside. She texted Calum McFee as soon as she got inside the car. Was he available to talk by phone?

Lachie and Cath MacKinnon had just arrived outside the house and waited for her to pull out so they could park in her spot, facing the wrong way. There was a line of cars and trucks parked along the roadway. An answer from Calum dinged up on her screen.

Gone fishing. This evening?

She couldn't wait that long. She called, soon as she got back to the little black-roofed house and had closed the door tight behind her.

"I'm in a river up to my knees, catching trout," he answered the phone. She could hear rushing water in the background.

"Alasdair MacPhail's not dead," she blurted out, "He's arrived back at the Skipper's House. Says it belongs to him. There's a party going on. The place is full of people."

"You're joking. Give me five minutes and I'll call you back."

Soon as he did, she told him everything. How Alasdair had shown up, driven from Glasgow with his granddaughter the day before, come over on the ferry. "He's been living in Canada all this time. In Alberta." How he had never drowned, but hadn't let on he was alive either. Had sneaked off the island instead. "He didn't want to live here anymore and he said that he thought Deirdre might kill him if he stayed." Fergus Alexander knew he was here. Word had got out that he was back and family had shown up from all over Sulla.

"Your mom is there, and Chrissie MacPhail. Her son, Rob, from the garage as well. Alasdair says he and Deirdre never got divorced and the house has always been his. He just let her stay there. But now she's dead, he wants it back."

"He owned it but he let her live on in the house, even although he says she tried to kill him?" Calum had moved into his Land

Rover. The sound of running water ended once he slammed the door shut.

"It looks like he got as far away as possible, soon as he could."

"Well, this is a bit of a mess." Calum didn't know what happened when someone was declared dead and their spouse had lived on in the house. "I'll have to check all this out. Did you find the title deeds?"

"I haven't seen them," she told him. "They were probably among Deirdre's personal papers. Iain Balfour took most of those back to Edinburgh with him just after she died. Alasdair's talking about going there to see him."

"This is interesting. If it ends up going to court we should maybe let Iain and his solicitor friend fight that battle."

"You think that might happen?"

"It could. Off the top of my head, the ownership of the house will need a court ruling. It's possible that you'll lose it. Neither you nor Alasdair should be living there until that's decided."

"He's there," said Elspeth. "And he says he's staying."

"Is he now? I expect the police will kick him out soon enough. One thing's for sure. You don't need to worry about the money from the books. Deirdre's own business dealings are yours and Alasdair can't claim those."

"I'm still going to get quite a lot of money." She told him about her conversation with Inga and how much more she was likely to earn from the filming of the TV series.

"They're doing six episodes? On Sulla? With four more series maybe to come?" She heard him whistle through his teeth. "They'll be filming there forever."

"That's a good thing?"

"It'll change things even more," he said, echoing what Sandy McQuarrie had said. "And it's all happening fast, on one wee island. But we'll just have to cope with it. Look, I'll head back to Oban and try to get as much work as I can done over the next couple of days."

"Sorry about the fishing," said Elspeth.

"Och, don't be. I'll find out what I can and I'll try to get back over by Tuesday. I want to meet Alasdair MacPhail anyway."

"He's great friends with your mother." Elspeth had curled up on the sofa, the dog beside her.

"They're second cousins. Grew up together. Mum's only two years younger, I think," he said. "Norman and Chrissie must be about the same age as him. Kate Mary will have known him too. She and my mother were in the same class at school."

"Alasdair calls her Nalda."

"Does he now? I've only ever heard my dad call her that. Has Fergus made any progress finding out who killed Liz Fraser?"

"Nothing so far that I've heard of. He showed up as soon as he heard that Alasdair was back but he left when the party got going."

"Sensible man. Maybe I'll buy him a pint and find out what he's got to say." Would she pick him up if he got on Tuesday's plane? He would need his car back. Was that going to a problem? She thought of the bike in the shed out back. Maybe she could ride that for a day or two.

He hung up. The only sound in the room was Wilma, softly snoring. Both Calum and Donalda's houses were empty. Being alone made Elspeth uneasy. She locked the doors and texted Jackie Buchanan. It was almost 5:00 p.m. Would she be stopping by to check in with her?

On my way, the answer came right back. By the time she had fed the dog, the police car was outside and Jackie was walking up the path.

"I've just been by your house," she said. "That's quite the party going on. The DI tells me that some old geezer that used to own it, someone they thought had died years ago, has come back and says it's his?"

"That's all true," Elspeth told her. Jackie had only lived on Sulla for the past few years. She hadn't heard all of the old story.

"He says your aunt Deirdre tried to kill him and he ran for his life? Never let on he was still alive until now, and it's been fifty years or more? Little wonder the DI's looking like thunder. Do you not own the house after all? You won't be able to sell it?"

"You still want it, after Liz Fraser was stabbed in the kitchen?"

"We might. We can live in the police house for as long as I've got the job," Jackie said, always practical, "but I want to quit in five years' time. Doug's business is growing and I could help him with that. We're going to stay here on Sulla. Love the life here, most of the time. So yes, we're still interested in your house. If it is still your house."

"It'll get sold anyway," Elspeth told her. "Alasdair MacPhail wants the money. Calum McFee says a court might have to decide who owns it, so it might take a while, that's all. Alasdair says he's going to move in. You've been by. Half the island's inside, celebrating him being back."

"I'm not going to stop that party unless I have to," said Jackie. "There's no need to piss folk off. But I can go there tomorrow and tell your uncle that ownership's in dispute and he and his granddaughter need to find somewhere else to stay. Thing is, you can't move in either." Elspeth remembered that Calum had said something similar.

"No problem," she said, "I'd rather stay here. Alasdair said that he might go to Edinburgh. My cousin there is Deirdre's executor. He wants to talk to him about the will. It could be months before we know who really owns the house."

"If it takes longer to get all that sorted out, I don't mind," said Jackie. "Doug and I can wait. Deirdre used to close up the place all winter when I first came here. I think the MacKinnons used to keep an eye on it for her."

Elspeth remembered Cath telling her so. She must have walked through the Skipper's House often enough. Perhaps she knew about the jade collection and could tell when she'd last seen it.

"Kimmy MacLeod says there's pieces of jade that have gone missing," she said. "She just noticed earlier today when she was cleaning. They were stored in a Chinese cabinet, up on the landing near the bathroom. They might be valuable. Kimmy wondered if someone was trying to steal them and Liz Fraser caught them at it so that's why she was killed."

Jackie reached into a pocket for a notepad.

"Tell me about it," she said, but there wasn't much else that Elspeth knew. Jackie would need to talk to Kimmy herself. "She's probably at the party, half smashed already." She put her notepad back inside her pocket. "I'll wait until tomorrow, when she's sobered up. I'll need to tell DI Alexander about this in the morning."

"The cabinet's upstairs on the landing," said Elspeth. "What if something like that happened to Deirdre as well? What if she found someone in her house, pocketing bits of valuable jade, and that person pushed her, so she fell? What if she was murdered, too?"

28

Jackie had rigged police tape back up by the time Elspeth arrived at the Skipper's House the following morning. Alasdair MacPhail and his granddaughter had been told to leave.

"They'll be okay. The family that's staying at the guest house are leaving today so they can move in there. I checked," Jackie said. "They've gone out visiting."

She would rather have been at church with her family but Fergus Alexander had been asked to lead the singing as a special guest at this morning's service and he had taken precedence. She had the work shift instead.

"Shouldn't he have kicked everyone out before the party ever got going?" Elspeth asked, remembering how quietly Fergus had left the house as the guests started to arrive.

"He thought forensics were done. We didn't know there might have been thefts related to the murder."

"But he knew that Alasdair had come back to claim the house and Deirdre had left it to me."

"Well," said Jackie. "Ownership is nothing to do with us. You'll need to sort that out in your own good time. Maybe he thought Alasdair was entitled to a welcome home party. He wasn't to know how many people would show up. But now the house is back to being a crime scene and it's a shambles."

The dishwasher had been loaded but more dirty dishes and glasses had been piled up on the kitchen table. Every single available plate must have been used. Someone had fried fish in the kitchen and left the frypan in the sink. Furniture had been moved around and the rug in the middle of the living room rolled up so people could dance. The big blue sofa had been shoved to the side.

Ainslie Goertzen had started to clean up. Two or three garbage bags were stacked at the kitchen door, but that was as far as she'd got before Jackie had shown up and stopped her.

"She said the party went on all night. We'll need to get Kimmy back in to clean this all up," said Jackie. "I've been by her house but she's so hungover she's useless. Is there anything here that still belongs to you? You should take everything with you."

There was nothing. Elspeth's belongings were few and they were all in Bernie Baxter's house. She had taken all the files she needed for managing the book festival from Deirdre's den.

"Will I get her computer back? And what's happening with her car?"

Jackie had no idea. "These things take their own time," she said.

Liz Fraser's overnight bag and toiletries all remained, however. Her little red Mini still sat in the garage. Her phone and computer had been taken to the mainland by the police.

"She had a partner in Edinburgh." Elspeth found it hard to believe that Jackie didn't know that by now. Maybe DI Alexander and his team hadn't thought it necessary to share the information with a local cop. She gave her Inga's contact information.

"Come and show me where that missing jade was," said Jackie.

They walked to the top of the stairs and along the landing to the cabinet where the jade had been stored. Jackie opened the doors in the front and lifted out one of the three large pieces that remained. The other two were bright green but this one was yellow, fading to brown, a fish, swimming among underwater plants, each scale meticulously carved, every line on the fins and the tail delineated. It was heavy.

"Kimmy said the ones on the top shelf were smaller. Lighter. Maybe easier to put in your pocket." Elspeth noticed a smaller object at the back of the bottom shelf, visible now that the big fish had been moved. She squatted down and reached in. "Look," she said, lifting it out. "Here's a little one." A tiny bird fed even smaller nestlings, the whole piece little enough to fit in the palm of her hand. The carving was detailed, the bird feathered, the little beaks rising from the nest. It must have fallen down from a higher shelf. Whoever had taken the others had missed it.

"I'll need to get Kimmy to tell me how full this cabinet was." Jackie put the fish back in place below two empty shelves and took the small piece of jade from Elspeth. "Will you look at this," she said. "All that work to make something this wee."

Elspeth was looking along the hallway. The only natural light came in through the stained-glass window above the stairs. The floor was polished wood. The two woven Indian rugs, each less than three feet wide but six in length, stretched along each end of the landing to the top of the stairs.

"Look." She pointed. "If Deirdre had come up the stairs and turned onto the landing just as somebody was helping themselves to her jade, it would only have taken two, three strides for that person to reach her and give her a good shove." She paced it out and faced Jackie from the place where the stairs ended.

"Uh huh," Jackie agreed. "I can see that." She placed the little bird back in the cabinet and joined Elspeth. Together they looked down to the landing below. "If she'd been facing someone and they pushed her, she would have fallen backwards. Or there could have been an argument. She could have walked away and then been pushed from behind. Only thing is, she could have grabbed the banister if she fell forwards and broken her fall."

"Would she have turned her back on a person she was arguing with?" asked Elspeth.

"Maybe not." Jackie had seen, at the time of Deirdre's death, how the rug was disturbed, the edge pushed aside. She hadn't read the results of the autopsy. It had been sent to DI Alexander in Oban, not to her. She didn't know if the break in Deirdre's neck showed whether it had been caused by a backward or a forward fall.

"Fergus Alexander isn't going to be happy if I tell him about this, but I suppose I'll have to," she said. "If she did fall backwards, they maybe need to check out her death again."

Red and blue light from the window illuminated them as they walked back down the stairs. The sun had broken through scuttering clouds and shone straight in through the coloured glass. Outside, they could hear waves splashing against the shore. Jackie peered through a clear patch of window.

"That's the MacPhails' boat," she said. "What's it doing out there?" She ran off down the stairs. Elspeth followed, Wilma at her heels.

Jackie was standing on the pier, the boat drawn in alongside by the time Elspeth had crossed the back gate and reached the grassy edge of the beach.

"I don't care what Alasdair MacPhail told you. Get that boat back to the harbour. You can't moor here," she shouted.

"It's his house now, Jackie. What he says goes," Rob MacPhail yelled back. He was standing near the prow, rope in hand.

"No, it is not. And this is a crime scene. It's off limits. You get right away from here."

Rob noticed Elspeth standing, watching. He glared in her direction then stepped back down into the boat to talk to a man at the steering wheel. That must be his brother, Norman, other son of Chrissie MacPhail, the less argumentative one. Elspeth heard the words "Canadian bitch" quite clearly.

"Right you are, Jackie," the more peaceable brother called up. He turned the boat around and soon it revved away back toward Tostaig, a wake spreading behind it, the noise deafening. The sun disappeared behind the clouds, the sky turned instantly grey and an unexpected gust of wind from the west almost threw Elspeth off balance.

"I'm going to tape this pier off as well. It belongs to the house. So does that patch of land you're standing on." Jackie strode up the incline from the pier. "By the time I've done that, the service at the kirk should be done. I'll have to go have chat with the DI."

The dog hadn't been walked and was looking hopeful. Elspeth took her along the beach while Jackie ran tape along the pier.

Elspeth was sheltered from the wind if she walked close to the dunes that edged the beach. The sea heaved in and out, green today, the colour of Deirdre's jade when it was close to the shore, darkening to that of bottle glass as it deepened. There were whiteheads on the crests of the waves. Elspeth kicked at the sand while she walked. It was too blustery to go far.

Her phone rang before she got back to the house.

"Hiya!" She heard Alasdair MacPhail's voice. "Are you busy?" He and Ainslie were just leaving the MacKinnon farm. Maybe he could buy her lunch?

The hotel and Annabel's café were the only two options that Elspeth could think of. She gave him directions to the café.

"Be there in fifteen," she said, and waved goodbye to Jackie.

"Look at this! Real food!" Ainslie Goertzen stood in the café, looking at what was on offer in Sandy McQuarrie's glass case. She had passed on the scones at the MacKinnons' house and now she was hungry, she said. Alasdair was outside, puffing on a cigarette. Ainslie wouldn't let him smoke in the car.

"Find us a table!" he had instructed. There wasn't much choice. Four of six tables were already occupied, none of them by anyone Elspeth recognized. These must all be visitors. She heard a woman with an English accent complain that she'd thought that their van would blow over last night. They'd leave on the ferry tomorrow, on their way to Tiree. The wind probably blew just as hard there, she complained. Her daughters were delighted. They were windsurfers.

Only two tables remained, one a two-seater. The other was close to Sandy's counter.

Ainslie ordered a salad. Elspeth said she'd have the same.

"With a bit of chicken?" Sandy suggested. "Local. Fresh roasted. Nothing like it."

They collected coffees from him, a black one for Alasdair. He had planted himself on the corner seat where he could survey the room and everyone in it.

"You'd never have got away with being open on a Sunday back when I lived here," he called over to Sandy. "This island used to be like the grave on the Sabbath."

Annabel and Sandy had dropped by the house last night while the party was in full fling, but they hadn't stayed long. Weekends were busy days. They needed their sleep. Annabel was serving tables. She found time to stop at theirs.

"Big party," she commented. "Is that why you're being evicted?"

"No." Alasdair rocked back in his chair. "The police say it's still a crime scene."

"So Fergus came and kicked you out?" Annabel was speaking casually but Elspeth could tell that she was fishing for information.

"It wasn't him." Alasdair was stirring brown sugar crystals into his coffee, watching them dissolve. "Some policewoman from around here did it. That DI that was talking to me yesterday left as soon as the party got going. Left us to enjoy ourselves." He grinned up at Annabel. His front teeth were white and even, all capped by a Canadian dentist.

"You were allowed to stay yesterday but now you can't? What's that about?" asked Annabel. "And why didn't Fergus tell you himself? Why send Jackie?"

"Because the DI had to go and sing at the church this morning." Elspeth offered an explanation.

Sandy slid salads across the countertop. "He did?" he said. "Wish I'd known. I wouldn't have minded hearing that."

"Tell me," Annabel interrupted, "which of you owns the house now?"

"Neither of us," Elspeth replied.

"Me," Alasdair answered simultaneously.

"Calum McFee says he thinks it might have to go to court," Elspeth remarked, once she was seated.

"That's Nalda's son? The lawyer? Maybe I should be talking to him." Alasdair had finished his coffee already and pointed to his cup. He could use a refill.

"I'm his client already," Elspeth informed him.

"See, Elspeth. That's what we need to talk about." He pointed a finger. She noticed that the knuckles were swollen with arthritis. "I just want what's mine. The house and the things that my aunt Megan left me. You're welcome to the rest. I don't want a single thing that belonged to Deirdre and that includes the money she made from those books she wrote. And that flat in Edinburgh that she bought after she acted like I was dead. You can have all the furniture in that room she set up for herself. That was never there before. It's too bad she knocked down the wall. I wish she hadn't done that. You can take away her clothes. Her jewellery. Her computer. Keep her car. Just let me have my house back and my pier. My bit of beach."

"Norman and Rob MacPhail came by in a boat this morning and tried to moor at the pier but Jackie Buchanan chased them away," Elspeth told them.

"Did she now? What's her problem? That's always been a MacPhail mooring," Alasdair grouched. "A boat there's not going to bother anybody. I had a good boat, once," he added. "I've been told that Deirdre sold it. After she pushed me off it into the Atlantic and left me there to swim or drown."

He and Ainslie were booked on the ferry tomorrow and in an Airbnb in Edinburgh that evening.

"Deirdre's flat is rented out so we can't stay there and your cousin Iain isn't offering to put us up. He's got a meeting set up with him and his lawyer, though. That's going to be interesting."

He would be back on Sulla soon. Maybe the police would let him back into his house by then. He was certain it was his. Meantime, he and Ainslie were going to go and meet up with Nalda. She was taking them to the Eventide Home to visit Kate Mary.

"And your cousin Norman?" asked Elspeth.

"I'll maybe give him a wave," he said.

The salads were eaten; the bill paid by Alasdair.

"You tell Nalda's boy I'm willing to let you have everything that was Deirdre's and maybe a bit more," he told Elspeth as he wobbled his way to the door, propped up by his cane. "Let me know if there's anything else that you'd like as a keepsake."

"You can have a keepsake and he's going to gobble up a house worth over £400,000 and another £50,000 worth of antiques?" Annabel said as they watched them go. "Does he know what it's worth? And that it's your share of Deirdre's estate? Don't let him do that."

29

Elspeth hesitated to go back to Bernie's house for the afternoon. If Donalda was not at home next door, she'd be entirely alone while she was there. She stopped by Jan's craft shop instead. It was small, converted from a garage, a big window knocked into a wall so Jan could display stained-glass panels against the light. Glass-topped cases held polished stone jewellery. She might buy something of Jan's to take back to her mother before she left. Jan waved from behind a counter, too busy attending to customers to talk, so Elspeth said goodbye and drove up to the north end of the island instead, Wilma riding shotgun at her side, looking out the window.

She had never explored that part of Sulla. It was hillier, craggy, with tiny inlets where the green sea crashed against the rocks, sending up salty white spume. Houses became fewer the further north she drove, the occasional cottage clinging to the edge of a bay, a patch of stony shingle at the door, the occasional stretch of sandy beach. Most of them had been renovated to accommodate tourists. Big windows looked out over the water. A couple of them had cars parked outside. Children were on a tiny beach, digging in the sand, sheltered from the gusty wind by a wall of rock. Hills rose on the other side, grass covered, rocks at the bottom. Streams of water ran down crevices to the sea.

The road clung to the shoreline, at times only two or three feet from the edge. At the farthest end, a lone white house stood sentinel. Elspeth stopped the car and got out, looking over skerries, the rocks that protruded from the water, stretching north, all the way to Skye, a faraway blur. The sky was blue, patches of white cloud scuttling across it. She'd have liked to walk Wilma but the wind buffeted her, so strong that it blew her breath away.

She turned the car south again and travelled down the western shore. The rocks there were smoother, the hills rounder, eroded by Atlantic gale-force winds, falling away into smooth boulders where it met the sea. It was still wild, more exposed, grand in scale. She preferred the tucked-in nooks on the leeward side, where the Skipper's House stood beside the long, sandy bay.

On Tuesday, Calum would come and claim back this car. Renting a vehicle from Oban was going to be impossible, unless she found one online and he brought it over for her on the ferry. She messaged him when she got home. They could try, he texted back, but one might not be available. Rentals were often booked in advance once tourist season was underway.

She went online and searched. Calum was right. Not a single rental car was available in Oban. The bike still lay in the shed behind the house. She took it out on the road. Riding it was okay when the wind was behind her but not so great when it hit her face on. Sideways, it was almost impossible. She'd only be able to ride on days when the wind dropped and she knew now that those were few and far between on Sulla.

A car zoomed past her when she was almost home. It stopped beside the three blackhouses. Donalda got out, waved to the people in the car and went into her own house. Alasdair MacPhail was the other passenger and Ainslie was driving. They didn't stop to talk. Elspeth didn't mind. Now there was someone next door to her and she was not alone.

She spent the evening working on the book festival. It was going to be hard to find accommodation for all the visiting authors if they couldn't use Deirdre's house. Now it seemed that ownership would be in dispute when they needed it, but maybe Deirdre's estate could be persuaded to rent it to the festival for that week?

She went to bed early and listened to the wind whistling though the telephone wires, gusting against walls that had held it at bay for generations, the dog tucked in at her feet. She fell sound asleep and woke hours later to the sound of loud banging on the front door.

She opened it, in her pyjamas, to find Fergus Alexander on her doorstep. A squad car was parked outside and a uniformed policeman she had never seen before was walking around Calum McFee's Peugeot, stopping to bend down so he could examine the paintwork with a flashlight.

"I need to know where you were last night," DI Alexander said without any explanation, his usual smile gone.

"Here," she stammered. "All evening. I didn't go anywhere."

"You can prove that?" he demanded, still abrupt. Elspeth had talked to no one but she had written emails during the evening. "Show me."

She led him to the kitchen, where her laptop lay on the table, and opened up her account. She'd emailed her cousin Iain just before 9:00 pm.

"After that?"

"I went to bed early. I've been asleep all night."

"No one can corroborate that?"

"Of course not," she replied, rattled by this line of questioning, wondering why he was asking, now that she'd got over her initial surprise. "But Donalda McFee lives next door. She knows I was home."

The uniformed constable appeared in the doorway.

"No sign of any fresh marks on the car, sir," he said, "but it's had its fair share of bumps and dents."

"We'll take it in, then."

"You'll do what?" Elspeth asked. "That's not my car. It belongs to Calum McFee."

"We'll let him know we've got it," the inspector retorted.

Donalda McFee walked into the hallway carrying Wilma. She kicked the door shut behind her.

"Your dog was out there running loose in the dark," she announced, and put Wilma down. She ignored the constable and confronted DI Alexander. "Just what's going on here?" she demanded.

"We're investigating the suspicious deaths of Alasdair MacPhail and a young woman that was with him. Their remains were found this morning in the car they were driving. They'd gone off the road, into the sea."

"They're dead?" Elspeth stood rigid, astonished. "And you think I had something to do with it?"

"Why would you think that?" Donalda demanded of the DI.

"Because it looks like they were forced off the road. Up near the northern skerries, just where the rocks are close to the road and the water's deep. This woman was seen driving around in the afternoon, looking."

"I went for a drive, that's all. I'd never been around that end of the island before."

"You stopped the car and got out, close to where this happened." The solitary white house that she had seen must be inhabited. Someone had been watching.

"I just stopped to have a look," she said. "I came home after. Rode a bike up and down the road after that, then I didn't go anywhere."

"She's driving Calum's car and it's been outside since I got home." Donalda McFee came to Elspeth's defence.

"Your house is built like this one? You sleep at the back? How would you know?" The DI turned his attention to Donalda. "This woman here could have gone out, middle of the night and come back and you'd be none the wiser." He addressed Elspeth once more. "Go and put some clothes on," he said. "I'm taking you in for questioning."

"I told you. I was here. I had nothing to do with this," Elspeth protested.

"You'd best do as he says," Donalda told her. "You need to have Calum here, I'll phone him and see how soon he can get over. Don't answer any questions until you've got him to advise you." Fergus Alexander frowned but Elspeth was grateful for Donalda's help and advice. "And don't worry about the dog. I'll keep an eye on her."

Minutes later, Elspeth was loaded into the back of the squad car. The constable drove and DI Alexander followed in Calum's confiscated Peugeot. They put her in an interview room at the Sulla Police Station. Calum would come in on the afternoon plane, she was informed shortly after. It was going to be a long wait.

Jackie Buchanan brought her an egg on a bun for breakfast.

"Just what is going on?" Elspeth asked.

"It's like this," Jackie explained. "Alasdair and Ainslie checked into the Harbour Guest House just after five yesterday. The owner does supper for her guests, so they ate and then they went off in the car, not long after seven. It was still daylight. They hadn't come back when she went to bed but she wasn't worried. She'd given them a key.

"There's a bodach, an old man, lives in the house up near the big northern skerries. He wakes early and goes walking. He was out just as the sky got light this morning and he saw tire tracks at the side of the road. He looked over and saw the roof of the car, just under the water. It had gone right over the edge. The road's pretty close to the sea there. They must have fallen four, five feet before they hit it. It's deep there. He called me, then I called the DI."

DI Alexander had summoned his team back to Sulla. They'd chartered a plane from Oban and been here before seven in the morning. He must have left them to examine the site and gone to find Elspeth straight away.

Calum McFee called and was permitted to talk with her.

"He's jumping to conclusions," Elspeth told him. "I went driving yesterday afternoon and I stopped at the north end of the island, where those skerries are, to have a look. Fergus has decided I must have been reconnoitring, looking for a place where the road's close enough to the edge that a car could go right over and the water's deep enough to submerge it.

"And he knows that Alasdair wanted his old house back. That I might lose it to him. It and all the valuable stuff that's inside it. So I have a good reason to want him dead. But I didn't. I'll get enough money from the TV shoot. He doesn't know that."

"You'll still be losing a lot of money, Elspeth. Close to half a million. You can see his point."

"I didn't want Alasdair to die! Or Ainslie? She'd just turned twenty. She didn't deserve this. Neither did he. Someone killed Liz and now they've killed them. It's got to be something to do with the house. I'm scared, Calum."

He agreed that she had good reason. She could be in danger. But no one would harm her right now, while she was safely tucked inside the police station. When did Fergus think that the car had gone off the road? Where had Elspeth been at the time?

"Alasdair and Ainslie went for a drive, just after seven last night. I was in Bernie's house. Your mom was right next door. Fergus thinks I could have gone out when she was asleep."

"I doubt that. She doesn't go to bed until after midnight and it makes more sense that this happened earlier. It could have been an accident and chances are it happened before it got dark. They wouldn't have been out sightseeing in the middle of the night, and how would you know that they were driving that way?"

"I didn't! Why is he so determined to pin this me?" Elspeth asked. "Is it just because I'm from somewhere else? There's all these old secrets on this island, like who helped Alasdair after he got to the shore, long ago, and kept quiet about the fact that he was still alive. Who was it that let Deirdre believe that she had killed him? Is it just easier to blame someone like me and not risk digging up any of that old dirt?"

"Fergus is going by the book," Calum told her. "You've got a strong motive and you were around. He could argue that my mother wouldn't have noticed you go off in the car. Not that that's true. She spots everything."

"He's taken your car in for examination," said Elspeth. "He won't find anything on it."

"It's mine, and he didn't tell me? You don't have a car and neither do I?" That created a problem for both of them. "I'm going to talk to Fergus and get him to release you. He can't hold you for more than twenty-four hours and he can't question you until I can get over there. If he won't return the car to me, I'll have to wait for tomorrow's ferry and bring the Land Rover over."

"Not until then?" Elspeth felt tears begin to well up.

"You don't need to be by yourself," he said. "Jan will put you up. Skye's over here in Oban at school for the week. She has a spare bed. I'll call and ask her."

The dog could stay with Donalda overnight. And Calum would be there by tomorrow afternoon, right next door.

It took another hour to get all that sorted out. DI Alexander appeared in the door of the examination room and grudgingly told Elspeth she was free to go. For now. He'd expect her to make herself available tomorrow afternoon at 4:00 pm, with her solicitor. He still had questions that needed answering.

Jan MacLeod was waiting by the front desk, deep in conversation with Jackie Buchanan that stopped abruptly when they saw Elspeth. She gave her a hug.

"Come on," she said. "Let's get you out of here."

The whole island was buzzing with the news of the latest deaths, she told Elspeth as she drove her over to Bernie's house to collect an overnight bag. The old man who lived in the white house up at the north end of Sulla had his binoculars trained on all the goings-on just along the shore and his phone at his ear. He was relaying an ongoing report on what was happening to the rest of the island. The site was swarming with police from the mainland, all dressed in their white plastic suits. Rob the Garage had shown up with a tow truck and pulled the car out of the water. A police boat had just come over from the mainland. It looked like the bodies would be taken away on it.

Elspeth packed her laptop and a bag. Donalda's car was in the driveway. She went next door and knocked.

"I can't believe it," Donalda said. "Alasdair's just come home and this happens to him? He's gone? Just like that? Your mother's going to be upset, too," she told Jan, who waited on the doorstep. "Are you going to tell her or am I?"

"She probably knows already," Jan said. "Word's got to have reached the Eventide Home. But don't worry. I'll go talk to her and set her straight, soon as I've got a minute.."

Donalda was pleased to hear that Calum would be back next door the following day, and she didn't mind if the dog stayed with her for now. "She'll be good company," she said.

Jan was good company too. Her house was half studio, half living space, a clutter that only seemed chaotic. Elspeth watched her move around her kitchen, brewing up coffee, finding everything that she needed with ease in spite of the mess.

She pushed aside paperwork that lay on a coffee table and heaped scattered stones from the beach into a bowl.

"Make yourself comfortable," she said, indicating a large, squishy armchair with a bright red slipcover. Stained-glass panels hung in all the windows, tinting the light in the room with warm colour.

Elspeth relaxed and told her everything she knew.

30

Elspeth slept well, exhausted by the day's events. She woke up in Skye MacLeod's pastel bedroom, the walls decorated with posters celebrating singers and bands she'd never heard of, photographs of Skye with her friends. She must have a boyfriend. He appeared in several of them, his arm wrapped around her.

She lay in bed and dozed, not looking forward to the day ahead and the interview that afternoon with DI Alexander. Here, she was safe and warm.

She'd told Jan, the night before, about the jade pieces that had disappeared from Deirdre's house and how Kimmy had suggested that a thief might have been disturbed by Liz Fraser, then stabbed her.

"Kimmy might just be right," Jan had said. They had drunk most of a bottle of wine by then and a fire blazed in a wood stove.

"I wondered if the same happened to Deirdre. If she found someone upstairs, rummaging around in the cabinet where she kept the jade, and that person gave her a shove."

"You think so? Have you told Fergus that?"

"He doesn't want to believe it. As far as he's concerned, the death was proved accidental and the case is closed, but Jackie Buchanan is interested. She thinks the autopsy results might show how Deirdre fell. If she went down backwards, it's possible that she was pushed. But that might all be forgotten now that they've got these new deaths to cope with. And the DI seems determined to make me some kind of scapegoat. The results from Liz's autopsy should be in soon. If they prove that she died after I left for Oban on the ferry that day, I'll be off the hook for that murder, at least."

"Let's hope." Jan had topped up their glasses with what was left in the bottle. They'd gone off to bed shortly after.

Elspeth dragged herself out from under the covers and looked out the window. The morning was bright and clear, the sun beaming down out of a cloudless blue sky, the sea, just across the road from Jan's house, a deeper blue flecked with silver, its only movement a slow, gentle pulse. No surging waves with crests of white foam today. The wind must have dropped.

It was too bad she didn't have the dog with her. She could have taken her for a walk but Wilma was with Donalda. A thought occurred to her. Donalda McFee and Alasdair were friends. He had called her 'Nalda'. Was it possible that Donalda was the person who had taken care of him when he had thought that Deirdre had tried to kill him? Could she have helped him leave Sulla without anyone knowing, even though the police and the islanders were searching for him? Had she known all along that he was still alive and kept his secret all these long years?

It meant Donalda would have known that the house did not really belong to Deirdre. That Deirdre had no right to leave it and its contents to Elspeth.

Donalda loved this island and its culture. The language, the traditions. Maybe she resented the changes that had come to the island. She had been kind and helpful to Elspeth, but maybe that was a way to cover up her real thoughts.

Elspeth could hear Jan moving around downstairs. She had said she'd have work to do this morning, first thing, sales to tally from the day before, supply deliveries to chase up. Jan had given her the house's Wi-Fi code.

She emailed Dave to tell him about the new developments but didn't mention that she was being questioned by the police about this. She would rather tell him about that face to face. Could they connect, online, tomorrow? He should be home, early in the morning if she tried to reach him at one, Scottish time. Then she sent a similar message to Margaret, her mother. Margaret had been here on Sulla shortly after Alasdair had gone missing. She knew that Deirdre thought she had killed her husband, but was that all?

"Let's go visit my mum," Jan said when Elspeth finally came downstairs mid-morning. "She needs to know what's really happening before she's told too much gossip." They'd have a good hour to talk to Kate Mary before the ferry arrived bringing Calum McFee with it.

Kate Mary had heard the latest already. Cath MacKinnon was visiting her and had told her all she knew. Cath came by regularly, she said. Her mother, Isa, and Kate Mary had been the same age and they had been friends. Cath knew all about the murders. She'd heard the plane come in early this morning and seen a police car whizzing by the road end near her croft house. She and Lachie had gone to look.

Police cars had been parked at the place where the car had gone over. She'd seen DI Alexander looking over the edge and a policeman had been directing traffic so she and Lachie hadn't been allowed to stop or talk, but they had heard what happened. Old Geordie MacLeod that lived near there had watched through his binoculars all afternoon and described everything. Rob McQuarrie had arrived and towed the car out of the water. It had been quite the job, water pouring off the car, hoisting it up onto the road. Lots of police had worked on it then a police launch had arrived and taken two body bags away.

"Is it true that Fergus Alexander had you locked up all of yesterday?" Cath asked. The question caught Elspeth by surprise, but she should have known that the island would know about that. Jan MacLeod noticed her confusion and jumped in with an answer.

"Elspeth wasn't locked up. He just wanted to talk to her then he got too busy," she said. "She's staying with me for now, so she'll not be alone. Just in case someone decides to come after her next."

"You think that might happen? Why would they do that?" Cath sat in one of the two available chairs in Kate Mary's room. Kate Mary occupied a comfortable recliner.

"Because now that Alasdair's dead, the house is probably going to belong to her again." Jan made sure the door was firmly shut, then sat down on the bed. She patted a place beside her where Elspeth could sit. "And the house has to have something to do with this, hasn't it? Everybody that's died has stayed there. First Deirdre, then Liz Fraser. Now Alasdair and that poor granddaughter of his."

"Maybe Chrissie MacPhail got it right and the place really brings bad luck," Kate Mary said quietly from her comfortable chair in the corner of the room.

Cath was frowning. "Deirdre wasn't murdered, though," she said. "That was an accident."

"Maybe it wasn't." Jan proceeded to repeat what Elspeth had told her, about how some jade was missing from the upstairs cabinet in the house.

"I've seen those," Cath said. "Deirdre showed them to me. She said she thought they were worth a lot of money."

"Well, someone's taken most of them away." Jan looked at Elspeth, expecting her to confirm the story. Elspeth had not intended to tell anyone else about the missing jade and the possible connection to the deaths in the house, but the news was now out.

"Kimmy that cleaned for Deirdre says that there were three shelves full, in an upstairs cabinet. Someone's helped themselves to a lot of those fairly recently. It's possible that Liz Fraser caught them stealing, and that's why she died. I can't think of any other reason for anyone to want to kill her," she said.

"Maybe the same thing happened when Deirdre died. Maybe she caught someone upstairs thieving. And she didn't fall by herself. She was pushed," Jan added, eager to add to the story.

"A whole shelf of notebooks that Deirdre wrote have missing too," Elspeth told them.

Cath MacKinnon's mouth hung open as she sat and listened, taking all this new information in.

"Do the police know about all of this?" Kate Mary asked.

"Jackie Buchanan does," Elspeth said. "She said she'd look into it. Listen, you mustn't tell anyone about this. It's police business and we don't know if any of it is true. We don't want to get another rumour going."

"Not a word," Kate Mary agreed and Cath nodded her head, but Elspeth was fairly sure that Lachie MacKinnon would be told all of this as soon as she got home. A few drinks in the pub and he would tell, too.

"How long will you be staying at Jan's then?" Cath was asking.

Not for long. Elspeth felt safer there, but Skye would be home by the weekend and would reclaim her room.

"I'll probably move back to Bernie's house in a day or two," she said. "Calum's coming in on the ferry so he'll be next door. And Donalda's there, too."

"I have to go. There's egg deliveries still to do." Cath stood and opened the door to leave. A caregiver passed by and cast a baleful look in Elspeth's direction.

"Half this island must think I'm the murderer," Elspeth said, once it closed again.

"Well, I don't," Jan told her.

"It's a strange thing," Kate Mary said, a faraway look in her eye. "Alasdair left us all those years ago, saying he had to get away or Deirdre would be the death of him, then he comes back here and a day later, he's dead."

"You knew he'd left? That he wasn't dead?" Elspeth asked.

The old woman smiled. "There was talk," she said. "Just whispers. There was a lot of speculation at the time. Most people thought he'd been washed out to sea and the fish had got him, but his real friends wondered about that."

Which of them might have found him? Donalda and her husband, Murdo McFee, maybe, but Donalda had been good friends with Deirdre. They liked to talk about books together and Donalda helped Deirdre collect stories from the islanders. She heard ones in Gaelic that Deirdre wasn't privy to and she told them back to her in English so she'd understand. So why would Donalda have let her friend believe that Alasdair was dead?

Chrissie and Norman MacPhail might have been in on it. Norman might have thought he'd get the house back once Alasdair was off the island for good. It was a MacPhail family house, after all, wasn't it? He wouldn't have expected Deirdre to stay, or that Alasdair would be declared dead. That he'd left a will leaving the Skipper's House to his wife.

Cath's mother, Isa, had been the same age as Kate Mary.

"Isa told me once that someone found Alasdair washed up on a beach, half drowned but not dead. They took him and hid him until he was better, then they smuggled him onto the ferry in the back of a van. They got him away without anyone knowing."

"Who did that?" asked Elspeth.

"I don't know. Isa wasn't saying." Kate Mary sat back in her chair and smiled sweetly. Elspeth wasn't sure that she believed her.

"Wasn't it cruel to let Deirdre think he was dead?" she asked instead.

"We weren't sure if it was true or not." said Kate Mary. "Isa sometimes had some daft ideas in her head. She could have made that story up, just to get a bit of attention. People do that sometimes, you know."

"Did you like Alasdair MacPhail?" Elspeth asked.

"Not really," Kate Mary admitted. "Alasdair was always a bit of a show-off. He was clever at school and there was an art teacher made a lot of him. Alasdair could always draw. That got him into art school. But he could be mean sometimes. He wasn't big so he couldn't fight like some of the other boys. Norman MacPhail and Murdo McFee picked on him sometimes, but Alasdair always had a good way with words. He'd get back at them that way.

"He and Deirdre argued a lot. They had a fight in the pub just a few days before he disappeared, about how he wanted to get back to civilization, he said. To be among artists again. She was having none of it. She wanted to stay here and write and she was the one making some money, she reminded him. He didn't like that. I thought it was odd that she wanted to stay and he wanted to go. He belonged here, on Sulla, but she didn't. We were all surprised that she kept coming back once he was gone. But you've got to remember, it took s[illegible] years for Alasdair to be declared dead. Deirdre couldn't get rid of the house and she was only here in the summertime. Donalda once told me that Deirdre believed Alasdair was still alive and he'd show up sooner or later."

"Or she didn't want to think that she'd actually killed him," said Jan.

"Well, maybe that too. Donalda always said we should be kinder to her. And, by then, all those books she'd written about Sulla were making our island famous. We had all kinds of visitors coming and tourism was picking up. Lots of folk, like Sandy McQuarrie's family, were thankful for that. Time passed and we forgot," said Kate Mary, "and now both Deirdre and Alasdair MacPhail are dead and gone. Maybe that's the end of the story and nothing terrible will happen to you." She smiled reassuringly at Elspeth. "You should go home to Canada as soon as you can. Sell the house to Jackie and Dougie Buchanan and leave us to ourselves again."

"I wish," Elspeth sighed. "But the house can't be sold for months yet. It might not be mine and DI Alexander wants me to stay. Liz Fraser died as well, and Ainslie Goertzen. I don't think Fergus will let me go until he knows what really happened This isn't over yet."

"And we need you here for the book festival," Jan chimed in on a more positive note. "Did you know that there's going to be film crews coming here, Mum? They're going to make a TV series about Deirdre's Mairi MacIntosh mysteries. Maybe we'll all get to be extras. I bet they'll need some old folks in it."

Kate Mary laughed at that. She wasn't as averse to change as she'd sounded seconds ago.

Elspeth and Jan had stayed longer than they intended. The ferry would be in by now, if it had arrived on time.

They wheeled Kate Mary to the dining area. Lunch was almost ready. Old Norman MacPhail glowered in their direction from a table and the staff behind the counter put their heads together and talked among themselves when they saw Elspeth. She was definitely suspected of being the killer.

They left and drove to the harbour. The boat was at the dock. Calum had disembarked long since, Colin the Harbour told Jan, noticing Elspeth sitting in the front seat beside her. He didn't say hello to her. He was noticeably less friendly to her than before.

Calum had probably driven home. Jan headed off in that direction.

31

Calum McFee's Land Rover was parked outside the police station at Balemartin.

"He must be in there, finding out what's been going on," Jan said as she drove by. "Will I drop you off at Bernie Baxter's house?"

Elspeth texted. Calum got right back to her. *Be home by one.* That wouldn't be long. Donalda's car was in her driveway, another one parked behind it.

"It's Chrissie MacPhail that's visiting," said Jan. "Are you going to be okay?"

"I'll be fine," Elspeth told her. She knew Jan needed to get back to her studio and get some more of her own work done. "I'll be back tonight, though, to sleep at your house if that's all right with you." She wasn't ready to spend the night by herself while a killer was at large and she did feel a pang of loneliness as she watched Jan drive away.

This was a rare windless day on Sulla. She could take the bike for a ride to pass the time until Calum arrived. She fetched it from the back shed and set off along the flat road, easy pedalling today, the green grass stretching on either side of her and the sea a shimmer of light in the noonday sun. She wished that she had a ball cap to shade her eyes, or sunglasses at least, but it wasn't too hot out. A perfect day for bike riding on Sulla.

She reached the path that cut across the machair to the cliffs at the south end of the island without seeing a single car. The weekend visitors had gone home. No one else was around. The worn path looked smooth enough for a bike but once she was on it, she found that the unpaved ground was bumpy. She hadn't gone far before she decided to abandon it and walk. There was nothing to prop it against but she could lay it down beside the path and pick it up on the way back.

She wasn't far from the cliffs. Birds were flying in and out of their nests, feeding their chicks. She recognized white-headed kittiwakes, black-headed gulls. Some smaller birds were maybe terns and big white ones might be gannets? Still no puffins.

The south end of Mull and Iona were clear to the east. Islay, further south, looked closer than last time she saw it. Visibility played tricks like those out here, when you were on a patch of land in the middle of the wide, open sea.

She thought about what she'd learned so far as she strolled. Kimmy MacLeod's theory about Liz Fraser's death might well be right. There was no reason other than theft for anyone to want to kill Liz. It was entirely possible that something similar had happened to Deirdre as well, but they might never know for sure.

Why would anyone want Alasdair MacPhail dead, though, and enough to kill his granddaughter as well? The Skipper's House probably had belonged to him. Deirdre had died before him and it was possible the house had never been hers at all. It could have been Alasdair's all along. If he died, it could possibly have become Ainslie's. He had said he'd use the money he got from selling it to pay for her to go to grad school. Was that why Ainslie had had to die, too? Had something been said at that party that someone had heard?

She was relieved to know that she might not own the house after all. She didn't want anything to do with it any more. All it had brought into her life was trouble. Perhaps Chrissie MacPhail and Kate Mary had been right when they said that the house was unlucky.

Wilma bounded up to her and dropped a ball at her feet. She looked back to see Donalda McFee striding towards her. Donalda waved.

"Chrissie's gone home. I saw you leaving on the bike and brought Wilma to meet you."

Elspeth picked up the ball and threw it for Wilma. "Calum's at the police station," she told Donalda. "He's coming back here soon."

"It'll be good to have him around. I can't believe what's happening on this island." They turned to walk back along the clifftop. “Alasdair MacPhail reappears from the dead and now he’s really and truly gone?”

“Did you know he was still alive?” Elspeth asked her. Donalda stopped in her tracks.

“Why would you think that?” she asked.

“Because someone did. They found him on a beach, half dead, and helped him recover, then they got him off the island and back to the mainland. Nothing like that could go on here on Sulla without people knowing.”

“Well.” Donalda resumed her walk. “There was a bit of talk, like there always is, but you don’t always believe what people say. Someone asked my Murdo if he had anything to do with it, but Murdo never could stand Alasdair. Chrissie would have helped him if she could. She always had a soft spot for Alasdair, but she was married to Norman and he hated him too. I think he would have been happy to see Alasdair drown.”

“You liked him, though,” said Elspeth. She picked up the ball and threw it again. Wilma caught it in mid-air and came bouncing back with it, tail wagging.

Donalda stopped again. “Yes, I did like Alasdair. And I grew to like Deirdre too. They were both interesting folk and I enjoyed their company. They brought some new life to this island and I was glad of it. I’m sad that both of them are gone, and I’m shocked that someone wanted to kill Alasdair and his granddaughter. I certainly had nothing to do with that.” She turned and walked away. Elspeth caught up and kept pace with her, aware that she had caused offence.

“Who’s been putting ideas like that into your head?” Donalda asked. “Jan MacLeod dropped you off, didn’t she? Have you been talking to Kate Mary?”

“We went there this morning,” Elspeth admitted.

“Well.” Donalda stopped walking. “Kate Mary quite liked Alasdair MacPhail as well. Maybe you should be asking her questions like these.” She pointed out over the sea to where a black bird had landed on a rock. “Look,” she said. “There’s a cormorant.” Her hand moved to rest in the small of Elspeth’s back.

They were standing close to the cliff edge. One push would send her right over the edge. Elspeth caught her breath. She said as normally as she could: “You used to make soup with them?”

"A long time ago. With potatoes." The hand disappeared from her back. "I never liked it very much." Donalda walked on. The moment passed, and Elspeth breathed easy once more.

I am getting paranoid, she told herself.

"This is a good wee dog." Donalda took a turn at throwing the ball. "I didn't think I'd get another one at my age but you need to find her a home. How about she stays with me? I wouldn't mind keeping her. And look, Calum's back." She waved in the direction of the road as the Land Rover drove by. "We should go and pick up that bike. Find out what he's got to say."

They walked quickly along the path, Elspeth pushing the bike, Wilma bouncing at their sides. There was no more ball-throwing.

Calum had good news. The post-mortem results were in on Liz Fraser's body. "She died within twelve hours of when you found the body," he told them, lifting a bag from the back of his vehicle. "You'd been gone on the ferry long before that, Elspeth. There's no way you could have killed her. Fergus has decided he doesn't need to see you today, after all. He knows all he needs to know about where you were yesterday."

"Well then, that's good to hear," said Donalda, and went back to her own house, Wilma trotting at her heels, off to her new home. At least that problem was solved.

"Liz's body is being sent to Edinburgh," said Calum. "Why don't you ask Inga if you can use Liz's car while it's here and get it back to her later, when all this business is sorted out?"

"Does Fergus say I still have to stay here?" asked Elspeth, pushing the bike between the houses, back to the shed. There was nothing she'd like better right now than a chance to get away from Sulla.

"Afraid so. He's still got you in his sights for the deaths of Alasdair and his granddaughter, but he's wavering. He knows perfectly well that it's probably the same killer as murdered Liz. Assuming that they were actually killed. It's possible that Ainslie drove off the road by accident."

"I think they were," said Elspeth. "It's too much of a coincidence, isn't it? He should find out who'll inherit the house now. It's not me. It never really belonged to Deirdre, not when Alasdair was still alive. Maybe it would have gone to Ainslie now, but she's dead too. So does it revert to the MacPhails? They were all at that party. Chrissie and her sons, Young Norman and Rob. Rob's tried mooring his boat at the pier, as if it's theirs already. Fergus Alexander needs to be finding out where both of them were last night, not me."

She propped the bike back inside the shed. Calum leaned against the door.

"You might be right," he said. "When Liz was killed, I thought it had to be something to do with the plan to film a TV series here. That one of the old diehards, someone that wants to see us go back to the good old days, had argued with her because of that."

"You don't think that's a good thing either, though, do you?" asked Elspeth.

He shrugged. "It's going to happen. There's no stopping progress, is there? Some people will benefit. There'll be film crews to house and feed. They'll hire locals as extras and people will get to see themselves on the telly Maybe this tourist boom that we're having isn't going to last and a TV series will give that industry a boost. Who knows? You'll go back to Canada and get your share of the profit and we'll never see you again."

"That's right," she said.

He turned away. She followed.

"You should tell Fergus what you think," he said, as they walked back to the house. "The thing is, pushing people to their death in a car is not how my MacPhail cousins would kill anyone. Rob, in particular, thinks of himself as tough. He'd punch someone out, not give them a shove."

"Liz was stabbed," she reminded him.

"There's that," he agreed, "but it's still not their style. It didn't take much strength to carry out any of these murders."

"So a woman could have done it? Is that what you're saying? Someone like me?"

"I've told you. I don't believe you did it," he replied. He'd left a briefcase on the doorstep of his house and went to pick it up. "I need to go and catch up on some work. I'll be next door if you need me." He reached his front door and then stopped. "We're both here tonight. How about we get together for dinner?"

"Sure," she said. She watched him go and realized that she liked Calum McFee, the more she saw of him. It was just dinner between neighbours. Client and lawyer. He was one of the few people around that she was sure had nothing to do with the murders, and he said that he believed in her. That was all this was, she told herself.

She needed to talk to Dave in Winnipeg. She tried contacting him but she got no reply. Dave was out and he hadn't replied to the last message that she had sent him. He was always out, never available when she needed him. Didn't he realize that this was important? And what was he doing that kept him away from home so much? Was something new going on in his life, just as it was in hers?

She called Inga Hansen, who sounded glad to hear from her. She had been told by the publisher that Liz's murder on Sulla had led to a spike in book sales. Creepy but true. She'd heard on the news that there had been more deaths, so it wasn't just Liz who had been targeted. Maybe they'd find the killer soon. Having Elspeth use Liz's Mini was fine by her, she'd check the insurance but she thought it would be okay. Elspeth could keep the car until the book festival. Inga planned to come to that. She could pick it up then. Or Elspeth could drive to Edinburgh when she was done here. Meet her Scottish relatives and Deirdre's publisher. Fly home to Canada from there. The police probably still had the keys to the car. She had a phone number for the Sulla Police Station. She'd let them know that Elspeth would pick them up.

Elspeth texted Calum. Could he drive her to Balemartin? He could, but he'd need to come right back home. He still had work to do. He stopped outside the police station while she ran in. Jackie Buchanan was there, no Fergus.

"He's out trying to discover if anyone knows anything about that missing jade," she said to Elspeth. "He thinks that's his best lead now. That it will take him straight to Liz Fraser's killer. So thanks for telling us about that." Fergus was no longer targeting Elspeth.

Jackie had received Inga's message and handed over the keys to Liz's Mini.

Calum drove through Tostaig, past the harbour and the hotel on the way to the Skipper's House so they could go pick up Liz's Mini. Two or three heads turned as they passed.

"I'm getting the evil eye," said Elspeth. "Maybe we shouldn't eat at the hotel tonight."

“That’s all right,” said Calum. “I’ll get us a decent bottle of wine and order something for pickup.” He smiled and shifted gear, his big hand close to her knee.

It was later in the afternoon, the sun over to the west, but it was still a calm day, the water cobalt, the sky baby blue.

“What’s that?” Calum said as he turned a corner and the Skipper’s House came into view. A thin grey plume of smoke was rising above the rooftop.

32

Cath MacKinnon's white van was parked in the driveway to the house. The smoke was rising from the back.

"That's got to be a bonfire," said Calum. But who was there? The house was unoccupied. They left the Land Rover at the roadside and hurried past the garage. There was a loud, swooshing sound, and the plume of smoke turned black. They could smell burning wood.

They opened the gate to the back garden. A large burning pyre had been built in the middle of the grass, at least six feet high. It contained items from the house, mostly pieces from the valuable hoard that Skipper MacPhail had brought back from his travels. Chinese chairs and side tables were heaped on top of one another, screens from Japan. The one with cranes on it that Donalda MacFee had coveted was almost gone. Pictures and wall hangings galore were piled up, the glass from frames shattered from the heat. Elspeth recognized the covering from Deirdre's bed and the Indian rugs from the upstairs landing, all smouldering. Megan MacPhail's treasured linens and silks added fodder to the flames.

The painting that Alasdair had made of Deirdre poked out, half way down, only recognizable by what was left of the frame, flames still rising from it. Another oily canvas must have been the source of the black smoke still rising above the house. One of Alasdair's drawings lay on the grass, half burned.

Out on the water, a boat was roaring out of the harbour and across the bay.

"Looks like Rob MacPhail's seen the smoke." Calum shaded his eyes to look.

"Look at this!" Elspeth noticed a heap of smashed porcelain lying beside the house. "It looks like it's all been thrown against the back wall." She walked closer and picked up a large fragment, one with a pale ivory-coloured glaze decorated with a few blue flower petals. It looked like it had once been part of the large vase which had stood on the landing.

"Watch out!" Calum shouted. Elspeth looked up just in time to see a chair emerge from an upstairs window and begin to tumble towards her. She jumped back as it crashed to the ground. A tall-backed armchair of intricately carved wood lay at her feet, two of its legs broken on impact.

All the windows at the back of the house were wide open. The one that Jan MacLeod had created was gone. In its place was a black void, edged with broken glass. Coloured shards spattered the ground below.

A face looked out of the window to Deirdre's bedroom. Cath MacKinnon, her hair dishevelled, glared down at them then abruptly disappeared from view.

"Cath!" Elspeth yelled up. "What are you doing?" There was no reply.

"I'm calling Jackie Buchanan." Calum raised his phone to his ear. Elspeth ran to the side of the house. The shed at the front contained garden tools. If she found a rake she could perhaps salvage some items from the blaze. She came face to face with Cath MacKinnon before she reached the gate.

Cath was wearing the yellow silk kimono that Elspeth had last seen lying flat in a wide drawer, carefully folded. Now it hung loose over Cath's old jeans and a washed-out blue sweatshirt. Dirt smudged her face. In her hand was a long black stick, thin and curved. She swung it at Elspeth. Elspeth ducked and fell as it whizzed over her head. Calum ran towards them. In her other hand, Cath grasped the head of a seated buddha. The statue wasn't big but it was solid. She raised it and flung it straight at Calum. It caught him squarely in the middle of the forehead and he dropped to the ground.

"Go away!" Cath screamed. "This isn't yours. Get out of here."

Elspeth rose to her knees. She watched in eerie fascination as Cath lifted the black weapon and unsheathed what she now recognized as a samurai sword. The blade was shiny steel. Elspeth made it up onto her feet and stepped backwards as the sword was raised, ready to strike.

"Cath! You put that down right now." Chrissie MacPhail's voice rang out behind them.

Cath's head swung round to look. Elspeth took the opportunity to jump aside. Chrissie was striding up the side of the house.

Cath dropped both sword and scabbard and fled. She jumped over Calum, still prostrate on the ground, the yellow kimono flapping behind her, then took off across the grass, straight toward the back wall. She almost crashed into Rob MacPhail, coming through the gate.

"What the hell is going on here?" he asked. He had headed right over on the boat, as soon as he saw the smoke and called his mother while he was at it.

"Just as well I came straight here," said Chrissie. "It looked like Cath was going to take your head off with that thing."

Calum tried to rise, blood dripping into his eyes. Elspeth ran to the edge of the fire and found a white pillowcase that had fallen wide of the blaze. She dropped to her knees beside him, wadded it up and held it to a gash on his forehead.

Rob MacPhail was on the phone.

"Cath MacKinnon's gone mad," Elspeth heard him say. "She's run off down the beach."

Chrissie toed the sword aside with her foot and went to help Elspeth. She inspected the cut on Calum's forehead. "You're going to need some stitches. You've taken quite a clout," she said. He tried getting to his feet, still dazed.

"Stay there." Elspeth looked behind her for more fabric. The piece she had used to staunch his wound was already soaked with blood. Cuts to the head bled a lot, she reminded herself. This might not be as serious as it looked.

The sound of an outboard motor roared out by the pier.

"She's taken my boat!" Rob pocketed his phone, turned and ran.

"What's that Cath gone and done now?" Chrissie left and went to look over the wall. "She must have gone straight down there to the pier."

"Look, there she is." Rob pointed. They could see the boat, kicking up a wide wake, roaring out into open water, yellow silk billowing behind the figure at the wheel.

A police siren howled and flashing lights approached on the road from Tostaig. Calum had managed to stagger to his feet. Elspeth found a tablecloth that was barely singed and replaced the sodden wad. "Hold that to your head," she told him "And lean on me. You're not steady on your feet yet. We need to get you sitting down."

The fire blazed on. Skipper MacPhail's treasure was going up in smoke.

A car screeched to a halt outside. Jackie Buchanan ran around the corner of the house, followed by a constable from Fergus Alexander's team.

"Are you okay?" She had a quick look at Calum's head. "Go sit down." The fire was burning steadily. "Lucky there's no wind," she said. "The house isn't in any danger."

Calum preferred to join the MacPhails at the wall, where they could watch the boat, further out from the bay, still travelling fast. A Kodiak was leaving the harbour in pursuit, a small fishing boat close behind it.

"How full is the tank on that boat?" Jackie called to Rob.

"Filled it yesterday," he shouted back.

"Look, she's stopping." Jackie pointed. They watched the boat slow down. The Kodiak and the fishing boat were closing in on it.

As it drifted to a halt, the yellow-clad figure stepped up onto one of the wooden seats. The silk kimono caught the sunlight as Cath MacKinnon placed one foot on the side of the boat, jumped overboard and disappeared below the water.

"Oh, shit," said Jackie Buchanan. Then she noticed Chrissie MacPhail marching towards the house. "Don't you go in there!" she shouted after her.

Chrissie walked back to where the rest of them still looked out to sea. The fishing boat had pulled up alongside the MacPhails' craft and one of the crew was boarding it. Rob knew the fishermen and reached for his phone.

"There's no sign of her," he reported back. "The current's strong out there. It'll carry her right down towards Islay if they don't find her right away."

"Can she swim?" asked Elspeth. No one knew. Another fishing boat and a smaller one with an outboard were on their way to join in the search.

The PC from DI Alexander's team was also on the phone, talking to his boss.

"He's almost here," he told Jackie. So was the doctor.

"Cath MacKinnon always had stupid ideas in her head." Chrissie MacPhail stood beside Elspeth, watching the boats circling out on the water. "But I never thought she'd do anything as daft as this."

"What kind of ideas?" asked Elspeth.

"Well, Cath's the daughter of Isa. Sandy McQuarrie's aunt. Used to be great pals with Kate Mary MacLeod. Isa's long dead and gone. She never was very strong. But way back, when we were all young, Isa took a liking to Alasdair MacPhail. She was already married, to John McFee. He was a feckless kind of man. Calum's uncle. Good-looking though. She fell for him when she was sixteen then found out what a mistake she'd made, and there wasn't much she could do about it, back then, so I can't say I blame her. But the problem was, she didn't know which of them had fathered Cath. And she went and told Cath that. I said to her once, you shouldn't have done that, Isa, but she said that she wanted Cath to know that she might have a better father than the one she lived with. And Cath believed her.

"I've heard Cath say that this house should be hers. And all those things in it." She nodded in the direction of the burning pile. The flames were dying down to a steady smoulder. "We told her not to be stupid, but she didn't pay attention. I told her more than once that this was a MacPhail house by rights anyway, and it should have gone to one of my boys."

Jackie had gone for a quick walk through the house. Now she came back and interrupted Chrissie.

"It's a shambles in there," she said. "She's thrown things around. But nothing structural is damaged, except for that window up there." She pointed her thumb up at the smashed stained-glass window. "At least she didn't set the fire in the middle of the house."

Rob MacPhail had found a broken table leg and was poking at the bonfire.

"Maybe we can get some stuff out of here," he said, and went off to find the rake. The PC went with him.

The doctor and DI Alexander arrived at almost the same time.

"I can stitch you up," Dr. Thomson told Calum, "but we need to get you over to Oban for an X-ray, soon as we can. You've taken a crack to the skull."

Fergus Alexander took command of the situation. Colin the Harbour had summoned the coastguard to help in the search for Cath MacKinnon. They were on their way. A full investigative team would be on Sulla soon, arriving by plane. Calum could get a lift back to Oban on it.

"I'm going with him," said Elspeth. DI Alexander didn't say that she couldn't.

Rob MacPhail had found a hose in the shed and hooked it up to a spigot on the back wall. He and the constable were managing to extinguish some of the fire. The smoke above the fire was turning into steam.

Fergus had contacted Colin the Harbour, still out on the water in the Kodiak. Colin was talking loudly against the sound of the outboard motor.

"We can't find any sign of her." They heard his voice ring out from Fergus's phone. "I think she's been caught in the current."

Lachie MacKinnon ran round the house and into the yard followed by the police constable.

"I couldn't stop him, sir," the PC blurted in the direction of DI Alexander. "He pushed me aside. Wouldn't listen."

"That's Lachie, Cath's husband," Chrissie MacPhail told Fergus.

"I know who he is." DI Alexander pocketed his phone and marched towards Lachie. He stood stock still by the coal bunker, looking at the fire, wondering where his wife had gone.

"Where's Cath? What's she done?" he asked. Fergus and the policeman both made to grab him.

Chrissie MacPhail's voice stopped them.

"You leave him alone, Fergus Alexander." She pushed her way between the DI and Lachie. "You too," she barked at the police constable. Then she said something to Lachie in Gaelic.

They watched as Lachie's knees gave way and he slid down the side of the bunker. Chrissie went down on her old knees beside him and talked to him in Gaelic. Tears began to roll down his face.

"Has anyone here got a hankie?" Chrissie demanded, in English. She turned so she could sit on the grass beside Lachie, their backs to the wooden side of the bunker, and they continued to talk. Jackie Buchanan supplied them with tissues. DI Alexander had his phone out and was recording the conversation.

"I'll tell you on the way to the plane," Calum whispered in Elspeth's ear. She and Jackie Buchanan were the only two present that spoke no Gaelic and had no idea what was being said.

33

As soon as they got into the car, Calum relayed what he had heard Lachie MacKinnon say. A large patch of gauze covered stiches on his forehead and he was quite alert once more, but he'd been told not to drive. Elspeth was at the wheel, taking it slowly, intent on listening to every word.

"He said that Cath's been helping herself to bits and pieces from the house for years. She sells it online. Boxes it up and goes over to Oban to post it so nobody will find out. Deirdre never noticed that they were gone."

"Not even when most of her valuable jade disappeared?" Elspeth asked.

"She wouldn't have known about that. It looks like Cath took those pieces recently. Before, she was more careful. She only took one or two things at a time. Small things that wouldn't be noticed. She and Lachie have had a key to the house for years. Deirdre asked them to keep an eye on the place when she was gone. She could go in and help herself whenever she liked, all winter long. But then Deirdre stayed in the house all year because of the pandemic and she couldn't do that anymore."

"So she needed the extra income?"

"You've seen their place. Lachie's not an efficient crofter and he drinks every penny he can lay his hands on. All Cath will have had was the money she gets from selling eggs. So she was able to make a bit on the side, until Deirdre stayed and that source dried up. Once Deirdre was dead she was able to help herself to the jade. She'd have got a lot of money for that. Make up for lost time. But then the word got out that Fergus Alexander knew the jade was missing. That the police thought that would lead them to the killer."

"We talked about it. Jan and I were visiting Jan's mother. Cath was there," Elspeth said. "So she must have thought that Fergus would find out she had them and think that she had killed Liz Fraser? But Cath? She wouldn't hurt a fly." The small terminal building was not far away. She pulled up outside.

A yellow plane was approaching the airport. Boats were still out on the water, within view of the harbour, searching for Cath. People were watching along the shore. Lachie had said that Cath couldn't swim at all. There was talk of recovering her body, rather than finding her alive. A dive team was on its way by boat from Oban, but there were fears she might have been swept away, far out to sea.

"You're right," Calum said. "It wasn't her that killed Liz Fraser. Or your uncle Alasdair and his granddaughter. It was Lachie."

"Lachie? He said so?"

"Confessed. We all heard him." They stayed in the car while the plane landed along a strip of green grass. "See, Cath wasn't the only person stealing from Deirdre. Lachie used to go in and help himself to a bottle of whisky now and then. He thought Liz had gone with you to Oban and decided to stop by on the way home from the pub that night. Walked right in. Liz caught him in the pantry, helping himself. Seems she lost it with him, was yelling that he must have shoved Deirdre down the stairs. She took out her phone so she could call the police and he just grabbed a knife, lying there on the kitchen counter. It was all over in seconds."

"But Alasdair? And Ainslie?"

"An accident, he says. When they were all at the party the night before, Cath made a point of introducing herself to Alasdair and he hadn't the faintest clue who she was. Acted like her mother had been of no interest to him at all. She couldn't believe it. She'd had this dream in her head all her life that her father was Alasdair and it might not be true. She went home and cried, Lachie said. So when Alastair and Ainslie drove by their croft the next night, Lachie got into his old van and followed them. He thought he would give them a bit of scare, that was all."

"He wanted to drive them off the road, just like he did to me and to Deirdre?"

"Sounds like it. But he didn't realize that Ainslie wasn't used to our roads or a left-hand-drive car. She must have panicked and swerved, just at the worst place. The car slid down the embankment and toppled into the water."

"And he drove away? Left them to drown?"

"Seems so." They left the car and walked into the terminal.

"So Lachie was responsible for all those awful things that happened to Deirdre? And the dead fish that was left for me?"

"Seems so."

"Did he kill her, too?"

"He swears he didn't have anything to do with that. Not him or Cath. It might have been an accident after all, Elspeth. Maybe Deirdre did trip and fall headlong down the stairs."

"But he did take her notebooks?"

"That's right. They were all lying on the kitchen table when he killed Liz. She'd been reading them. He could see that Deirdre had written in them and he'd heard tell in the pub that the police knew about the notes that he had left to annoy her. He scooped them all up and took them home. Burned them, just to get rid of them. He thinks that's what gave Cath the idea to start a bonfire of her own. He's blaming himself for that."

Donalda McFee was waiting inside the building.

"I came to see you off," she said, and lifted the corner of the gauze on Calum's head to look. The doctor had stitched the cut. He felt fine, Calum insisted, but Dr. Thomson still insisted he go for an X-ray.

"Who's picking you up off the plane in Oban?" asked Donalda.

"A friend," he replied.

"He tells me nothing." Donalda rolled her eyes and sat beside them.

"Lachie MacKinnon?" she asked. She knew already who the murderer was. "I always thought he was a bit useless. Fancy that. I hope they get that poor wife of his out of the water before she's dead and gone too."

The plane was taxiing to a stop in front of the building. There wasn't long to talk.

"So, Mother," Calum asked. "What's the real story about how Alasdair MacPhail managed to leave Sulla all those years ago?"

"Well." Donalda sat up in her chair. "We all promised but I suppose there's no harm in telling any more. It was Isa who found him, half drowned on the beach. She was married to John McFee, your uncle, Calum. Not a good man, not like your father. She couldn't take Alasdair home so Kate Mary and her husband, Angus, took him to their house instead. Alasdair was perfectly fine once he got dried off but he asked us not to let on that he was still alive. That was hard, because everyone was searching for him, but he was adamant that he needed to get away from Deirdre without her knowing. We found enough money between us to get him to Edinburgh. He still had friends there from art school and he wanted to get back to them. Kate Mary and Angus put him in the back of a van they had and took him to Oban on the ferry, then they saw him off on the train. He'd shaved his beard off and he was wearing a suit that had belonged to your grandfather. He was a small man so it fitted. He looked quite different."

"Did he write to anyone after? Or phone?"

"Not really. The postmistress here watched every letter that came in and out of the mailbag and she was a right gossip. So was the telephone operator. All our calls were directed through her back then and she wasn't above listening in. She'd have told in a minute.

"He got one of his friends in London to drop us a note, to see if we could find his birth certificate and send it to him there. It was November by then and Deirdre was gone back to Edinburgh. Isa had a key to the Skipper's House in those days. She went in and found it, and his passport. Kate Mary went over to Oban and mailed it to London from there."

Four police had climbed out of the plane and were walking across the runway to the building, carrying bags of equipment.

"So you all knew he was alive and helped cover up the fact? You were all in on it and you let Deirdre think he was dead?" Elspeth asked.

"She tried to kill him." Donalda's voice hardened. "She didn't deserve our sympathy."

"You told me you liked her," Elspeth said, surprised.

"Och, well. Time passes." Donalda was interrupted by the arrival of Jackie Buchanan and the young constable, come to pick up the police team. Jackie waved as they escorted them out the front of the building to their cars.

"I don't know what Fergus needs all those police for now," Donalda said. "He'll be able to write up his report and go home.

There'll be no trial. Case closed, that'll keep him happy." The prop plane sat on the runway, engines still running so it could take off again as soon as they boarded.

"She's probably right," Calum said as they walked out onto the runway to see him off. He had no idea who the Skipper's House would belong to now. Most likely it would go to some descendant of Alasdair MacPhail though, not to Elspeth. He'd had at least one daughter in Canada, the one who had parented Ainslie. There could be other grandchildren living in Alberta.

"I don't mind one bit," Elspeth said. She didn't care to ever set foot in the house again. Too much tragedy had happened there.

On the short trip to Oban, high over the sea, they passed over a police launch, carrying the dive team to Sulla. The pilot flew lower and dipped his wings so they could see the boat. A diver waved up to them.

"I wonder if they'll find her," Elspeth mused. There was no doubt in anyone's mind that Cath MacKinnon was dead, but they also knew that people had assumed Alasdair MacPhail had drowned all those years ago, and they had been wrong about that.

The friend who waited to meet the plane was a woman called Sally Kerr. She taught music at Oban High School. She hugged Calum, then she examined his bandage.

"You feeling all right?" she asked him. "Let's get you to the hospital right away. You could have concussion and not be aware of it. Thanks for taking such good care of him," she said to Elspeth. "Can we drop you off somewhere?"

Elspeth had come along because she had thought that Calum might need her help. Obviously he did not.

The Oban airport was a few miles out of town. Elspeth sat in the back of the car and listened to them talk as Sally drove. The whole story was retold. They dropped her where she asked, at the tourist kiosk on the bay.

Her usual Airbnb was booked for the night. She found a room in a big old hotel near the ferry terminal. It was comfortable and clean and it had efficient Wi-Fi. She logged on. There were messages. The whole of Sulla was buzzing with the news.

Jan let her know that there was still no sign of Cath. The divers were at work. Elspeth called her.

"Lachie's at the police station. Charged with murdering Liz Fraser and of forcing Alasdair and Ainslie into the water and leaving them to die. They're still hoping that Cath's body will show up. Everybody's wondering why she didn't burn the house down, if she wanted to destroy everything in it, but Donalda McFee says that she was like Chrissie MacPhail. She thought the house was ill-fated, so she didn't want to have it. It was all the fancy stuff that was in it that she liked. Isa, her mother, used to tell her stories about them, the ones that Megan MacPhail had told her classes in the school at Sulla. Cath grew up wishing she could have things like that.

"She kept some, you know, in a cupboard in her own house, fans and dolls, things like that. I suppose she set fire to the rest to make sure that no one else got them."

"Do you think Alasdair really was her father?"

"I don't think so. That was just another fantasy. Maybe they'll do a DNA test and find out for sure."

Elspeth went for a walk around Oban Bay. The evening was beautiful, the water calm, boats riding at anchor. There were tourists walking by. She blended right in with them. She ate fish and chips, sitting on a bench. Every move she made on Sulla was scrutinized and talked about. Here, she enjoyed the anonymity.

She got back to the hotel and went to the bar for a drink. A message from Calum said that he was fine, no worse than a mild concussion but he had to stay at the hospital overnight for observation. He hoped to catch tomorrow's regular flight back to the island. Would she be on it?

She texted back. She'd booked a ticket for the ferry already, first thing in the morning.

Another message was waiting for her, from Annabel. Sandy McQuarrie was out on a boat helping the searchers. He'd just let her know that the dive team was still out in the water, but there was no sign of Cath MacKinnon. They were fairly sure she was gone, swept away by the sea.

Elspeth sighed. She drank what was left of her wine. She wished she could leave all this behind, go back to Winnipeg. Catch a train in the morning to Glasgow instead of going back to Sulla. Take the first ticket available to Canada. Anywhere in Canada. She could get home from there.

But she knew she couldn't go. Not yet. She was a part of what had happened out on the island. Her passport was still there, too, in her bag in Bernie Baxter's blackhouse. She needed to get back on that boat tomorrow and help with the cleanup.

34

Elspeth walked downhill in the dark to the ferry early the next morning. The street lights were still on, the glow from the town and the remaining stars reflected in the water at the harbour. It was Thursday morning and the boat did not look busy. She was surprised to see Calum McFee standing at the top of the gangway, talking to a man in a suit. He introduced him. The valuer who was supposed to assess the contents of the Skipper's House had finally put in an appearance.

"Most of the contents are gone?" he asked. He'd need to have a look at what was left but he'd have to ask the police for access to the house. He went off to call his manager and inform him of the situation.

The gauze that covered the gash and a swollen lump on Calum's forehead had been replaced by a plaster and the skin around it was turning purple.

"You are going to have a black eye." She looked up at it. "Weren't you going to wait for the plane?"

"I've got a thick skull," he joked as they went to the cafeteria and bought coffees, but he did have dark shadows under his eyes. "I couldn't sleep in that hospital. All the lights and sounds kept me awake. People kept coming and going. So I decided to check myself out and catch the boat with you."

They found window seats in the observation deck, facing one another, a large single-pane window between them. It was still dark outside, the lights from the boat dancing on the water but the sky was growing lighter over the hills behind the town.

Calum had kept himself busy during the long night by finding out more about Alasdair MacPhail and his family, he told her. Ainslie Goertzen had social media accounts. So had Alasdair. He had a daughter and Ainslie was one of three siblings.

"Don't be surprised if the house goes to them." Calum yawned, lack of sleep catching up to him. "The best that we can hope for that they'll decide Deirdre was entitled to half and you'll get that. It's going to take months before that all gets sorted out. Just don't count on it being yours."

"I don't know that I want any of it." Elspeth sank deeper into her chair and pulled her jacket around her, chilled at the memory of all that had happened at the Skipper's House the day before. The engines on the boat whirred as it began to move away from the pier. "I don't want to go near it, ever again."

"Maybe you'll change your mind once it's all cleaned up. It'll look entirely different now that most of Skipper MacPhail's hoard is gone. The newer furniture in it, all the things that Deirdre bought, belong to you. You should get all that back."

"What'll happen to Deirdre's car?" she asked.

"Well then." He rubbed his eyes, wincing as his fingers brushed the swelling on his forehead. "It seems it's been sent to your cousin in Edinburgh since he's Deirdre's executor."

"That's all right. I can use Liz's Mini for now." It was still in the garage at the Skipper's House. Retrieving it would mean going back.

"Yes," he said. "But the Volkswagen was Deirdre's and it should be yours. We'll need to get it returned."

"It's too bad Cath burned the painting of Deirdre. I hope there's one of the drawings left that Alasdair did of her when they were young and happy. I'd like to have one of those."

"We can ask, but don't get your hopes up." Calum had phoned Fergus Alexander last night to get an update. He had talked to his mother as well. She would pick them up off the boat when they reached Sulla. "Cath did a pretty good job of trashing everything she could lay her hands on. They've searched Lachie and Cath's house. They found a cupboard full of dolls, fans, saris, Japanese tea sets that she kept for herself. Kind of pathetic, isn't it? There's the remains of a bonfire out behind their barn, too. A whole bunch of twisted spiral coils and some burnt scraps of paper." They both drank their coffee and gazed out the window. The boat moved out across the bay, the sea a gentle swell. This would be an easy crossing to Sulla.

"The thing is, Deirdre only had basic insurance on the house. I told her more than once that she should take out extra coverage for the contents but she just laughed. Said everything was safe where it was. Who would want it, anyway. Little did she know."

"So it's all gone?" said Elspeth.

"Almost. There's what Cath stole. Some of the jade was safely tucked away in the back of the MacKinnons' van. She hadn't had time to sell it yet. That's worth something. The police have taken it all as evidence."

"They're not mine, anyway," Elspeth said. "They belong with the house. The notebooks that contain the manuscripts will still be there if Cath didn't burn them. I hope so. I think I'd like to keep them."

"You'll get them back if they are, but it's going to take a while. Lachie will go to trial for the three deaths. Murder, in the case of Liz. Culpable homicide for Alasdair and Ainslie."

"But not for Deirdre?"

"No. It looks like it really was an accident. Lachie insists neither he nor Cath had anything to do with it. They didn't know that she was dead until the day that Cath stopped by and found the body."

"But he did threaten her. And me."

"Fergus isn't interested in that, so he hasn't asked, but I suppose so. You know, Lachie was a lost soul from the start. The only son, so he inherited the croft, but that wasn't what he wanted. He loved the sea. He should have been a younger son, like Rob MacPhail, gone off to see the world. What a sad case this is." He drank a mouthful of coffee, looked at her across the rim of the paper coffee cup and changed the subject. "But you'll be staying for a while? There's still the book festival to come."

"I suppose so, but I think Deirdre's ashes must be gone," Elspeth said. "I left the urn in her bedroom window, the one where we both saw Cath looking out. Maybe she smashed it against the wall and threw the ashes into the fire."

"That's too bad." He frowned, then yawned again. "We know that Alasdair didn't drown at sea, so you won't be going out in a boat and throwing them into the water after all. Maybe it's best this way. There'll still need to be some kind of memorial at the festival for Deirdre, though, won't there?"

"For sure. I'll need to stick around for that. And you guys are still paying me to help manage the festival."

"That's not a problem, Elspeth. You can go back to Canada if you want to."

"Well," she said and stretched. The sun had come up now. The waves sparkled outside the window and the hills of Kerrara were clearly visible, lights still shining from the occasional house as they passed. "I was thinking about that." She had been awake most of the night, too, the events of the day running in her head, aware that she couldn't leave Scotland yet.

"Bernie Baxter's going to need his house back by the end of the month. I could get most of the festival work done by then. Maybe I could go on a road trip for a couple of weeks after that. I've hardly seen this country, and it's where I was born. I could drive Liz's Mini to Edinburgh and get together with my Scottish relatives. Spend a couple of days with Inga Hansen and meet Deirdre's publisher."

She pulled her feet up onto the seat, getting more enthused about the idea as she talked. "Then I could rent a little camper van, and go to Carnoustie, where I was born, to see my granny Balfour's old house. Drive all the way up to Inverness. Take the tourist route back to Argyll. Then I could come back here and park the van in someone's driveway for the last couple of weeks while I do the book festival. After that it's off, back to Canada."

"You were born in Scotland?" he asked. "So you could live here if you wanted? You've got citizenship?"

"I suppose so. I was two years old when we moved. I am going to go home," she assured him. "I've got a show to design for a theatre company in Winnipeg. I need to get back to work again. I might have some money coming to me, quite a lot, maybe, but it's not going to be the huge amount it would have been if I'd got the house. That's okay. I like what I do."

"And there's Dave," he said.

"I'm not sure where Dave and I are at any more." She looked out the window, avoiding catching his eye. "But I need to find out. I'm supposed to talk to him sometime later today. He has no idea what just happened here." She would need to talk to her mother as well. Fill her in on the whole sorry story.

The coffee was done. She lowered her feet back down to the floor and stood. Crumpled the paper cup and reached for his.

"Who is Sally Kerr?" she asked.

"Sally?" He handed her the empty cup, a slow smile creeping over his face. "She's married to Alec Kerr. I've known him for years. We go fishing together. Sally's just a friend."

She felt her face turn pink. She'd got that wrong. But it changed nothing. She would go back home to Winnipeg. She and Dave had been partners for fifteen years. She thought they might be drifting apart, but that would need to be worked through.

"I'm going to go up on deck to get some fresh air," she said. "You look like you need to sleep."

"Sorry." He yawned again. "I thought the coffee would keep me awake but it's not working. We never did do that dinner," he said, as she turned away. "How about tonight?"

"You bought last time," she said. "It's my turn. My place? I'll order a takeout. You can bring the wine."

"I'll do that," he said. "Wake me up when we get to Sulla. See you later."

Elspeth dumped the paper cups in a container and went out onto the foredeck. The boat was just passing Mull, a cluster of tourists waiting to see pretty Tobermory as they sailed by. She went to the other side of the boat and stood alone at the rail, where the water stretched, uninterrupted to the horizon. Somewhere out there was Canada. Home, or was it? She had no idea whether she wanted to be with Dave any longer. Meantime she could get to know Calum McFee a little better. He's been married twice, already, she told herself. Then she realized that the same was true of her. She pulled out her phone and found the number for the Tostaig Hotel.

"Elspeth!" Donnie, the hotel manager, sounded glad to hear her voice. "Are you on your way back?"

Yesterday, she had dreaded returning. Now, she was more optimistic. There was an evening with Calum McFee to look forward to. Three weeks to enjoy being on the island, with no more threat of danger. Seven whole weeks to meet her relatives, see more of this country that she barely knew.

"How's Calum doing?" Donnie was asking. "Is it true that Cath MacKinnon smashed his skull in? That it's fractured? That they had to take him to Glasgow?'"

"Not a chance," she laughed. "You've got that all wrong. He's got a bump on his head and black eye and he's on the boat right now, with me."

"Grand! Good to hear that. You know they found Cath MacKinnon? A fisherman from Iona picked her up early this morning."

"She's dead?" Elspeth asked.

"Long gone. They're saying she had some teeny wee dollies from the Skipper's house stuffed in the pockets of her jeans. She'd been wearing some yellow silky thing from the house and it was shredded to pieces. Now, what was it you were phoning about?"

"I wondered what you've got on the menu for tonight," she asked. "I was thinking about picking up dinner."

"Just a minute. I'll put you on to Frieda." Elspeth needed time to recover from his news. She had liked Cath MacKinnon and was sorry that her life had ended like this.

She could hear him talking to whoever was on the other side of the bar while she waited for Frieda to come to the phone.

"Calum's on his way back here on the boat with the Canadian," she heard him say.

"That right?" There was the usual bar laughter.

Elspeth didn't mind. There was nothing malicious in the sound this time. It almost made her feel like she belonged, a little. Don't kid yourself, she told herself. You'll never be an islander, any more than Deirdre was. But she and Sulla had some history now. She maybe didn't need to leave forever.

She found a seat where she could see the grey sea swell, all the way to the horizon, the prow of the boat cutting through the waves. She'd stay here for the rest of the trip. Watch Sulla come into view and see the Skipper's House from the sea once more. Go wake Calum up once they approached the harbour at Tostaig and tell him that they had found Cath's body. That the case was resolved. And then she'd have to wait and find out what would happen next.

Acknowledgments

It's over six years now since Signature Editions took me and my books on board and I couldn't be more grateful to be in their capable and expert hands. Karen, Ashley, Terry and all of the many people it takes to put my books together, thank you! And thanks for having faith in this new series.

Thanks also to Doug Whiteway, my patient, thoughtful and thorough editor, who makes my books so much better.

Kirsty Macdonald and Ann Atkey have been with this book since the beginning. They read it first and gave me detailed notes, chapter by chapter, and they have listened to me talk it through, from when it was just an idea to now, when it's a published novel.

I want to thank Christine Hannah, for advice about forensics, Nikki Philp for answering my questions about legal issues, and Andrew Minor, as always my trusted advisor on the RCMP. Thanks also to my dear friend, Diann Bennett, in Auchtermuchty, for keeping me up to speed on all things Scottish.

About the Author

Raye Anderson is a Scots Canadian who spent many years running theatre schools and presenting creative arts programmes for arts organizations, notably at the Prairie Theatre Exchange in Winnipeg. She now calls Manitoba's Interlake home, where she is part of a thriving arts community.

She has published four books in the Roxanne Calloway Mystery series: *And We Shall Have Snow* (shortlisted for the 2021 CWC Best Crime First Novel and the 2021 WILLA Literary Award for Fiction), *And Then Is Heard No More*, *Down Came the Rain*, and *Sing a Song of Summer*. Her work has taken her across Canada, from the Pacific coast to the Atlantic coast, and as far north as Churchill and Yellowknife, as well as to the West Indies and her native Scotland.

Eco-Audit
Printing this book using Rolland Enviro100 Book instead of virgin fibres paper saved the following resources:

Trees	Water	Air Emissions
3	1,000 L	207 kg